HUMANITY

ANDREW SPENCER

ISBN: 0-9906994-0-4
ISBN-13: 978-0-9906994-0-8

DEDICATION

This book is dedicated to my biggest fans: my wife and children. Thank you for always believing in me, even when I don't. Every day I watch as you all adore this man you see as husband and father, and every day I am so humbled in looking at him through your eyes that you make me aspire to be more like him.

ACKNOWLEDGMENTS

To my mother Dyanne, thank you for passing on some small measure of your talent to me. I still wish I had the ability to write descriptive prose as you do, but I guess we all have to work with the gifts God gives us. One of the most pleasant surprises that writing this book brought was the experience of sharing the process with you.

To my wife Chris, thank you for the endless days and nights when you carried the load for both of us so I could pursue this dream. Thank you for always believing in me. Most of all, thank you for being the person on this Earth who looks out on the world through a similar lens to me; you make me feel sane and more importantly, understood. Also, thank you for the rainbow – it was brilliant.

To my youngest children Maddie and Brody, thank you for always looking at me like I am a superhero. You don't understand yet, but one day you will know how much strength and courage it can give you when your child looks at you like you can do *anything*. Because of you, I can.

To my oldest daughter Ariel, thank you for being so patient with me while I was busy writing this book. I know you are a married woman and you understand, but my heart still cringed every time I saw that a day of writing had gone by that I hadn't spoken to you. Thank you for being so sweet and not making me feel bad about it.

A special thank you to my beta readers: my wife, my mother, Tom and Deana, and Leslie. Your feedback saved me several embarrassing mistakes and made this book much better than it would have been. Most of all, thank you for encouraging me; you may not know it, but there were several times when your words were what made me keep writing and not languish or leave this book to collect dust while I pursued other things.

Lastly, to all of those who are probably not reading this sentence because like me, they skip past the Acknowledgments and go straight to the story, thank you for buying this book. I hope it brings you enjoyment – but most of all, I hope it makes you think about something – anything – you may not have thought of yet. If it accomplishes both of those objectives, then it was all worth it.

i

FOREWORD

This book is a work of fiction. But to say that it is *only* a work of fiction would be to only tell half the story.

I have to say, researching this book was just as fun as writing it. Even being an avid student of history, mythology, and world religions, I found myself uncovering patterns in the writings of our ancestors that I had never known or even expected.

I say this because I want you – the reader – to know that I did not make this story from *nothing*. I made it from *something*. Consider it a work of speculative fiction that sprang from some Basic Truths I either already knew or discovered while researching the book.

Basic Truth 1: Guess what? That stuff we call mythology? They didn't call it "myth"ology in the age when it was prevalent. They called it religion. It was their religion, and they believed in it as strongly as we believe in ours today. Mythology is our modern, condescending term for the deeply held spiritual beliefs of our forefathers. It was never about *myth*. It was and has always been about *belief*.

Basic Truth 2: When you look into our past, you start to notice that some very interesting characters keep popping up in different places, at different times, with different names.

Basic Truth 3: When you look into our past, you also start to notice that many stories you may have thought were specific to one religion or mythology were actually very common, and have been repeated throughout time and across all civilizations. It's a very humbling and awe-inspiring moment when you start to wonder if maybe – just maybe – there is some universal truth behind them all. Or behind everything.

Basic Truth 4: You can learn a lot – and I mean *a lot* – by studying where the words in our language originated from.

Basic Truth 5: Whether in the realm of science or belief, we all have a tendency to think we know more than we actually do.

Read. Enjoy. When you come across a reference to something ancient and find yourself wondering if the author (that's me) made it up or if it's true, I encourage you to look it up. You'll often be amazed what you find. And remember...it all begins with opening your mind...

1

The yellow police tape made a fluttering sound as it rippled in the breeze, still draped around the edge of the small rectangle of grass in front of the dorm building. Meghan's broken body had been discovered there in the early hours of the morning. The tape stood out as a bright yellow ribbon in the dim shadows of dusk as Aletheia approached the stairs to the building. For the hundredth time that day, she wondered as she walked past if she had been the one who pushed her roommate to her death.

She was tired; her will depleted from having to carry her numbed body and mind through the events of the day. She had woken at four in the morning to the sounds of police sirens and hysterical classmates pounding on her door. Images of the remainder of the day flashed through her mind; she could still see Meghan's mother's hands, trembling as she asked Aletheia in a broken voice about her daughter. She could still feel the dry lines of salt on her cheeks, making the skin feel tight and crusty where the tears had streamed down. She had been too shocked to wipe them away.

The events of the day had left her feeling empty, but the tiredness had already been there. Night after night of fitful, restless sleep had taken its toll. She had been having the disturbing nightmares for some time now, always with the same theme. Today it was as if it had all come to a head; as if some master plan to break her had finally come to fruition. Try as she might, Aletheia hadn't been able to reconcile Meghan's violent demise with the dream she had experienced the night before, with her pushing the girl over the porch railing to her death six stories below. She could still see the scene in her head as though it were playing like a movie in front of her.

Aletheia mounted the concrete stairs to the old building, placing each foot in front of the other without thinking. Adam walked beside her like a silent guardian. He had been there to comfort her the whole day, as he always was. As they entered the building, he waved several other people away that tried to approach. Aletheia didn't notice them. She was focused on the tingling in her chest where it felt like her heart had been ripped out; it was a feeling of pain that she didn't have words to describe. She navigated listlessly through the halls of the building she knew so well, taking old wooden stairwells up and up.

The initial chaos of what had happened had turned the entire day into a surreal blur. The only part she could remember was the first ten minutes, before another girl in the dorm led her downstairs to the front of the building. The ache in her heart had hit her when she first saw the sheet-covered form. Tears had erupted out of her; wrenching, heart-wracking sobs bursting forth from her core like a raging torrent of pain and hurt. She and Meghan had been best friends since they first moved in together.

Aletheia had never experienced a significant death in her life. Her grandmother had passed when she was young, but the woman had been very old, and had lived a full life. Aletheia remembered it as a sad moment.

But not like this, she thought. Her grandmother's death had felt *right*…part of the natural order of things; the tapestry of life. Meghan's death felt…wrong. Like a vicious tear in that tapestry, ripping through fabric and destroying the beautiful picture it weaved in a garish display of disregard for the work of the weaver. Her friend was not supposed to die this young, and certainly not like this.

And it may have been me who did it. The thought hit Aletheia's heart like a stone dropped in water, sinking deep into her and leaving a wobbly pit inside her stomach even as her mind refused to accept the possibility. She loved Meghan; they got along better than Aletheia had ever gotten along with anyone. They went everywhere and did everything together, like two peas in a pod.

I would never hurt Meghan. Except maybe I did. What if I'm not a good person? What if I'm sick? What if there's something inside me that is broken, and I can't remember what I did? She tried to shake off the thoughts, but they came on anyway. It all came flooding back.

The door to the common porch on her floor of the dorm was open, letting wisps of the cool night breeze into the hallway. Rounding the corner, she could see Meghan, standing at the railing and looking up at the stars. It was quiet outside. The girl stood unaware anyone else was now on the porch with her, and Aletheia guessed she was deep in thought about something.

3

Thoughts...images of Adam flitted across Aletheia's mind, but soon subsided as she moved forward, slowly approaching her friend. Meghan's lustrous black hair hung in loose curls down her back. She had always had such beautiful hair. She was in her pajamas, or what served as them – a pair of Victoria Secret sweats and the old, worn Maroon 5 tee shirt she often wore. It had been given to her by her ex-boyfriend. She had never gotten over him. Maybe that was why she wanted Adam for herself.

Aletheia felt herself rush forward then, closing the distance between her and her roommate's back in a split second. Meghan's cry was muffled, somehow, as she lurched forward over the railing and started to fall. It sounded like it came from a hollow can; a split second muted scream that stopped abruptly. Moving forward, Aletheia looked down over the railing to see Meghan's broken form on the ground below.

Aletheia pushed the memory of the dream from her thoughts again, as she had tried to do so many times that day. She and Adam slowly walked down the hallway to the last door on the left. Stopping in front of it she paused and stared at it. On the other side of that door was her room. *Their* room. All of Meghan's belongings were behind that door; her clothes, her books, her personal items. All memories of a life that would never be again. Aletheia wasn't sure if she was ready to see it all. She felt Adam's hand touch her shoulder, gentle but strong, and gathered her resolve. Sliding the key into the lock and turning, she pushed the door open and forced herself to step through. Adam followed and closed it behind them. Her gaze immediately fell upon the tall glass on Meghan's nightstand.

Images flooded her mind. Memories of her and Meghan,

laughing and drinking at the bar that night; stumbling home and not realizing until they got back to their dorm room that they had carried their drinks with them the whole way. Aletheia sunk down, her butt hitting the wooden floor hard, and covered her face with her hands. Adam sunk down beside her and held her as she cried, and they stayed that way for a long time.

She wasn't sure how much time had passed, but she knew that her tears were gone again – cried out for the second time that day. She sniffled, and Adam got up and got her a tissue from the desk.

"Do you want me to help? I can get some of your stuff for you, if you're ready. Or do you need more time?" he asked.

"No. It's okay. I'm okay." She pushed herself to her feet and reached up to place her hand on his shoulder. "Thank you."

"I just wish I could make it better."

Adam reached out and hugged her then; a strong, firm hug that made her feel safe, if only for the moment. His hugs were always like that. He wasn't the biggest guy she had dated – he stood maybe six inches taller than her and was lean and athletic – but he was the strongest man she knew. His hugs felt like a vice grip, if a vice grip could hold her gently. She inhaled his cologne deeply; it smelled like citrus and spice and comforted her. Had it been a different day it would have stirred up other feelings in her as well. Adam went over to her side of the room and started gathering some of her things. They had decided she would stay with him at his place for a few days. She couldn't bear the thought of staying in her room.

It didn't take long to gather what she needed – in truth she already had quite a few items at his place anyway. Adam meticulously packed the small duffel bag; everything he did was meticulous. Aletheia nearly smiled as she watched him. She knew he was self-conscious about it around her because he thought it bothered her. Adam could laugh and have fun as much as any of the many college friends she had, but when he was serious he turned into a machine; everything he did was exact and precise, and always according to a plan. On a different day she could have laughed watching him count out how many pair of underwear and socks she might need. Although it did grate on her at times – Aletheia was not a planner – Adam never seemed to realize how much she loved it about him, and wouldn't trade his quirks for anything.

"I'm guessing you don't want your textbooks or any school stuff. You're not going to try and do homework, are you?"

Aletheia shook her head. "No, I can't even think of that right now."

"How about your journal? Maybe it would help?"

Aletheia thought about it for a moment, but decided that she didn't want to remember the day or the night before in any detail. Besides, she didn't think she could bear to read what else was in that journal. Not after what had happened.

"No...I'm good. Maybe when we come back."

Adam finished packing the bag for her and Aletheia distractedly added a few more items to it before nodding to him that she was done. Zipping the bag shut, Adam hoisted the strap onto his shoulder and moved to the door, waiting for Aletheia. As they were about to leave, she headed over to Meghan's desk. It smelled like her here; a mixture of vanilla and flowers. She reached down and picked up a beaded bracelet that lay there, feeling the small, transparent plastic beads in between her fingers. Meghan had bought it at the open-air market one Saturday when they had spent the whole day together. It had been sunny that day, and they had a great time eating good food, laughing, and shopping together. *She always loved the sun.* It was a happy memory, and Aletheia wanted something happy to remember her friend by.

2

Aletheia was quiet during most of the car ride back to Adam's house. The rumble of the Camaro's engine increased as it turned a corner, something she would not normally have even registered. The leather seat felt firm and cold as her body pressed back into it with the acceleration of the car. She stared blankly out the window as the lights of businesses and houses flashed by, lost in thought about the night before.

Adam had stayed in her room, up late studying for his history exam. She remembered that Meghan had gone to bed first, and Aletheia had curled up on her narrow twin bed next to Adam, falling asleep soon after while he had read by the focused light of a small lamp on her nightstand. The nightmare had come again, and in greater detail than usual. This time it had been her pushing Meghan over the railing; it had been other ways on other nights. She had killed her best friend in every way she could imagine in her dreams.

The next thing Aletheia remembered was being woken up by Adam – still in his clothes from the night before – to the sounds of sirens outside and someone pounding on the door. Aletheia had woken up groggy and disoriented, and Adam had gotten out of bed to answer it. When he opened the door, Lyssa – a friend of hers and Meghan's – stood there with tears running down her face. She looked panicked and distraught. Aletheia woke up more quickly at the sight of the girl, came to the door next to Adam, and put her hand on her arm.

"Lyssa...what's wrong?"

The other girl's voice cracked as she spoke the words. "It's Meghan. She's dead." She broke down as she said the last, unable to say more, and Aletheia's face twisted up in confusion.

"What are you talking about?" She turned around to wake Meghan and have a good laugh over the news, and saw her friend's bed empty. The sheets were rumpled and tossed aside as though she had slept in the bed and gotten up out of it, and Aletheia's confusion grew. She spun around to look at Lyssa, glancing back and forth from the bed to the girl as she spoke.

"No...she was just here. She fell asleep before we did last night. We just need to find her – I'm sure she's around here somewhere." Lyssa just shook her head, gently took Aletheia's hands in hers, and looked her steadily in the eyes.

"No, Lee. She's gone. I'm so sorry. She jumped off the porch last night. They found her..." The girl trailed off and started crying again, embracing Aletheia in a tight hug. She could feel Lyssa's body shake slightly with each sob as the news sunk in. Aletheia felt the tears well up in her eyes and a pit form in her stomach. She broke the hug and grabbed the girl by the arms, panic in her voice.

"Are you sure? When? How did this happen? Where is

she?"

Lyssa looked at her sympathetically and said to her softly, "Come on. But...it's not easy to see."

She led Adam and Aletheia through the hall and down the flights of stairs to the ground floor of their dorm. As they got closer to the front of the building, Aletheia realized the large, wooden main doors were open and she could hear a commotion coming from outside. Several girls were standing in the doorway, looking out. She saw a flash of red, then blue...red, then blue repeatedly in the doorframe. Lyssa led them past the other girls onto the first floor porch. As Aletheia passed them, she saw looks of shock and disbelief on their faces, and a few glistening eyes and tear-streaked cheeks. Lyssa led them down the stairs off the front porch. The commotion got louder, and now Aletheia could make out the sounds of men talking to each other and to the people in the crowd, giving directions. Aletheia followed the stares of the onlookers to the point they were looking at. Turning her head to the left, she saw it: a form...a body...lying on the ground, shrouded in a sheet. By the shape of the form under the sheet she could imagine the angle and position at which it was laying. At that moment everything from the night before came flooding back. Memories of the dream; of pushing Meghan, of watching her fall, of watching her land in exactly that way. The last words she heard were Adam's beside her – an exclamation of shock – and then she was shaking violently as a guttural scream of denial poured from her lungs.

After the initial wave had hit her, it had taken Adam and Lyssa a long time to calm Aletheia down. The rest of the day became a collage of conversations, including the police asking her and Adam if they could answer any questions. She had been a mess at the time and Adam had graciously done his best to answer the questions for her, explaining to the officer that she was the victim's roommate and was very distraught. The officer had seemed understanding, but Aletheia couldn't shake the feeling that he had looked at her weirdly during his questioning, and it made her mind race, wondering if there was something the officer suspected that he was not telling.

Aletheia was so lost in her own memory that she didn't even notice where they were. It was only the motion of the car stopping that brought her back to the present and announced that they were at Adam's house. She sat motionless in the passenger seat as Adam got out of the car and retrieved her bag from the back. He came around to her side of the car and opened the door to let her out, and then held her hand as he led her from the circular dirt driveway up the walkway to the small house. It wasn't much to look at – just a small one-story fixer-upper set back behind the trees on a modest lot – but he owned it, which was much more than most men in their twenties could say. It was even more impressive when she thought about where he had come from and what he had been through in his life; for all intents, Adam should have probably ended up in rehab, or jail, or a cemetery plot. He had stayed out of trouble, unlike the rest of his family.

Adam unlocked the front door, the high-grade lock looking out of place on the shabby blue-painted steel. She hadn't understood half of what he had said about it; something about it being "bump-proof". Aletheia honestly thought Adam was paranoid when it came to anything related to safety or security, but she patiently let him do the things he needed to do. She knew and understood his need for constant vigilance. Aletheia guessed that if she had grown up in one of the worst neighborhoods in Los Angeles and had a convict for a brother, she would be paranoid about safety too. Even though he hadn't spoken to him in years, Adam was always worried his brother would show up at his door, bringing trouble and violence with him.

Adam shut the door behind them and turned on the kitchen lights, immediately bringing her bag to his bedroom and helping her get unpacked. After they had settled in, Aletheia told him she needed to call her mother. Adam plopped down on the couch and turned on the television as she took out her cellphone.

"Hi, Mom. Yeah. I...I had a really bad day today. No, it's not. It's Meghan..." Aletheia's voice trailed off as she walked into the other room. It was a long while before she came back in the living room.

"How did that go...telling your mom?" asked Adam.

"As well as it could. I just want to be next to you and...not think for a while."

"Of course," he replied, smiling. "Come on." He patted his hand on the couch next to him, inviting her to sit. Exhaustion took Aletheia shortly after she sat down on the couch, and she fell asleep on Adam's shoulder to the muted sounds of reruns they had seen a dozen times before.

Aletheia woke some time later when she felt herself moved as Adam shifted on the couch. He was leaning forward now, listening to and watching the television intently. She managed to squint at the TV through heavy lids that were stubbornly resisting her attempts to open them. The news...Adam was watching the news. She leaned forward next to him and peered at the screen. A female reporter – a blonde woman tightly wrapped in a gray rain jacket – was reporting live from the front of her dorm building. Adam looked to her, and she could see the shock in his face, his eyebrows raised behind the moppy brown bangs that partially obscured them.

"What is it?" whispered Aletheia.

"The police...they found a witness who saw Meghan when she...when she died. They're saying it wasn't a suicide now. They're saying it was a homicide." Adam looked to her as if the whole world had gone mad. He sounded confused and sad. "Somebody murdered Meghan? Why would that even happen? Who would even want to?"

The scene on the television then changed to a woman being interviewed on the street – a homeless woman, by the looks of her. She was wearing a soiled scarf over her hair, the front of which was streaked with shades of brown and blond and rested above a dirty, tanned face. She was talking to a reporter that must have been behind the camera.

"She was just up there..." she said, as she pointed up at what Aletheia guessed was the porch of her dorm building. "She was just standing at the railing, and this other girl came out and just pushed her right off. Saw the whole thing. Horrible."

In her groggy state the words and their implications took a minute or two to sink in for Aletheia. Her mind tried to come up to speed quickly to process them.

Somebody murdered Meghan. A girl...pushed her. Aletheia's hand went to her mouth, trembling as she held it there.

"Oh my God." Images from the dream once again flashed

through her head; of Meghan on the porch, of her rushing at her, of Meghan falling to her death.

"Oh my God," she said again, more emphatically. Her head started spinning. It started spinning and did not stop, no matter how she tried to clear it or make sense of what she had just heard. She could feel her own pulse beating in her neck. The police had an eyewitness, and they said it was a murder.

Someone pushed her. Aletheia couldn't bear the thought of it. She was starting to lose her grasp on what was real and what was not again.

Did I kill Meghan? Why? There's no way. There's just no way... Adam's words brought her attention partially back to the moment.

"Are you okay? I know...I can't believe it either. Who would want to kill Meghan? She was so sweet; she never hurt anyone." He dropped his head to her level and looked in her eyes.

"Don't worry. Maybe it's a mistake...maybe the eyewitness is confused...or lying to get attention. She looks like a homeless lady off the street. Nine times out of ten they're untreated mentally ill people." He looked back at the screen and then to Aletheia again.

"Even if someone did do that to her...the police will figure it out. They always do. Nobody gets away with anything anymore." Turning his attention back to the television, he added, "If somebody did do that to Meghan, I hope they fry her and she burns in hell."

The world swam and spun as her mind raced, her hands and voice trembling.

"I need a minute," she said as she pushed herself off the

couch and lurched unsteadily for the bathroom. Closing the door behind her, she leaned back against it and looked at herself in the mirror. She could feel the ridges of the hard wood panels in the door pressing against her back; it felt like the only solid thing in her world. The sound of Adam's voice told her he was just outside the bathroom.

"You okay?"

Aletheia tried her best to steady her voice and sound calm as she answered him. "I'm...I'm okay. I just need a minute to process this. I'll be fine." *I will not be fine. I'm losing my mind.*

Adam's consoling voice came from the other side of the door. "Okay...take your time. I'm here if you need me."

She waited until she was sure he had walked away from the door and then turned back towards her own reflection in the mirror. *I can't believe this is happening. If I didn't know better myself, I would even think I pushed her. I couldn't have. Could I? What the hell is happening to me?* Still standing in front of the vanity, Aletheia placed her face in her shaking hands and sobbed as quietly as she could manage. Her mind threw thoughts at her rapid fire, cycling back and forth between guilt and innocence.

She couldn't help the *other* thoughts that now came unbidden to her mind. She hadn't thought the *other* thoughts in a long time, but since the nightmares had started they had crept back in. Meghan's death had just driven her over the edge.

I could do it. I don't want to, but I could. It would make it all go away. I just want it all to go away. I'm tired. I want to sleep. I want to go to sleep and not wake up. If I found out I did that to her, I would just end it. Just end it once and for all. I don't want to live like this anymore.

The thoughts brought her back in time, back to her teen

years before she had gone off to college and met Adam. Those were dark times for Aletheia, filled with counselors and prescription pills, and people tilting their heads when they spoke to her and asking her "how she was feeling." Once she had fought and clawed her way out of that dark place, she had sworn she would never go back. She had done well, too. Getting away from home had been good for her. Meeting Adam had been good for her too. Sometimes Aletheia felt stupid for being such a mess and even considering suicide when her life had been such a cakewalk compared to his, but none of that changed the way she felt.

No, that's not fair...he has never been through anything like this.

Aletheia felt so alone. She wished so badly she could tell Adam that the other thoughts had returned, but she felt like she couldn't. Adam knew everything else, and it had made her feel better to have someone to talk to about it. He knew about her past depression and her thoughts of suicide when she was a teen. He knew about the nightmares she was having. Not the ones involving killing Meghan in various ways, of course; those she felt she shouldn't mention because they made her look jealous, insecure, and crazy. The other nightmares, though – the ones that always involved the dark figure that stalked her and followed her every step – she had told Adam about those. He had been so sweet about it, to the point of staying awake in her room one night while she slept and standing guard over her to show her there was nothing to be afraid of and there were no such things as bogeymen.

It was different now though. She knew she needed to tell Adam about the other thoughts and about the nightmares causing them for her own sanity. She knew she needed to tell him because their relationship was built on trust and she needed to trust him with it, even if it looked horrible. She had the opportunity to do it multiple times in the last twenty-four hours, but she just couldn't bring herself to. *What if something clicks for him and he looks at me differently? What if he wonders if I did it just like I do? What if that makes him see me as a different person? What if it makes him not love me anymore?* No. She couldn't tell him. Not yet.

Looking at her face in the mirror Aletheia saw dark circles around her eyes; puffy bags earned from lost sleep and hours of tears. *I look like hell.* Wiping away her tears, she turned on the tap. Cupping her hands she let the cold water fill them, leaned forward, and brought it up over her face, over and over. The water was refreshing and washed away the tears. She drank some, from her hands, and tried to calm her breathing. It tasted cool and clean and she tried to imagine it washing all the horrible thoughts and images out of her mind. She knew she had to get herself under control. Maybe she just needed more time to think, to try to make sense of it all. Drying her face on the hand towel, she turned and left the bathroom and went back out to join Adam.

3

They had decided to go to bed, so Adam went through his ritual as he did every night: he made sure all the outside lights were on and checked all the doors and windows to make sure they were locked. He had been so proud of himself when he had reinforced the door jambs and installed the shatterproof film on his windows; it made him feel like he was doing what he could to prepare himself. After all, life was hard and bad things happened. As far as Adam was concerned, when they did the reason things usually went south so quickly for people was because they hadn't been prepared. Most people instead liked to pretend that those things didn't really happen to people – liked to keep their heads in the sand and keep humming their happy tune. Adam knew better.

Two empty pizza boxes lay cockeyed on the coffee table, lids open, their bottoms decorated with blotches of grease like an abstract painting. The boys were laughing at something funny the talk show host on the television had said, just two brothers

18

having a good time while Mom worked another late shift. Adam looked over at his brother James – the tattoos, the muscles, the wife-beater shirt and all the other markings that advertised him for what he was – and saw nothing but the laughing, smiling face of the little boy he had grown up with. Adam would never admit it – his brother would never understand – but he missed these moments. He missed just hanging out with his older brother, playing and laughing and running through the neighborhood when they were both young and innocent. He missed getting into trouble together; not the type of trouble that James got into now, but the type that they had gotten into back then that resulted in their mother smacking their butts with a hairbrush and them pretending it still hurt. That had all changed when James had dropped out of school. He had still insisted that Adam finish, always wanting his younger brother to stay on the straight and narrow, but as a role model James hardly set a good example.

The boys continued to laugh at the talk show host's sarcastic rant until the loud crash stopped their laughter short. Adam and James both swung their heads around towards the door to the apartment where the crash had come from, but by the time they realized what was happening the men were already on them, beating them viciously with punches and kicks, and pistol-whipping them across the mouth, face, and head. Adam tried to fight back, as did James – growing up in a bad neighborhood they both knew how to handle themselves well in a fight – but it all happened too quickly. The attack was so sudden and violent that before they could respond they were overwhelmed. It seemed like the beating went on forever, until all either of the brothers could do was curl up in the fetal position and try to protect themselves.

Adam's head was clear – he had never been knocked out and it served him well as he was able to keep his wits about him – but he could taste blood in his own mouth. In fact, he could taste and feel a lot of blood welling into his mouth, and it was hard to breathe. He wondered then if he or James could reach one of his brother's guns – James always kept several guns in the house – but it seemed all but impossible. The men were armed, and there were at least four of them from what Adam could register in the chaos of the moment.

Eventually the beating stopped; at least, the incessant beating did. Adam felt the cold steel ring of a gun barrel pressed to his head as he lay in a ball on the cushions, the man shouting obscenities at him and threatening to spray his brains all over the couch. He didn't look up, but he could tell from the sounds around him that James was in the same situation, being held down at gunpoint with an occasional kick or punch put in for added measure. The man yelling at James was asking him where something was, and making it very clear that if he didn't tell him he was going to watch his little brother die. James was yelling something back; not in the commanding voice his brother had grown since joining the gang, but in a voice that sounded more like the brother Adam remembered when he got scared. He could hear the sounds of the apartment being torn apart around them, and a few moments later a yell from the other end of it where the room he shared with James was.

Some words were exchanged then between James and the man by him. Adam couldn't make them all out, except for the last part. "You keep your mouth shut, or we'll pay another visit when your mama's home." *Then Adam heard the man spit on James, and they were gone. It happened so fast that Adam barely realized they had left. He stayed where he was – in complete and utter shock – for a full minute after they were gone, not really sure what had just happened. When he finally looked up, he saw his brother's bloodied face looking back at him, terrified.*

Adam and his brother had never been the same since that night. In the aftermath, there had been a lot of emotions, and they had changed from day to day. One minute they were frightened little boys once again in a big scary world together. The next they were just happy to be alive. But those emotions had been shorter-lived than Adam would have wished. James' thoughts and feelings had quickly turned to fury and revenge, and before long he and his friends were tracking the men down who had done this to make them pay. At first, Adam had gone through the same emotions; had even considered joining his brother and their friends in teaching them a lesson. He had no tolerance for people who preyed on others – had no compunctions with putting a bullet in any of the men who had done it, especially if they were a threat to his mother. It was only when he had found out what it had all been about that his feelings had changed. Getting targeted for no good reason was one thing; getting targeted because it was well known that you had a stash of drugs and money was another. Adam had been young and naïve, and hadn't fully understood what it was his brother did to make money until then. That had been the beginning of the end of his relationship with James. Adam had simply not been able to forgive him for putting their mother and their little family in that kind of danger.

Shaking the thoughts from his head, Adam checked the lock on the front door last. *Buying time...just buying time. By the time anybody gets through that door...I almost feel bad for anyone who gets through that door.* He shook the thought away and it was immediately replaced by thoughts of Meghan. For the thousandth time in his life, he wondered why people did the things they did to others. Heading into the bedroom, he took a deep breath and let it out as he slipped into the covers beside Aletheia, pressing himself up against her back and spooning her. As he placed a kiss on the back of her head, he thought to himself, *At least I can protect this one. God, if nothing else, help me protect her and let us live a long, happy life together.* His eyes closed as he drifted quickly off to sleep, while a foot away Aletheia's lay open, deep in thought.

The next morning was quiet. Aletheia slept in very late, having finally fallen sleep in the early hours of the morning. At least there had been no nightmares that night. She felt very safe with Adam, in his house. She wasn't sure exactly why, but she felt safer there than she had in her dorm room. Ever since the nightmares had begun, she had started to get a very creepy feeling in the dorm. That had been a large part of the reason why Adam had stayed over many nights in the last few weeks. Having nightmares like that left her feeling like she always had to look over her shoulder.

She woke to find Adam's side of the bed empty, the sheets and blanket rumpled. The golden morning light was streaming in through the curtains, rays of it slanting across her eyes as she moved into their path and telling her brain to wake up. She swung her legs down over the side of the bed and twisted herself up into a sitting position. Her jaw cracked as a large yawn forced its way out of her, and she got up and headed towards the kitchen. She knew where he was; when Adam wasn't studying, working, or with her he was always in the same place. She considered popping into the garage to say good morning but decided to give him his space, knowing it was his way of working through his emotions. Meghan had been his friend too.

Deciding to wait for him to eat breakfast, Aletheia called her mother again and told her about the developments of the night before. Her mother was shocked and begged her to come home. She was concerned that there was a serial killer preying on college girls and that she would be in danger. *So typical...always worrying about crazy things.* It took Aletheia some time to reassure her that she was indeed safe and there was nothing to worry about. After she finished talking, she hung up the phone with an exasperated sigh and called Lyssa to check in on her.

It was good to talk to Lyssa; nice to share her feelings about what had happened with another girlfriend who understood. Adam was supportive, but he wasn't good at actually talking about things. After a while, the conversation turned to the news story from the night before and the idea that Meghan had been murdered.

"I know, it's crazy. They're here now going through her stuff for clues," Lyssa said.

"Who's there?"

"The police. They're in your room right now, putting Meghan's stuff in boxes."

Aletheia's heart started beating frantically in her chest and her head became dizzy. Before she could stop herself, she blurted out, "You don't think they went through my stuff too, do you? Those are my personal things!"

Lyssa paused for a moment on the other end of the phone. "Uh…no, I don't think they'd do that. They're looking through her stuff to see if they can find any clues as to who might have pushed her."

Lyssa's answer did little to calm her nerves; inside her head Aletheia was doing her best to talk herself down and remind herself that Lyssa was right. Just because some bad dreams had made her question herself didn't mean the police thought she had done anything wrong. She had a hard time concentrating on the rest of the conversation, and after a few minutes said goodbye and hung up the phone, images of policemen dusting her room for fingerprints running through her mind.

Thud. Thud. Thud. Sweat poured down Adam's forehead from his scalp, threatening to drip into his eyes as his fists thudded into the heavy bag over and over again, rocking it with each blow so the chain it suspended from clinked wildly. He quickly reached up and wiped his forearm on his brow to keep the sweat from stinging his eyes before connecting with the bag again. His tightly corded muscles were long since sore, his arms shaking not from effort but from simple exhaustion. The eight miles that morning had gotten his blood flowing and helped clear his mind. The workout that followed had taxed him; he had not stopped until his muscles could no longer move the weights. Two and a half hours into the workout came the heavy bag. He ignored the trembling in his arms as a minor inconvenience.

Thud. Thud. Thud. Images of every bully who had ever tortured him as a boy drove him on. Images of every predatory criminal he had encountered in the city, each one a threat to him and those he cared about. He hit the bag harder. Images of his brother. Images of his father. Scenes of his father beating his mother flashed through his mind. His brother trying to intervene and being thrown into a wall. Adam could still feel the strong, calloused hand around his throat, squeezing just enough to make it hard for him to breathe. He could still feel his feet starting to tingle as they dangled off the floor; could still feel the broken plaster on the wall behind his back dig into his shoulder blade as he was pressed against it. Rage welled inside him and gave him renewed strength. The chain clinked faster as the bag jerked against it as if trying to break free. The world was unfair. The world was pain. *Thud. Thud. Thud.*

Adam knew he had a rage inside him – an unhealthy, toxic rage – as surely as his brother did. He had learned to use the images during his workouts to bring out the rage in a safe place. He had stopped working out at the gym because the men had laughed at him and told him he was going to kill himself working out the way he did. They hadn't understood Adam. He wasn't working out. He was *training*. When he had explained it to them, they had asked him what he was training *for*. It was a question he hadn't been able to answer easily. Sometimes things only made sense in his own head.

Adam was training for when *something bad* happened. He didn't know yet exactly what the something bad would be, but he knew it would happen nonetheless. He couldn't change the world and make all the bad things go away. All he could do is be ready. He needed to be strong. Fast. Smart. He needed to be able to fight harder, run longer, handle more pain. At some level, Adam understood these weren't rational needs. He was just a regular guy, and regular guys didn't need to be any of these things. Except he did.

The thudding had reached a crescendo, the heavy bag rocking and swinging from the center beam of the old garage as Adam unleashed all his fear, all his fury, all his pain on the canvas. Seconds turned to minutes, his breath coming in gasps as he refused to let himself stop; making himself believe that every blow was the difference between life and death for someone he loved. Finally he stopped, hitting the bag one last time for good measure. No one else understood. Adam couldn't have cut down his workouts because...he *needed* them. They were the only place he could release the hurt inside him. They were how he stayed sane.

He let himself pant for only a few seconds, and then made himself stand up straight and take a single deep breath, inhaling slowly through his nose and exhaling through his mouth despite his lungs and brain screaming to him that he should be gulping air. He let go of the last of his rage as he stripped the thick gloves off his hands and threw them aside. Leaving the tape on his knuckles for the time being, he sat down cross-legged on the mat and placed his hands on his knees. Closing his eyes, he felt himself move away from the painful, dark place he had been and into a more peaceful one. It usually took a long time to work out the anger inside him, but when he finally did, an amazing thing happened. He felt...*clean*. The moments at the end of the workout, after he had purged himself of all the demons that haunted him – rage, humiliation, fear – were the most peaceful moments he felt in his life. Adam let his guard drop completely and emptied his mind. He floated in the emptiness. He just...was.

In that moment, Adam felt like he was the person he was supposed to be before all the *bad things* had changed him. The rage and the fear were not his true self; they were like ugly scar tissue built up over the purer soul underneath, and he wore that scar tissue like armor. Lee had noticed it; she said it came down over him when he felt threatened and turned his face to stone. Adam had tried to explain it to her but it was hard to.

In his mind, he understood: sometimes the only way you could survive was to turn off your emotions and not let yourself feel. Sometimes, when you were dealing with someone who wanted to hurt you – not just physically, but mentally and spiritually *hurt* you – the only thing you had left to protect yourself was to turn off all your emotions and endure whatever came your way. When you couldn't feel, you couldn't be hurt, and when they couldn't hurt you, they couldn't control you. Sometimes, it was the only way to *win*.

When Adam finally felt his true self emerge, it felt like a tingling feeling of power and joy and purity rising up inside him until it burst from his core like an exploding star. He felt *light*. He felt centered. He felt connected to others and to God in a way he usually did not. He sat with his eyes closed, inhaling slowly and deeply, and as he exhaled all the stress, pain, and doubt he had been holding melted away with the light that filled him. He stayed that way for a long time.

4

The next morning they both woke late. The previous day had been uneventful, both needing the quiet time to process the death of their friend and not feeling up to much else. Sleep had been hard to come by for both of them. As they sat in the kitchen eating their breakfast, their conversation was interrupted by a sharp pounding on the door. Adam gave Aletheia a quizzical look that told her he wasn't expecting company before shrugging and getting up to answer. As always, he peeked out the peep hole before unlocking the door, and saw two men in suits standing on his front step. Before he could ask who they were through the door one of the men put his hand in his trouser pocket, moving his jacket aside just enough for Adam to see the glint of a badge on his belt.

He turned to Aletheia as he unlocked the door and said, "It's the police. Maybe they found out some more information about Meghan's death." Aletheia's breath caught in her throat. She wanted to run, but there was no way to. Not now. She didn't even have time to react before the door was open and Adam was talking to the two officers.

The men at the door showed Adam their badges and gave him their names – both detectives, apparently. They then made sure they were talking to the right people, just like Aletheia had seen in the movies. She stood frozen in fear, her heart beating out of her chest, waiting for them to say what she knew was coming – that she was under arrest for the murder of Meghan Young. Instead, the detectives asked Adam if they could come in, and he obliged. When they came inside they introduced themselves to Aletheia as well.

"Good morning. I'm Detective Reese, and this is Detective Marsh." The man who spoke looked to be in his early fifties, with gray showing in his brown hair and a stern face that looked worn; perhaps from years of smoking. His partner was younger – Aletheia placed him in his late thirties – and looked more like a salesman than a police officer. Slick black hair framed a well-groomed face. Glancing at his clothes Aletheia realized *everything* about the man was meticulously well-kept. She introduced herself warily, taking their outstretched hands in hers to shake them as if reaching out and petting a pair of poisonous snakes. Adam asked them if they would like to sit down.

Instead of accepting, Reese simply said to them, "There have been some new developments in the circumstances surrounding your friend's death. We were wondering if the two of you would be willing to come down to the station and answer some additional questions."

Before Aletheia could answer – before she could even react – Adam had already answered for them. "Of course we will. Anything we can do to help. Do you need us to come down today?"

Aletheia thought her heart was going to leap straight out of her chest right then and there and give her away. Part of her wanted to scream – scream out of sheer panic and frustration – at the world, at God, at the detectives, at Adam. She knew in her heart she couldn't, but she wanted to.

He doesn't know...he doesn't understand. He thinks we have nothing to hide. He doesn't know what I've been hiding all this time. But them – they know something.

Detective Reese glanced at her as if he could read her mind. "Actually, if you two could come back with us this morning we can take any statements we need now."

Adam looked to Aletheia, but she couldn't respond. In fact, it was all she could do at that moment to not throw up her breakfast in front of the three of them. Her stomach churned and her fingers tingled as though she had fallen asleep on her arm. Adam must have mistaken her expression, or simply been oblivious to any danger, because he turned back and said, "Umm...sure. We can do that, if you don't mind waiting a bit. We both still need to get dressed."

Aletheia could barely hide her distress as the next twenty minutes blurred together. She didn't remember getting dressed; couldn't even recall a single turn on the ride to the station. Even knowing that she wasn't under arrest, sitting in the back of the police car and watching the back of the two detectives' heads through the steel cage was a little too close to Aletheia's fears for her to remain calm. By the time they got to the police station, her hands were shaking so badly she had to hold them in front of her and wring them until her knuckles were white just to keep it from being noticeable.

Inside, the station, she and Adam were led back into

administrative areas, through cubicles and past other detectives and uniformed officers. The walk seemed like it took an eternity, and each step of the way Aletheia felt as though every police officer she passed looked at her knowingly, as though they all could spot a guilty person on sight. They finally found themselves in a small hallway with a few doors leading off to their right.

"Okay Mister Parker, Detective Marsh will take your statements. Miss King, you can come in here with me and make yourself comfortable."

If the fear she was already feeling weren't enough, the detective's words hit her like a brick. Aletheia felt faint and dizzy at the thought of being separated from Adam for questioning. Her head whipped from the officer to Adam, panic visible on her face, then back to the detective.

"Is that really necessary? I thought…I thought we would be giving you our statements together?"

Detective Marsh smiled and said, "Sometimes when people are answering questions together they get influenced by each others' details and it affects their memory of events. We find we get much better information if we take statements separately. After all, we all want to figure out what happened to Miss Young."

His partner looked to Adam and Aletheia and nodded, but one look at Adam's face told Aletheia there was going to be trouble. His expression had changed from cooperative and innocent to suspicious and angry in an instant. She knew what he was thinking; Adam knew enough about these types of situations from his brother to know when something wasn't right. She also knew she couldn't let him say anything. Adam may have been a nice guy, but when he didn't trust someone, he didn't mince words. Besides, there was no way he would leave her alone if he felt like she was scared or nervous.

Aletheia was stuck in a bind. Seeming too nervous about being questioned alone would make her look even more suspicious, and she couldn't afford to look any more suspicious than she did. If she was innocent – and everything in her being and all of her sanity depended on that hope – then she had to act it. She took a deep breath and interrupted Adam as he opened his mouth, no doubt to start questioning them about what they were doing.

"No…I get it. That makes sense." She turned to look Adam in the eye. "It makes sense – you should know, from all your psychology classes. People's memories get clouded by other people's stories." Adam held her gaze for a second, just long enough to let her know he was on guard and didn't like the situation one bit. She breathed a small, indiscernible sigh of relief when he nodded and slowly walked away with the other detective. As she entered the room, she watched Adam's back as the detective led him to a door down the hallway. As she entered the room and the door closed behind her, it was the most alone she had ever felt in her life.

The room was as plain as the hallway had been. Fluorescent lights bathed unadorned, off-white walls in a dull glow that made everything seem drab and bleak. There was a square table in the middle of the room with a manila folder resting on it. Two wooden chairs were pulled up to it on opposite sides. As expected, there was a mirror on the opposite wall which she knew someone else must be watching her through. Detective

Reese pulled out a chair for her to have a seat, then made his way to the other side of the table and sat down. Aletheia couldn't help but be conscious of the mirror – she felt very conscious of the eyes on her as she sat.

Reese smiled at her – it looked like the smile of a shark that smelled blood in the water. He seemed like a cold, hard man; the kind of man who would arrest his mother for breaking the law because it was the right thing to do. He was probably a very good cop, but he scared the hell out of Aletheia. He reached into his jacket and pulled out an audio recorder, and placed it on the table between them before activating it.

"Let's get started, shall we? Tell me about your relationship with Miss Young..."

The first few minutes were very straightforward. It was a blessing that he repeated to her many of the questions she had already answered two days ago. It gave her time to calm down. Even though she was still nervous and trembling, the repetitive questions started to make her wonder if she had overreacted to everything. *It's not like they know your dreams. Maybe it really is just more routine questioning.* She felt herself relax, the tiniest bit.

"Did Miss Young have any enemies? Anyone she had made angry, or that might have a problem with her or want to hurt her in any way?"

"No...no. Meghan was nice to everybody. Everyone loved her."

The detective gave her a hard look, then a quizzical one. "What about your boyfriend, Adam? Did he...*love*...Meghan?"

Aletheia's olive cheeks flushed red. "Umm...what? Love her? Like, as a friend...yes, we both did? Is that what you mean?"

"I didn't mean anything in particular. How is your relationship with your boyfriend? Are you two getting along well?"

Aletheia's mind raced, trying to understand why the detective would be asking her that. It was such an odd question that she didn't quite know how to respond. "We're doing...great...why do you ask?"

"What about Adam and Meghan? What was their relationship like? Were they close?"

Aletheia's head was starting to spin again, trying to keep up with the changes in direction from Reese's questions. "I mean, they were close...yes. Like I said, we were all friends...I'm sorry, I don't understand what any of this has to do with Meghan's death?"

"Just trying to get to know Miss Young. So tell me, did the two of them ever date?"

Detective Reese was staring at her now, hard, and Aletheia could feel her hands getting clammy and sweaty. She was starting to feel sick. "No...they never dated. They didn't know each other until I introduced them."

"Oh. I was just wondering. They're both good-looking young people. It'd be understandable if they were attracted to each other."

Aletheia just sat and stared at him, and tried to swallow the lump in her throat. He looked at her and nodded, then continued. "So tell me, where were you, exactly, between three and four am on the night of Miss Young's murder?

There it was – the question she had been dreading. The question they only asked people when they already suspected the person was guilty. It hit Aletheia like a ton of bricks, making her heart sink into her stomach and her stomach rise into her throat all at the same time. She felt as if she would throw up from the size of the lump in her throat, but she swallowed it down and made herself answer as best she could. "I was in bed, asleep, with my boyfriend." ...*dreaming about killing her in exactly the same way that she died...or was it a dream at all? Could I have been sleepwalking? Did I do this and block it out? Do I have another personality or something?*

"You were in bed, asleep, between three and four in the morning that night?"

"Yes." Her mouth felt dry.

"Aletheia, how did you and Meghan get along? Did you two ever fight?"

"No...not really. That's one of the things I liked most about her. We got along great."

"Did you have any reason to be angry with her on that night?"

Aletheia's heart was pounding so hard now she could hear it in her ears. "No. Why would you even ask that? Do you think I killed her or something?"

Reese didn't pause for a second; he seemed to be getting more and more direct with his questions by the minute. "So it didn't bother you that Miss Young was in love with your boyfriend, Adam?"

Oh my God! How could he...how could he know I dreamt about that? "What are you talking about? Meghan wasn't in love with Adam!"

"Really? Because she says otherwise."

Aletheia knew she must have looked very confused at that

moment, but Reese doggedly persisted anyway, opening the manila folder in front of him and pushing it over to her. As he turned the photocopies towards her so she could read them, she immediately recognized them as Meghan's handwriting. "What is this?"

"It's her journal. You want to read it yourself, or you want me to tell you what it says?"

Aletheia pulled the papers closer, looking down and reading the script. It was hard to do – not because the writing was unclear; Meghan's handwriting was neat and pretty – but because it was a piece of her friend, talking to her as if from beyond death. She read the words silently to herself.

Had another dream about Adam last night. It was amazing...he was...amazing. I don't understand why I keep having these dreams. It was funny at first but now...I just don't know. I don't understand why I can't get him out of my head – I keep seeing him, even during the day. He just pops into my thoughts, all the time. I don't feel like I'm in love with him – he feels like more of a brother to me – but maybe I am? Am I? Maybe I am and I don't realize it? What the hell is wrong with me? I am such a horrible friend. Get yourself together, Meghan...Lee is your best friend! You would never do that to her in a million years, never, ever, EVER! Just get him out of your head!

I don't know...maybe it's not about him. Maybe it's just because he's the first guy I've gotten close to since Mark. Maybe that's why I'm so confused. I just hope it passes. I can't ever tell Lee. I can tell her anything but this. She loves him so much – she would never forgive me for this. She would kill me if she knew.

Aletheia stopped reading and put the papers down. *She would kill me if she knew.* She knew she was in trouble; really big trouble. She looked across the table at Detective Reese.

"Look...I know this looks bad. I get it. But I had no idea she thought about Adam that way! I swear! And I didn't kill my friend! I loved Meghan – I would never hurt her. You have to believe me!"

Reese sat silent and stared at her – a cold, icy stare of a man who had been lied to a thousand times and seen crocodile tears on at least half of those occasions. He lowered his voice and said to her, "You know what I believe, young lady? I believe you. I believe that you didn't know about this...at least not until that night. I believe that you found out that night – the two of you argued, and you pushed her. Maybe you didn't mean to push her over the railing and kill her – maybe that part was an accident. If it was, I suggest you come clean right now and tell me, because it will go a lot easier for you if you do."

It was more than Aletheia could bear. She broke down and cried. She had never felt so trapped, so defeated in her life. They thought she killed Meghan, and truth be told there was part of her that wondered if she had too, even if she couldn't fathom it. As she sat there and wept, Reese kept badgering her, kept hammering at her to confess. He went back and forth between yelling at her and soothingly offering her options to confess to a lesser crime. Her head was spinning, her vision blurred with tears, Aletheia didn't know what was going to happen next. Somewhere inside her, though, her stubborn resolve sparked to life.

No! I didn't do this! I would never! Her fear turned to anger and determination. She thought of Adam, and wondered what he was going through then. That thought proved to be her saving grace. In that moment, wondering what he was experiencing, she immediately knew what he would do if he was being accused. Steadying herself, she wiped her tears as Reese watched her, finally now silent.

He probably thinks I'm going to confess. Well screw him.

"I didn't kill Meghan. She was my best friend and I loved her. If you don't believe me…don't. Am I under arrest, or not?"

Reese stared at her for a long time before he answered. "Not at this time. Not yet."

Aletheia nodded, composing herself as best she could for a woman who had just fallen apart in front of a complete stranger who held her life in his hands.

"Then I'll be leaving now. I won't be answering any more questions without a lawyer."

Reese took a deep breath, and let it out, his disappointment evident. He nodded his head slowly and got up from the table, and silently led her out the door. Before releasing her into the waiting room, he looked her in the eyes with that icy stare and said, "Don't leave town."

Aletheia returned his stare as best she could, and then turned and walked out of the waiting room, and all the way out of the building as fast as she could. Spotting a small coffee shop across the street she raced to it, and when she got inside, bee-lined to the restroom. Hurrying inside it she locked the door, sank down against the wall, and cried.

5

Adam looked across the table at Detective Marsh. He had decided that he did not like the man; he reminded him of a corporate yes man who was all smiles and niceties while he slowly set you up for a fall so he could advance. Adam tried to shake the feeling – it really wasn't a fair assessment, but nonetheless it was the impression he got from him. Still, he was determined to cooperate with the police as much as possible. Even though he was getting a bad feeling about the way the police were behaving, Adam had seen James take his own situation from bad to worse more than once by not cooperating with them. Marsh sat down across from him and took out a voice recorder and set it on the table, pressing the keypad to turn it on.

The detective's questions were standard – how long have you known the victim, what is your relationship to her, did you know of anyone who would have had a reason to harm her – the usual questions, at least from what Adam knew. He answered them as straightforwardly as he could, stiffer in his responses now that he felt on guard. He found himself getting irritated with the redundancy of the questions – many of them were the same ones he had answered when he had given the police a statement two days before. He told Detective Marsh so, and the man nodded knowingly.

"I know…my apologies. The same questions over and over get frustrating, but it's all just standard procedure." Adam rolled his eyes in frustration, and Marsh noticed. He stopped asking questions for a minute then, and leaned back in his chair, looking at Adam.

"Okay then, let's see if there's anything else we need to know that we haven't already asked. What was Miss King and Miss Young's relationship like?"

Adam's eyebrow lifted at the question, and he paused before he answered. "What was it like? I don't know, like best friends. They were inseparable. Like sisters."

Marsh nodded as Adam answered as though that had been exactly what he had thought too, but continued on. "They ever fight? Ever seem…catty, with each other? You know how women can be."

Adam felt his spine stiffen at that question. He was liking this man less and less by the second. "Catty? No, they never got 'catty' with each other. Like I said – they got along great."

"So they never fought? Never argued?"

"No. Why do you ask?"

Instead of answering, the detective just continued to ask questions. "How about you? What was your relationship with Miss Young like?"

Adam was actually caught a little off guard by that. "I told you…she was my girlfriend's roommate. We were friends. Not as close as the two of them, but good friends."

"You and her ever date?"

"No...I met her through Lee. I didn't know her before that."

"Too bad...she was a really beautiful young woman. That was why I asked before...about Aletheia. Having a friend that pretty be so close with her boyfriend – it's amazing she never got jealous. My wife would kill me if I spent time with a girl that pretty."

The hair was raising on the back of Adam's neck. He didn't like this line of questioning. "Yeah, Meghan was really pretty. And so is Lee, and I love her, so I wasn't really interested in cheating on her with her friend, if that's what you're getting at."

"No...I wasn't saying you were cheating. I was just saying women get jealous. But hey, not a bad problem to have, right – having two beautiful women in love with you?"

Adam exhaled sharply, getting visibly annoyed now. "No, that wouldn't be a bad problem to have, I guess, but I wouldn't know. I only have one – Lee."

Marsh put a surprised look on his face. It was obvious to Adam the man was playing a game with him. "Oh, you didn't know? Miss Young was in love with you, Adam. It says so right in her journal. She had dreams about you all the time." Marsh seemed to have stopped moving now and was watching him intently.

Adam's face screwed up in confusion – a much more genuine expression of surprise than Marsh had been able to muster. "What are you talking about? Meghan wasn't in love with me. Meghan was still in love with her ex – they broke up like six months ago. What do you mean, she wrote it in her journal?"

"You don't believe me? Fine – take a look for yourself."

The detective opened a file folder on the table that Adam hadn't really noticed to that point. *He must have been planning to spring this on me all along...* Marsh pushed a small stack of photocopies across the table to Adam and sat back, watching the young man as he read the handwriting recorded on them.

Had another dream about Adam last night. It was amazing...he was...amazing. I don't understand why I keep having these dreams. It was funny at first but now...I just don't know. I don't understand why I can't get him out of my head – I keep seeing him, even during the day. He just pops into my thoughts, all the time. I don't feel like I'm in love with him – he feels like more of a brother to me – but maybe I am? Am I? Maybe I am and I don't realize it? What the hell is wrong with me? I am such a horrible friend. Get yourself together, Meghan...Lee is your best friend! You would never do that to her in a million years, never, ever, EVER! Just get him out of your head!

I don't know, maybe it's not about him. Maybe it's just because he's the first guy I've gotten close to since Mark. Maybe that's why I'm so confused. I just hope it passes. I can't ever tell Lee. I can tell her anything but this. She loves him so much – she would never forgive me for this. She would kill me if she knew.

Okay, tomorrow's a new day. Maybe it's time for me to start dating again. I need to get Adam out of my head. Mark too. I need to move on. Maybe moving on from Mark will help me stop obsessing about Adam...who knows. I just hope I don't have another dream tonight. They certainly don't help any. I wonder if he's really that...

Adam pushed the papers away with a start, not wanting to read anymore. He could feel the color in his face; feel the heat rising in his cheeks. He was confused, embarrassed, and off-guard. If he didn't recognize Meghan's flowing script, he wouldn't have believed she wrote it. Marsh just stared at him like a bird watching a worm.

"Look, I know this looks weird, maybe even bad…but I had no idea. We were close…we were friends, but…I had no idea she felt that way. It's probably just like she said – her heart belonged to Mark. She was probably just confused."

Marsh looked at him, and the look of surprise on his face this time seemed more genuine. "Huh. Well, maybe you didn't know…but what about Aletheia? Did she know? Women have a way of sensing these things."

Adam hadn't thought of that possibility. He was a very smart guy, but he wasn't always the quickest when it came to picking up on people's emotions. Lee, on the other hand, was very perceptive when it came to people. *Did she know about this? Could she have sensed it? How the hell did I miss it?*

"Not that I know of…she never said anything like that…never acted jealous or anything. Besides, you don't know Lee – even if it were true, she would understand that it was just about Mark, and she would work through it with Meghan. It's not like Meghan was going to act on it."

"You're right. I don't know Aletheia…but are you sure *you* do?"

Adam's jaw tightened and he looked Marsh square in the eye. His words were slow and deliberate. "Yes. I am."

Marsh nodded. "Tell me again what you were doing the

43

night of the murder." It was the first time the detective had openly referred to Meghan's death as a 'murder' since they had started talking.

"I'll tell you, but not again, because this is the first time you've asked me. I was in Lee and Meghan's room, in the bed with my girlfriend."

"And Aletheia?"

"I just told you, she was in the bed with me."

"Can you verify that she was in the bed between the hours of three and four o'clock in the morning?"

"Yes, I can."

"How? She could have gotten up while you were sleeping. It seems like a stretch to me to say you can verify that she was in bed the entire night."

"Why don't you just come out and say it? Is she a suspect?"

"We haven't ruled her out yet."

"What do you mean you haven't ruled her out yet? I just ruled her out for you!" Adam's anger got the best of him, his voice raising with his temper at the detective's unending stream of implied accusations. He looked at Marsh again, and was immediately incensed by the look of smug satisfaction on the detective's face. Adam understood the man was just doing his job – just following a lead – but Marsh didn't know everything. Adam took great pleasure in relating one more fact to the detective that would throw a monkey wrench in all of his smug theories.

"Actually, I was up studying for my history exam all night. I never fell asleep. Lee was in the bed with me the entire time. And I am willing to testify to that, asshole."

The tiniest flicker of anger crossed Marsh's face at the last word. It was gone in an instant though, replaced by a look of patient determination, like a man chipping away at a something he knew would eventually break.

"Really? So tell me, if you were awake all night, how come you didn't see Miss Young get up and leave the room? Or did she fall six stories out of her bed?"

"You've seen the room, detective – they have armoires separating their two sides, for privacy."

"You didn't hear her get up?"

"iPod. I like to study to music."

"Would you be willing to submit to a polygraph? If you're telling the truth, you've got nothing to hide."

Adam had watched his brother go down this road before as well; he had also read too many psychology textbooks to fall for the ruse. Polygraph machines weren't good predictors of deception like they claimed to be; instead, they were simply a device for interrogators to get more information out of the people they were questioning.

"Why, so you can have me take it and then lie to me about the results and tell me I 'failed' to see if I confess under the pressure? No thank you. There's nothing to confess. I'm not lying. Lee didn't do it."

"I see." Marsh grew quiet and stared at Adam for some time, nodding his head gently. He looked like he was about to ask another question, but by now Adam's anger had caught up with his initial shock; his brain had caught up with his adrenal system. Before Marsh could utter another word, Adam said, "I think we've answered enough of your questions. I don't think I'll be answering any more without a lawyer. Am I being detained? Because if not, I'm done here."

Marsh's face changed instantly from the range of emotions he had displayed during the interrogation to pure business. "Very well." The detective got up to open the door for Adam to leave, but before he could leave the room, Marsh put his hand out and placed it on Adam's chest, stopping him.

"You know, you seem like a decent guy. Maybe you didn't know about Miss Young, or your girlfriend, or the little cat fight they were having over you. Maybe you had nothing to do with any of this. Hell, who knows – maybe you nodded off that night and you really never did see her get up out of that bed. Just understand one thing: if you lie to protect her, we'll figure it out. And when we do, you'll go down with her. You've got your whole life ahead of you, and if you tell the truth, one day you won't even remember loving her. But if you lie to protect her, you'll remember her every single day as the girlfriend who wasn't worth ruining your life for. Think about it."

Adam returned the detective's stare with a cold, hard one of his own. "She didn't do it. There is absolutely no doubt. I know, because I was there all night, and I was awake the whole time. And while you sit here harassing us, whoever did do this to Meghan is out there getting away with it. Now please take your hand off my chest. I don't like being touched."

Marsh nodded and took his time taking his hand away, perhaps just to prove a point, and led Adam out to the waiting area without saying another word. When they got there, he told him he could wait for Aletheia there.

Before he left, Marsh added, "If your memory becomes clearer, call me. Oh, and don't leave the area."

Adam ignored him and walked away, wondering if the man believed him.

6

Adam took a seat and leaned his head back on the wall, closing his eyes and trying to get his thoughts together as he waited for Aletheia. He wondered how everything had changed so quickly – it seemed like just yesterday that everything was normal and he and Lee were having lunch with Meghan and laughing over her frustrations with one of her professors. It was hard to believe that over a mere four days, she was dead, and Lee was now on the verge of being arrested for her murder. He was roused from his thoughts by the vibration of his phone in his pocket. Taking it out, he saw a text message from Aletheia.

at the coffee shop across the street. when you're
done come over

Hopping to his feet he shot a text back quickly.

on my way

As Adam walked out of the building he started to worry. He had been so angry and shocked at the whole ordeal – so upset about the detective's accusations and their long-term implications – that he hadn't had a chance to think about what

Aletheia's questioning must have been like.

If they think she did it...

Adam picked up his pace and hurried out into the street. Just across from the station he saw the small coffee shop, and he rushed across the streams of moving traffic to get there. Pushing through the door, he scanned the room and saw Aletheia. She was sitting alone in a back corner, watching for him, and when she saw him she nearly leapt to her feet. Adam closed the distance to her in a blink and within seconds they collided in a tight, desperate hug. Aletheia tried her best to hide her tears from the other patrons but Adam could hear her gentle sobs, feel her body jerk with each one as it burst from her.

"Come on...let's go someplace we can talk."

Aletheia nodded and grabbed her purse before leaving the shop with Adam. A few of the other customers looked up, but only for a moment. She picked up her pace and walked as fast as she could out the door.

When they got outside, Aletheia said, "I just want to go home."

Adam nodded and called a cab company as they walked the few blocks to a nearby park he had seen before when driving through this part of town. After he hung up the phone, a thought dawned on him. *They must have thought she would confess. That's why they gave us a ride to the station – they weren't planning on her coming back.* He reached down and held her hand more tightly. They soon arrived at the park and sat down on a bench together. Aletheia was trembling, staring at the ground in shock.

All Adam could say was, "I know what probably happened to you in there, because I know what happened to me. We can talk about it at soon as we get home, okay?"

Aletheia nodded in agreement, knowing that to utter one word about what had happened at that moment would be to unleash a torrent of thoughts that were raging inside her. If she started, who knows what she would say or how loud she would say it.

If the time waiting for the cab to arrive had seemed long, the cab ride itself felt like an eternity. Aletheia and Adam remained silent the entire ride, each not daring to say a word and staring out the window. The cab driver tried to make small talk with them, which made it even worse. Adam did his best to reply, although he was sure he made no sense at all at least twice. All the while, if the cabbie could have seen the seat between them in his rearview mirror he would have seen two people holding hands and gripping each other's so tightly that it looked like they might break them. When they got to the house Adam paid the cabbie and sent him off, and then ushered Aletheia inside.

The minute he closed the door she spun around and threw herself into him, sobbing as she blurted out, "They think I did it! They think I killed Meghan! Adam, they're going to try to send me to prison!"

Adam held her tight, trying his best to console her, although he really wasn't sure how. He couldn't dispute what she said. It certainly looked like she was their prime suspect, and if so, it was only a matter of time before they showed up with a warrant for her arrest. The thought made him feel sick. Half of him wept with Aletheia; he couldn't help some tears from coming to his eyes at the thought of what she was going through. He was afraid. The other half of him – the half that had brought him through a hellish life in the slums – was already turning to stone. He would not let this happen to her. His mind was already racing, planning on how he would protect her and what they should do to prepare themselves.

After a while, Aletheia's sobs lessened and her tears started to subside. Adam got her some tissue and helped her to a seat at the kitchen table.

"We'll figure this out together. There's always a way. Guilty jerks get away with crimes everyday – I'm sure we can figure out how to keep two innocent people out of jail."

Aletheia looked at him blankly through red, bloodshot eyes. "What do you mean, two? Why would you go to jail? They didn't say anything about you being part of it to me. Did they threaten you too?"

Adam nodded his head and said, "They think I'm covering for you. I'll explain in a minute. But first, tell me what happened. Tell me everything."

Aletheia took a deep breath and started telling Adam what had happened in the interrogation room. Her voice shook as she started to recount the ordeal, but as she continued she got steadier and calmer; it felt good to share it with someone. When she got to the part about Meghan's journal she hesitated, revealing it to him piece by piece. Aletheia watched him carefully as he listened.

When she had gotten it all out, Adam nodded his head solemnly and said, "I know. They told me too. They showed me her journal." He looked at her with an earnest expression. "Lee…I had no idea. I mean, I never got any type of vibe like that. I hope you don't think…"

Aletheia shook her head, managing a weak smile. "Of course not. I know, Adam. I didn't know either. She never said a word to me. I can understand why – I don't know if I would have told her either if the situation had been reversed." Adam nodded in understanding as she added, "But that doesn't make it look any better. They think her and I went out to the porch while you were asleep and she told me. They think I got mad and pushed her."

Adam shook his head. "I know! It's crazy! I tried to tell him but the smug bastard was so sure he had it figured out. He thought I was lying." Adam noticed then that Aletheia was shaking again, this time so badly that he could see it beyond just her hands. He leaned forward to take her hand and to his surprise she pulled it away.

She looked down at her lap and said to him, "Adam…I have something to tell you. I'm not sure how."

He looked at her with his head tilted like he always did when he thought she said something odd or funny. "Don't be silly – you can tell me anything. What is it?"

Aletheia took a deep breath and forced herself – it was very hard to do – to look in his deep brown eyes. She loved those eyes. "There's something I haven't told you. I didn't want to say anything because I thought it was nothing. I thought it was just me being crazy. But now I'm really scared." Her voice broke when she said the last words, and Adam pulled his chair closer and locked eyes with her.

"Lee, you don't have to be scared. I'm right here, and I won't let anything happen to you. What is it?"

She looked at him then, a small, sad smile crossing her lips. *This could be the last time he looks at you like this. If you did this, Aletheia, this might be the last time you ever see him – at least, the him you know. What if you're guilty and he realizes he wants nothing to do with you? What if he hates you? Would you blame him?* Aletheia forced herself past the thoughts running through her head. She was a good person: she believed in telling the truth and in being held accountable. She would do the right thing.

"Adam, you know the nightmares I've been having?"

"Yes, of course. What about them?"

"Well, I only told you half of it."

"What do you mean?"

"There have actually been two recurring nightmares. There's the one I told you about, and one other." She paused, gathering the last shred of her strength to tell this man what was sure to make him look at her the same way that detective had – like a vicious monster. "In the other one, it's me and Meghan. And when I'm with her, I feel like…like she wants you for herself. And in every dream…I kill her, Adam."

Adam's face looked shocked, but the look changed to sympathy in seconds.

"Oh, Lee…"

Aletheia cut him off before he could even say whatever sweet thing he had been about to say. "Wait. I need to tell you the rest. The night that Meghan died...was killed – the night she was killed – I had the same dream. Every time I have it, I kill her in a different way. But that night..." She let out a big sigh before she continued, resigned to her fate like a prisoner on death row who has realized they are out of appeals. "…that night I dreamed that I followed her out onto the porch, and pushed her off. I saw her land on the ground below. I saw her die. I even knew how she landed, Adam."

Adam looked at her horrified. Aletheia's heart broke in that moment; her worst fear realized. *And there it is…the beginning of the end. Not going to stop now. He's a good person – he deserves to know the truth.*

"Adam…I swear to you…I don't remember doing it. I don't remember pushing her. I don't even feel like I did it – I mean, why would I? I loved her…and I didn't even know about her feelings for you. But you need to know that…maybe I did. Maybe I did and I'm just going crazy. Maybe I've lost my mind. How could I do something like that and not know it?" She looked to him for just one sliver of hope…anything. She needed something. She had nothing else left. Instead of looking at her with concern, his horrified look had turned to confusion. He looked at her now as thought she was crazy.

"Lee…are you serious? Are you really worried you did this?"

As she nodded in agreement, Adam's mind raced back over the last few days and it dawned on him that he had never told her. There had never been a time or a reason to, especially considering he had no idea she was carrying around this fear and this burden.

"Lee, listen to me." He smiled as he looked into her beautiful, green eyes. He loved those eyes. "You didn't kill Meghan."

Before he could finish, she burst out at him, her pain and fear coming through in her voice. "How do you know? How do you know I didn't?"

"Because…that's what I'm trying to tell you. It's the same thing I told that detective. You didn't do it, because I was right next to you all night. I was awake the whole time, studying for my exam."

"Yeah, but you don't know. What if you drifted off? What if I got up in the night and did that while you were asleep. It wouldn't have taken long. What if I'm sick?"

Adam interrupted the panic-stricken words that were flowing from her mouth. "Lee! I had my headphones on, so I guess I never heard Meghan get up and go out on the porch – but you were asleep next to me the entire time. All the way up until they found her in the morning. I think I'd know if you got up right next to me. I didn't fall asleep. Not once."

Aletheia's face was a mask of confusion. She wondered if he was just saying it to protect her, but she knew Adam and that wasn't something he would do. He was very honest, especially with her. Yet none of it made sense. Adam kept at her, seeing her confusion and realizing she needed a little more prodding to truly accept her innocence.

"Hey – listen to me. I know the dream freaked you out – it would freak me out too – but you couldn't have possibly done it. I was right there the whole night. Don't you get it? It would have been impossible. I was in your bed, watching you. You were having nightmares again."

Aletheia's shoulders slumped, her brain finally accepting defeat. Adam would never lie about something this big, even to protect her. Actually, the more she thought about it, that wasn't true. He would lie to the police, or to anyone else; but he wouldn't lie to *her* about it.

I guess I didn't do it. Why am I surprised? I'm not a murderer – I would never do that. But that doesn't explain the nightmares. She shook her head left to right, trying to make sense of what she knew. It was like trying to put a puzzle back together when it was obvious the pieces didn't fit; they didn't even seem like they came from the same puzzle. It felt like there were two stories unfolding: one the story of an innocent girl, and the other the story of a guilty one. And the dreams didn't fit the story she had now. The one where she got to be innocent.

Adam – seeing that he had finally gotten through to her – leaned forward and grabbed her in a big hug. She hugged him back, her eyes welling up, only this time with tears of relief. She still was in a lot of trouble, but at least she wasn't losing her mind. At least she wasn't a murderer. When they finally let go Adam took her hand and held it.

"Do you mean to tell me that you've been walking around for four days wondering if you pushed Meghan over that railing?" His face contorted into a mask of emotion. "I'm so sorry...that must have been awful. And then with them interrogating you at the station like that, and you wondering if you did it?"

She sat back up, brushing the brown curls out of her eyes. "It wasn't fun." They both sat there for a few minutes, quietly digesting all the things they had been forced to absorb in the last few hours, both good and bad.

She finally broke the silence and said to him, "I still don't understand the nightmares. I mean, they're the reason I thought I might be guilty. I thought I was losing my mind. It just doesn't make any sense. Why did I dream that? Why did I dream that on that night? And how did I know how she landed?" She looked at Adam, perplexed. "I feel like I saw her death."

Adam's mind went to work on logical explanations right away. "I don't know...it could just be a coincidence. How many ways can a person land?"

"Yeah, but think about it. Even if I were having those dreams for a while, what are the chances I would have dreamed about…it…happening that exact way on that exact night? It's just creepy."

"I don't know. Maybe you're psychic? I don't believe in ninety-nine percent of the people who say they are, but it's possible. That *is* pretty crazy."

Aletheia shrugged. "I don't know anything anymore. I really don't understand, but I don't like it. It feels…creepy. Especially when I think of the other dreams I've had too. I feel like I'm in some sort of horror movie."

Adam exhaled. "I don't know what to tell you. I don't understand why this is happening either, but I'm in it with you."

Aletheia bit her lip, a little harder than she intended to, and looked down in her lap. "Adam…do you believe in stuff like that? Like, supernatural things?"

Adam thought about it for a moment and said, "Yes and no. I don't believe most of the stuff people claim to have seen. People are liars, and the ones that don't lie are usually confused. But in general…yes, I believe in that stuff."

Aletheia nodded. "I know this sounds crazy, but…what if I'm being haunted or something?" She looked up at him and continued, "I mean, I keep having nightmares about this dark figure chasing me, and about…killing my best friend…and then she dies the exact same way. Before I was so scared I was going crazy – that it was coming from inside me –I didn't even think about the alternative. What if it's coming from…the outside?"

Adam looked at her. "You really think that?"

"Do you have a better explanation?"

Adam thought about it. He wished he could answer yes – could tell her what it was and how to make it go away – but he couldn't.

"No. I'm sorry…I don't."

Aletheia just shook her head in confusion. "Me either."

Before she could continue, Adam looked at her and said, "Listen…I know there are a million other things on your mind right now, but we have to starting thinking about protecting you. We need to find you a lawyer and we need to find one quick. I don't like where all this is going."

Aletheia understood and agreed. She added, "I know we do but I don't even know where to start."

He looked at her and said, "Maybe my brother's lawyer?"

"Your brother's lawyer is in California. What can he do to help?"

"Maybe my brother's lawyer can recommend someone good up here? He might know someone."

Aletheia nodded, still deep in thought about the bizarre string of recent events. "Okay…while you call him, I'm going to call my mom again."

Adam was surprised when a human voice answered the line at the attorney's office and not a recording. Asking the receptionist for his brother's lawyer, Adam was told he was in court that afternoon but that he could leave a message on his voicemail. He left all the pertinent details – those he felt comfortable sharing by phone – and his contact information and hung up. In the other room he could hear Aletheia's panicked voice. He could tell by the tone of the conversation that her mother was upset and was upsetting her as well.

7

It was a long time before Aletheia came out, visibly shaken from the call. "My mom's freaking out. She has to work tonight but she wants to come see us in the morning."

Adam nodded. "Sure. Of course."

"She's calling my uncle. I'm not really sure there's much he can do to help, but he's always been there for me. Who knows...with his job, maybe he can help find out what really happened to Meghan and clear this up. He has contacts at nearly every police station in the state."

As if on cue, her cellphone rang in her hand, the contact name "Alex Mann" displaying on the screen. She eagerly answered it.

"Uncle Alex?"

The gravelly voice on the other end immediately made her feel better. At ease. Safe. "Hey Pigtails, your mom tells me you're in trouble. What's going on?"

Pigtails. Her uncle had been calling her that since she was a little girl and her mother used to put her in pigtails for school. He had always thought it was cute. Aletheia had many fond memories of her uncle, of sitting on his lap and playing with his mustache, which even then was as gray as his hair. He had been there for her throughout her life after her dad had died when she was a baby. Although his job as an investigative reporter kept him away traveling all the time – he worked for a large news company – he had visited her and her mother a lot when she was a child. He always made it a point to check in on them, see how Aletheia was doing, and make sure they had everything they needed. Any time she had gotten into trouble, he had always found a way to come see her and help her out.

Aletheia started spilling every detail she could think of to her uncle, with the exception of the dreams. She didn't want to tell him about those. Aletheia valued her uncle's approval very much. She didn't want to give him any reason not to approve of her – not that he ever had. Besides, now that Adam had made her realize she hadn't done this – that she couldn't have – she didn't think it was important.

Best to just leave that detail to me and Adam. She told her uncle everything else – everything she had been through in the past few days, including what had happened to Meghan, the eyewitness, and the awful experience with the police they had been through today. She even told him the details about Meghan becoming obsessed with Adam and writing about it in her journal, and how the detective had accused her of becoming jealous and doing this to her friend as the result of a fight over him. Alex just listened on the other end of the line as she spoke. *Knowing him he's probably memorized every last word and detail I've said already.* When she was done relaying all of her story to him, or at least all that she could remember right now, he blew out a long sigh into the phone, and then he spoke.

"Well, kiddo…you are in quite a bind there. I'm really sorry about your friend. Losing someone is never easy, and it's ten times worse when it's unexpected."

She tried not to think of her father. Although she had been just a baby, she knew how hard it must have been on him to lose his only brother.

"The first thing I'd say is they're not telling you all the evidence they have. In my experience, the only way they'd go after you like that is if they already think you did it and had at least some evidence to back it up. Now as to what that evidence is…seems pretty flimsy to me to just assume that based off the journal stuff. You said there was an eyewitness?"

"Yes. She was on the news. She looked like a homeless woman or something."

"Well, that'll help you if it goes to trial – the fact that she's homeless, I mean. But if I had to bet, I'd say they showed her some pictures of girls in your dorm and she identified you. That would explain why they locked in on you already. Listen, kiddo – don't worry. I have one thing I absolutely have to take care of tomorrow and then I'll be on the first flight I can get out there. Everything's going to be fine."

Aletheia breathed a sigh of relief as soon as he said he was coming. Even though she wasn't sure how he could help, just knowing he was there made her feel safer. *He'll know what to do. He always knows what to do. The man has literally been in war zones. Besides, he covers this kind of stuff all the time – he'll know who to talk to.*

Alex's gravelly voice spoke again on the other end of the phone. "Now listen…I'm going to tell you three things. First, I need you to do something. I need you to get a good lawyer, right away. I know a few there in Seattle who are top-notch. I'll send you their names and contact info. You get the first one you can get a hold of and tell them you're my niece. Tell them I'll be covering the bill – and this is no time to argue about that. Second, I want you to know what's probably going to happen from here. They're probably going to get a warrant to search your places. Your dorm room...maybe Adam's place too. Just be prepared. When they search, don't get in their way and don't make a scene or they can arrest you. Make sure you don't consent to let them search anything not on the warrant, but if they do just note it and stay out of the way. It's a lot easier to keep you out of jail for now than to get you out of jail once you're in. Understand?"

Aletheia nodded as she spoke. "Yes. We were just in the middle of trying to find a lawyer when I called Mom. I'll do both of those things."

"Good. And third," he took a deep breath before continuing. "Now listen, I don't want you to panic – like I said, everything will be fine. But you need to know that sometimes these things happen slow and sometimes they happen fast. It all depends on what they think they have for evidence. If, by some chance, it happens fast and they come with a warrant to arrest one or both of you before I get there – don't worry. Just try to stay calm and do what they say and don't answer any questions without your lawyer. I'll do everything I can to get you out. Understand?"

"I understand." Aletheia trusted her uncle, but the thought of being arrested and going to jail to stand trial for a murder she didn't commit terrified her. Her uncle's voice kept her from succumbing to her fear for the moment.

"You okay, kiddo?"

"No...but I will be. I'll be okay. I didn't do it, so even if it takes a long time to sort out it'll be okay."

"Okay then. You hang tight. I'll be there as fast as I can. Love you."

"Love you too."

Aletheia hung up the phone, feeling calmer than she would have thought, given the circumstances. She guessed it was all a matter of accepting their situation for what it was. A few days ago, the thought of being accused of murder was terrifying. Now that it had actually happened, it was still scary, but her brain had shifted to adjust. Once Aletheia was off the phone she filled Adam in on everything her uncle said.

When she was finished, Adam said, "Wow...well, I'm glad he's coming out here. I hope he can help. That's pretty scary. Like you said, though, I guess the thought of sitting in jail awaiting trial and then getting found innocent is a lot different than the thought of going to jail for life. We'll do what we have to."

Adam thought for a moment and then added, "If they are going to search this place, I hope they don't take my guns. I can't hide them...that'll just look suspicious. I have a permit so they know I have them."

Aletheia had never liked that Adam had guns in his house. Not that he had many; a couple of handguns that he had told her about and even showed her in an effort to help her not be afraid. He kept them for home defense, in two small safes with fingerprint locks – one by his bed and one in the living room. It was all very James-Bondish to Aletheia, but again, she knew what he had been through and why it was important to him. At least he handled them safely; Adam had taken all the gun safety and home defense shooting classes he could find. She knew if the time came when he ever had to use them he would use them responsibly.

Adam looked at her and said, "I can't imagine there'd be anything, but is there anything in your room you want to get out of there in case they search it? It might not matter. I'm guessing they're going to search here – and my car too – but who knows?"

Aletheia thought about it and shook her head, "Nothing I can think of. If I stay over awhile I'll need some more of my clothes and stuff eventually, but that's it. I guess we could go by tomorrow morning…"

Aletheia's words were interrupted by the ding of an incoming message on her phone. She looked at the screen and saw a text message from her uncle with the names of three lawyers in Seattle and their contact info, just as he had promised.

After calling the first one and leaving a message, they found luck with the second. His name was Matthew Donovan, and as soon as his secretary told him who had referred them he called them back personally and made himself available to see them the next morning. They took the appointment, which immediately made Adam feel relieved. In his mind, the more prepared they were, the better.

Aletheia barely slept that night, tossing and turning in the sheets but getting little actual rest. Adam's restlessness next to her told her he was having difficulties of his own. Although the initial tidal wave of panic when they found out she was a suspect had subsided, it had been replaced by a more constant, relentless state of anxiety. It was as though a dark and ominous cloud had descended on their lives and they could do nothing but wait for the storm it brought. Every sound, every creak, every bump in the night flooded her mind with images of police bursting into the house to arrest them. She spent the entire night thinking the door was about to come crashing in any minute. It was a long time before sleep finally took her.

She woke late in the night, roused by the sound of something moving in the other room. Adam lay asleep next to her, his quiet, steady breathing telling her he had finally found deep sleep. The sound again...she knew she had heard something. Scared, she gently shook Adam's shoulder, trying to wake him.

"Adam...Adam, wake up," she whispered. "I hear something." Adam groggily opened his eyes and looked at her. It took a moment of her whispered pleas before he registered what she was saying, but as soon as he did, he shook his head to wake up and sat bolt upright in the bed.

"Stay here," he whispered. Reaching over to the small safe on his nightstand, he placed his fingers in the grooves that held the scanners and it opened. He took out the revolver inside and quietly rolled out of the bed. Aletheia watched as he slunk silently to the bedroom doorway, peeked out, and then disappeared into the other room. She heard a series of thumps and what sounded like a whimper, and then...nothing. It was quiet outside the bedroom doorway. She stopped breathing then, straining her attention towards the other room to hear something...anything. Unable to hear any sounds, she considered calling out to Adam but she was too afraid to. Rolling quietly out of her side of the bed, she looked around the room for something to defend herself with. The only thing she saw was the pair of samurai swords Adam had displayed on his wall.

That's weird...I thought he kept all his martial arts stuff in the garage? Not having time to overthink it, she crept over to them as quietly as she could and slowly – eternally slowly – slid the smaller one out of its sheath. *Waki-something. That's what he called it.* She grabbed it with two hands on the hilt, not having any idea how to use it except to stab or swing, and tip-toed as quietly as she could to the doorway.

Just as she moved out into the hallway, a dark form crashed into her. She screamed, and as she screamed she reflexively thrust out straight forward with the blade in her hand. She felt it – and heard it – slice through flesh as it ran through whatever was in front of her. Panic-stricken and blind in the dark, she kept her wits about her enough to hold tight onto the hilt of the weapon and pull it back out. As she did, it made the same sound it had when she had stabbed out with it. It sounded like slicing a large piece of meat for cooking. Whatever it was she had stabbed crumpled to the floor with a thud. She stumbled back against the doorframe as her hand fumbled up the wall to her right. Trembling, she managed to find the light switch and flip it up. The hallway filled with light.

She looked down in horror at Adam, lying on the hallway floor. He was bloodied and battered, his nose splattered across his face. On his stomach, a patch of blood was getting larger and spreading across his white t-shirt where the sword had entered his body.

Aletheia screamed, a scream of complete terror and pain ripped from her very soul as she fell to the floor, gripping the man she loved and crying to him how sorry she was. She didn't even feel the sword fall from her grasp; didn't hear its clanging as it hit the hardwood floor. She looked up frantically for help, and that was when she saw it. A shape – that was the only way to describe it – a shape of blurry darkness rushing towards her. Before she could react she was flung up against the doorway, held there by something large that she could feel but could not see. As she screamed she saw the blade lift off the ground in front of her as if by some unseen force. She heard the now familiar sound of it shearing through flesh as it hurtled forward and skewered her against the wall again and again. Each time the blade pierced the taught flesh of her stomach it sent jolts of searing hot pain through her abdomen. Somewhere in front of her she thought she heard a deep, guttural growl.

Aletheia woke screaming, Adam's hands on her shoulders, gently but firmly trying to shake her awake.

"Lee...Lee! Wake up. You're having a nightmare." She looked at him and shook uncontrollably, backing away like a scared animal for a moment. Adam moved forward and took her in his arms, rocking her back and forth as she trembled. "It was just a dream. It was just a dream. You're fine...you're right here with me."

It took some time for her to shake off the effects of the dream. Adam turned on the light on his nightstand. She looked at him – Adam – sitting right there in front of her. He was whole and healthy and alive, not bloodied or hurt. She turned her head towards the wall. No samurai swords hung there – not even a holder. *Right...they're in the garage.* A glance at Adam's nightstand showed her the small gun safe there, unopened.

Adam looked at her and said, "Another one? Are you okay?"

She just stared blankly and said, "Yeah, I'm okay. It was just so real. I'll be alright. I just need to shake it off." Adam hugged her then, and she buried her face in his chest, inhaling the smell of him in an attempt to bring herself to a happier place in her mind. Coming up for air, she hugged him back and put her chin over his shoulder. Opening her eyes again, she looked at the hallway and noticed that the light was on.

"Did you turn on the hallway light?"

Adam pulled away and turned to look at the lighted area outside the bedroom door. "Yeah...I turned it on when I got up to use the bathroom. Sorry – I must have forgotten to turn it off again."

Aletheia looked at the hallway suspiciously.

Adam saw the look and said, "Would it make you feel better if I checked the house?" With that, he got up to go out and inspect the rest of the house. Aletheia grabbed his arm and stopped him. The similarity to her nightmare was too much for her to bear.

"No...I'll go with you. We'll go together."

They walked through the entire house together, going from room to room and turning on lights as they went. After clearing the entire place, Adam looked to her and said, "See? There's nothing here. Everything's fine."

Aletheia conceded, feeling better at least that they hadn't found anything. But it still did not settle her mind completely. She wasn't sure if anything ever would.

8

It was near dawn before Aletheia found sleep again. She felt as though she had barely slept ten minutes when Adam woke her.

"Sorry, sleepyhead…time to get up. We've got to get to the lawyer's."

Aletheia groaned and turned over, forcing herself to roll out of the bed. She was so tired…the kind of tired that could make a person not even care about going to see the attorney who might be able to keep her out of jail.

Jail. The concept of that place stuck in her mind as she wrestled with her brain to wake. There were few things that terrified her as much as the thought of that. She had watched one too many reality prison shows to ever want to go to that horrible place. The fear she felt when thinking about it was finally enough to motivate her to roll out of the bed and force herself to stand.

A quick shower later and she and Adam were sitting and eating breakfast together. Adam looked up from his cereal between bites and asked, "We should have an extra twenty minutes if we leave right after this. You know what you need from your place? You need me to make you a list?"

Aletheia chuckled in her head. *Of course he wants to make a list.* "No...it's fine. I just need some more clothes for now." Her brain went over everything in her room, trying to think about her daily routine and remember anything she may have forgotten.

Adam popped his head up from his eating as if he had a revelation. "Oh! If they look through all your stuff, maybe we should hide those pics we took of you a couple of months ago? You know...*those* pics?"

Aletheia blushed over her spoon when she realized what he was talking about. "Oh God...I hadn't even thought of that! Thank you. I wouldn't want those jerks...eww..."

Adam nodded his head. "I know...anything else you can think of you wouldn't want them to find?"

"I don't know...my personal stuff I guess. My journal, my..." the bran flakes suddenly lost all taste in her mouth. She might as well have had a mouth full of dirt. The spoon felt heavy in her hand.

Adam stopped eating and looked at her concerned. "What? What is it?"

Aletheia put her hand to her mouth, covering it. "Oh no...oh no..."

"What's wrong?"

She looked up at Adam. "My journal...we've got to get my journal."

He looked at her and relaxed a little. "Oh! You scared me for a minute there. Of course we can get your journal. I wouldn't want those guys reading my personal thoughts either."

She cut him off. "No, no, no...my journal! The dreams I've been having, Adam. It's all in my journal! The dreams I've been having about Meghan, all of it...it's all in there. If they see that, they're never going to believe me. There's no way!"

Adam's eyes popped open a little wider when she told him about the dreams being recorded in there. His face darkened. "Oh...man. Okay, we need to get that out of your room and hide it somewhere. Better yet, we should just burn it in the fireplace," he said, motioning over his shoulder to the living room.

Aletheia nodded, getting up from the table and quickly rinsing the bowl in the sink. Adam was hastily scooping his last bites of cereal into his mouth. They practically ran out the door. Adam drove as fast as he felt he could to her dorm building without getting pulled over. Pulling up in front of it, they noticed two police cars parked in front of the building – one marked and one unmarked. They looked to each other worriedly. Adam slammed the car into park.

He turned it off and hopped out quickly, Aletheia mirroring him on the other side of the vehicle, and the two ran up to the building. Adam led the way, racing up the old wooden stairs, taking them three at a time all the way to the sixth floor. Even with her adrenaline flowing, Aletheia was breathing heavy and her heart was racing by the time they reached her level. She could feel the pores on her skin opening in preparation to sweat. Adam looked like he had just gotten up off the couch.

He looked at her and said, "Okay...deep breath. Let's not look nervous."

She nodded in agreement and took a few deep, shaking breaths. Adam took one large one, closed his eyes, and exhaled slowly. When he finished, he looked about as calm as a Buddhist monk. *I wish I could do that. Maybe I should take him up on that offer to teach me to meditate.* Adam gave her a glance, making sure she was ready, and as soon as he saw that she was he reached out and opened the wooden door and they walked out into the hallway as calmly as they could manage.

Moving down the hall, it became more and more obvious to Aletheia the further they got that they were too late. There were people lingering in the hallway, close to her room but not too close, watching her doorway like onlookers at the scene of a car accident. As she got closer, she could see that the door was open and had police tape stretched across it. Aletheia steeled herself and strode up to it, Adam following. When she got to the door she was stopped by a uniformed officer who was standing just inside the room.

"Whoa...you can't come in here. This is a crime scene. Come on...move along, or step back and keep your distance."

Aletheia stopped and said, "I live here. This is my room." She tiptoed and peeked over the officer's shoulder. Her room was full of activity. There were officers and a couple of men in suits taking pictures and putting items in boxes.

The officer at the door stopped short of the standard response he had been about to give her and cocked his head at her. "Hold on a sec." He then leaned back and shouted, "Reese! Come here!"

Aletheia's heart sunk at the mention of that name. She tried to control the fear welling within her, leftover from the last experience she had with this man. He had truly scared her then. She took another deep breath. *I won't be scared now. I won't!* The detective walked over towards the door and immediately recognized them.

"Miss King. Mister Parker. What can I do for you? Did one of you remember something else that you wanted to share with me?"

Aletheia could feel Adam beside her. Looking over at him, he looked like a hunting cat ready to spring. She knew that look, and she could see by the stony expression he wore that he was angry. When Adam was really angry, he didn't yell or scream. He just went blank, like a sheet of ice. *Of course he's angry...this is the first time he's seen Reese since I told him how he treated me. He wants to punch him in the face.* Aletheia pushed any fears of what might happen if Adam let himself indulge in that fantasy from her mind. She didn't have time to manage him at the moment.

"What's going on here, detective? I need to get in my room."

"I'm sorry, Miss King, but you'll have to wait. You can wait here in the hallway if you'd like."

"I need to get some things and I'm running late for an appointment. It'll just take a minute."

"That's not going to happen. We have a warrant to search this room. You can't remove anything from it until we're satisfied that we've completed our search." Reese got an inquisitive look on his face. "What is it that you were hoping to remove?" The emphasis he put on the word 'remove' made it very clear what he was implying.

Aletheia looked the detective squarely in the eye. Her stomach was in her throat, but she refused to let this bully of a man see her intimidated. She remembered her uncle's words. "You have a warrant? Can I see it?"

Reese's lips formed a flat line in his mouth. He reached into the pocket of the blue blazer he was wearing and produced a folded piece of paper and handed it to Aletheia. She opened the document up and read it. It was a jumble of headers, addresses, and titles, and a bunch of legal jargon. Aletheia understood it well enough. It gave them permission to search her room for evidence in connection with Meghan's death. It looked official, and it had a judge's signature on the bottom.

She handed it back to him, and he folded it back up and placed it in his pocket before asking her again, "So what was it you said you wanted to remove from the room?"

"Just some clothes." Aletheia fought hard to not swallow repeatedly. Her mouth had suddenly gone dry and her words were making a smacking sound when she spoke.

The detective nodded. "You look pretty stressed. You need these clothes…urgently?"

Taking it as a reminder that any signs of nervousness on her part would likely be viewed as further evidence of guilt by the man, Aletheia steadied herself. "No. But I'm running late for an appointment."

Reese simply shrugged. "Well…you can come back when we're done and collect any items you need." Aletheia looked to Adam, wondering what he was thinking, but her boyfriend's face was a stoic mask. *Knowing him he's probably wondering if he can storm in there and take them all out before they shoot him.* She could almost laugh at the tragedy of it all. She was truly and rightly screwed.

Keeping her composure despite the dread filling her, she replied to the detective, "Fine," and turned to walk away. Before she could take her second step she heard Reese's voice behind her.

"Miss King! You said you had an appointment. Might I ask where and when?"

Her uncle's voice filled her memory for the second time during the encounter. She didn't turn around. "If you have any more questions for me, you'll have to talk to my attorney." With that, she walked away down the hall. *Now I just have to hope I have one.*

Behind her, Reese watched her back for a moment and then looked to Adam, who was still standing there. "It's still not too late for you, kid."

Reese's comment was met with a stare from Adam that was so cold it even seemed to take the grizzled detective by surprise. His face an emotionless mask, Adam simply turned and followed Aletheia down the hallway, walking briskly to catch up.

Aletheia felt Adam come up beside her, not wanting to look back and see the stares of the other people in the hallway as she stalked off. She had recognized most of them as they had approached the room, and when she had first turned away from the detective she had seen the looks on those faces. They were not the looks of friends who knew and supported her. They looked down, or at each other, or even straight at her as she had passed, whispering to each other. They were the looks of people who thought they were seeing a monster unveiled; as though they didn't even know her at all. With every step she took, the same words echoed through her mind over and over again. *Shit, shit, shit, shit, shit!*

9

"I'm screwed." It was at least the fifth time she had said it in the car as they drove to the lawyer's office. "I am so screwed. They're going to read my journal and they're going to read the parts about my dreams and they're going to arrest me. What am I going to do?"

Adam tried his best to calm her and still pay attention to the road. The traffic in downtown Seattle was thick this morning. "I know it looks bad right now. But look – it's not going to do us any good to panic. Let's just get to the lawyer and see what he has to say. This Donovan guy – your uncle said he was good, right?"

"He just said all three of the ones he was sending me were good. I don't know anything about this guy in particular." She looked at Adam then, her face paler than he had remembered. He had seen her scared before – many of those nights she had nightmares she woke up in sheer terror – but this was different. She had the look of a trapped animal. She looked desperate. "Adam...do you think..."

He looked at her now, listening intently. Adam could sense that she had something important to say. "What is it?"

Her face screwed up, as though she was trying to comprehend something that made no sense to her but that she knew she had to consider. "Do you think I should run?"

Adam looked at her with wide eyes. "Are you serious?"

She shook her head. "I don't know. I mean...I don't know what else to do. They think I did it, and they have all this evidence, and...I'm sorry. I know it's crazy. I'm just talking crazy. I just don't know what else to do."

Adam watched her as carefully as he could while still driving. "Look...I understand. I'm scared too. Let's just talk to this lawyer first before we get ourselves even more freaked out than we need to be. He's probably been doing this awhile – maybe it's not as bad as we think. We're not lawyers, right? We don't know if what they have is even a lot of evidence or not."

Aletheia nodded her head absentmindedly. "I know. You're right. I'm just scared. I don't want to go to jail."

Adam took his right hand off the steering wheel and reached over to grasp hers in it. "Hey...look at me. I'm not going to let anything happen to you, okay?"

She smiled resignedly; it was the best she could muster. "Okay." Aletheia was silent for a minute or two before she started to talk again...about the case, about everything that had happened. She needed to think; to figure it all out. She needed to think out loud. Adam did his best to help her process it all. Soon they were pulling into an underground parking garage and then riding the elevator up to the eleventh floor of the building.

It's certainly a nice office. That's got to be a good sign,

Aletheia thought as she looked out the window behind Mr. Donovan. He had a beautiful view of the Seattle skyline. His furniture was all dark, polished wood and glass, with the exception of the comfortable-looking black leather chair he sat in. It didn't look like the office of an unsuccessful lawyer.

"So you are Alex Mann's niece? It's a pleasure to meet you. I'm Matthew Donovan. You can call me Matt." He flashed them a boyish grin.

Aletheia and Adam introduced themselves. Once the introductions were done, she asked, "So…how do you know my uncle?"

It wasn't just his grin that was boyish. He reminded her of a boy scout, actually, from his clean-cut short brown hair to the pinkish hue of his cheeks. "Your uncle's a damn good investigator. We met on a case I was working on. He helped me set an innocent man free who had spent the last fourteen years in prison." He then smiled and added, "He's a good friend." Matt's tone changed slightly then, and he seemed to get more serious. "You're here in my office, and that means you or someone you care about is in trouble with the law. Now tell me…what's going on?"

Aletheia looked at Adam and he nodded. They had discussed this in the car and agreed that she should tell this man everything, even about the dreams. After all, if he was to help them, he needed to know. Besides, Adam understood attorney-client privilege from all the messes he had been through with his brother, and he had assured Aletheia that anything she told Matt could never be used against her. She started telling Matt her story, from the beginning. He sat and listened intently the entire time, taking notes on a lined pad of paper in front of him with an expensive-looking pen. He would occasionally ask her to clarify a point here or there, or would turn to Adam and ask him questions when her story included him. Other than that, he just listened and let her tell her entire story from beginning to end. When she was done, he bit his lip and looked up at the ceiling for a minute, seemingly trying to reason through everything that had happened. He then exhaled and looked at them both.

"Well, first of all, let me say that I am very sorry for your loss. It's easy to forget about that in times like this. I hope you're both giving yourselves some kind of outlet to process that grief."

Aletheia and Adam were surprised to hear that kind of empathy from a lawyer, but they thanked him nonetheless. He continued on. "So...let me make sure I am summarizing the evidence you think they have against you accurately. Correct me as I go if I'm missing something. They have your journal which details dreams you had been having for the last few weeks where you kill Miss...Young because you think she is trying to steal your boyfriend. They have the victim's journal which details the fact that the victim had in fact been obsessing over your boyfriend during the same period. They have you within say, one hundred feet of the crime scene at the exact time of the crime. They have an eyewitness who saw the crime occur and said it was done by another woman around your age. And you think this eyewitness has, albeit mistakenly, identified you as the killer."

He looked to the two of them and Aletheia and Adam both nodded their heads. Aletheia was pale. *It sounds so bad when you say it all at once.*

Matt continued. "Okay, now your alibi. You say you were asleep in the room when the crime occurred. The only person who can corroborate this is your boyfriend, and he has. Adam –

you are prepared to testify that you were awake the entire time?" Adam nodded his head. "And she never got up and left the bed?" Adam shook his head. "No. She never even woke up."

Donovan got up and walked around the back of his chair, his chin in his hand. He was deep in thought. He turned to them both and said, "I want you both to understand that you can feel safe telling me anything. I am willing to represent you, and as your lawyer nothing you say to me can be used against you in court. I also want you to know that it is my duty to defend you to the best of my ability whether you are guilty or innocent. All people deserve a fair trial and a full defense." Adam let out a deep breath. He knew where this was going, because he had heard a similar speech before. The man then looked at Aletheia and continued what he was saying. "Aletheia, I need to ask you this once, and please do not be afraid or offended. Did you do it?"

Aletheia looked at him, sad that she even had to answer, but earnest nonetheless. "No. Of course not. I would never do that to anyone, and she was one of my best friends."

Matt smiled at her and said, "Good." He then looked to Adam. "And you, Adam. I need to know…are you telling the truth about never falling asleep? You never drifted off…not even once?"

Adam looked the man straight in the eye. "No. I was awake the whole time. She didn't do it. It's not even possible."

Matt nodded and smiled. "Good. Okay, so here's the way I see it. All the evidence they have is circumstantial, with the exception of the eyewitness. Now, if she did identify you from a photo that would normally be pretty damning, but didn't you say the murder occurred at around three or four in the morning?"

"Yes, that was what the police said."

"So we have a single eyewitness identifying you in the dark, on a porch six stories up from the other side of the street. On the other hand, we have your boyfriend lying in the bed next to you swearing you never left the bed. That's a decent alibi. Testimony of a spouse or a loved one regarding an alibi is normally taken with a grain of salt, as most people would be willing to lie to protect someone they love. But as long as you are a reliable witness, Adam, it should be enough to introduce reasonable doubt." He then asks Adam directly, "It's not usually an issue, but is there anything they could use to discredit you as a witness? Have you ever been convicted of a felony, or perjury, or lied under oath?"

Aletheia was watching Adam as Matt asked him his questions. His face changed the minute the last question had come out. He now looked like a deer in the headlights. She had never seen Adam look that way before. "Adam? Have you?"

Adam's shoulders slumped. "Dammit. I can't believe my family and their crap never stop coming back to haunt me. I'm sorry Aletheia." He turned towards the lawyer to explain, not able to look in Aletheia's eyes right then, which were wide open in surprise. "I lied under oath once…and I was caught. I was a minor at the time, but I don't know if they expunged it or not. It was my brother James – the idiot – the first time he got into really bad trouble. He needed an alibi, and I lied for him. He was my brother, and I was young. It was so stupid. I got caught – he was identified by like, four other people at the scene of the crime. I got a slap on the wrist, but it was on my record. Aletheia, I'm sorry."

Aletheia just looked at her boyfriend, surprise and

disappointment on her face. "Why didn't you tell me?"

Adam shook his head. "It never came up. You know how much crap there is in my past, and I just never got to that story with you yet. And when all this happened, I honestly hadn't thought of that or how it would affect this until now. I'm sorry."

Matt let out a sigh. "I see. Well, hopefully it's been expunged. If it hasn't we'll have it expunged as quickly as possible, but that may not happen in time. If they find it before we do, even if it gets expunged they can still find witnesses from that case to testify against your character. I'm not going to lie to you...it's not a death blow, but this hurts your defense. Your alibi rests on a witness that has lied under oath before to protect a loved one."

Aletheia saw the redness in Adam's cheeks. It was not often she saw him embarrassed or ashamed. She reached over and held his hand tight. "It's okay. It'll be okay."

Matt then looked at Adam and added, "You also said you had a lot of issues in your past. Anything I need to know about. Ever been arrested or convicted of anything?"

Adam shook his head. "No. Nothing. I try to stay out of trouble. My family – they're another story. My dad's in jail for life. My brother is in and out. My mom's been the cleanest, but she has...drug problems. She's been arrested a few times for it, and she's been to rehab."

Aletheia chimed in to defend him, "Adam's a great person. He pulled himself up out of all of that and now he's a college student, and a homeowner, and a good citizen."

Matt relaxed a bit and looked at them both and said, "Well...that is a good thing. You should be proud of yourself, Mr. Parker. I work with a lot of people who have backgrounds like yours. Most don't make it out. That will help if they try to call your character into question."

Donovan spent the last few minutes with them going over details and next steps. When they were finished and about to leave, Aletheia turned and asked him one last question. "Matt? In your opinion…what are the chances that they're going to arrest me and charge me with this?"

He looked at her then, and his voice softened. "Well, Miss King, I think that is a strong possibility that you need to prepare yourself for. For now, I hope you feel a little better. You have one extra person on your side today, and I can assure you, I am very good at my job."

Aletheia nodded and walked out of the office, thanking the man for his help.

The ride home in the car was quiet. The two of them could not stop thinking about the lawyer's answer to her last question. Adam in particular was deep in thought. *I can't believe it. I'm the only one who could have protected her and I can't even do that.* He looked over at Aletheia's thoughtful face. *Well I don't care what it takes. I will find a way. I'm not going to let her rot in jail for something she didn't even do.*

When they got back to the house, Aletheia's mother's car was already there, and the woman was leaning against the side of it looking at her cellphone. When she saw them pull in the driveway, she put her phone away and walked over to Adam's car. Aletheia got out and her mother embraced her tightly. Tears flowed freely from both of their eyes. After a long time, she finally let go and gave Adam a hug as well. He hugged her back, glad to see Aletheia have more help than he could give alone.

"I'm glad you're here, Janet. She needs all the support she

can get right now."

The older woman smiled at him and said, "I'm glad you're here for her too."

They went inside and talked for a long time. Aletheia told her mother about everything…everything except the dreams. Of all the people in her life, her mother was the last person she would tell about the dreams. She knew if she did, she would try to press her again to start seeing a psychiatrist, to start taking the medication again. Those were the last things Aletheia needed. Still, it felt good to talk to her mother. Like her uncle, her mother made her feel safe – like everything was going to be okay. Even if she knew it wasn't.

Later that evening, the three of them were eating dinner when Aletheia's phone rang. She looked down at it and as soon as she saw who it was, quickly touched the screen and brought it to her ear. "Hello? Uncle Alex?"

"Hey there, kiddo. You doing okay? You hanging in there?"

"Barely. I'm starting to freak out a little. Mom's here, though…that's helping a bit. We met with the lawyer this morning. Matt Donovan – that's who we chose. Not really 'chose', I guess…he was the first one who could see us."

"Good. You're in good hands. He's a good lawyer and an even better man. What did he have to say?"

"Well, he said he'd represent me…and Adam. He sounds like he believes us. But it wasn't all good. He said there's a good possibility they're going to arrest me, maybe soon. That's why I'm freaking out."

Aletheia could hear the exhale on the other end of the phone. She knew her uncle enough to know that it meant he was worried. The few times she had seen him worried in her life, it had always been for good reason. He didn't worry over minor things. He said, "Alright then, I'll be on the first plane out there tomorrow morning. You hang tight, okay? Tell your mother I said hi. Love you."

"Love you too."

Aletheia's mom stayed for some time after dinner, helping clean up and just being there to give support to her daughter. Eventually she said her goodbyes to them and hugged her daughter tight, again not wanting to let go. Promising to return tomorrow to visit and to see Alex, she left. After she was gone, Adam went through his usual routine, securing the entire house, and then he and Aletheia retired to the bedroom.

Being in the bedroom again made Aletheia think of sleep, which in turn made her remember her dream from the previous night. The day had been so chaotic, with one crisis presenting itself and then another, that she hadn't really had time to think about it or even tell Adam. She looked over the bed at him, watching him as he pulled down the comforter and sheets.

"Adam, I want to talk about the nightmare I had last night."

He paused fluffing his pillow and looked at her. "Okay…tell me about it." Adam plopped himself down on the bed, leaning on one arm and listened as Aletheia sat down on the edge of her side and spoke.

"It's been bothering me all day. It was the dark figure again…" She continued on until she had told him all the details of the dream. When she was finished, she added, "The last time I dreamt I killed someone they actually died. I'm scared for you."

Adam smiled at her and shook his head. "Well, I'm not. Don't you worry – I'm not going anywhere. And I'm not afraid of any bogeymen."

His bravado did little to ease her mind, but it at least felt good to share it with him. The nightmare had shaken her even more once she had been awake and considered what it might portend. "Just be careful, okay? Maybe don't use those swords of yours for a while. Just the thought of one of them near you makes me nervous now." *Or near me.*

Adam nodded. "Of course. They will stay locked in the garage, okay?"

Aletheia nodded, her worry about his safety and her own relieved the tiniest bit. Adam turned on the TV for a half an hour or so to help them put their thoughts in a different place before going to sleep, but it helped little. Fear and worry weighed heavily on both their minds, and it was a long time before they finally drifted off.

10

They were awakened in the early hours of the morning by loud knocking at the front door. Adam slowly opened his eyes; a quick glance at the blinds told him it was still early. No light crept in around the edges and between the slats yet. Adam looked at his phone, and then to Aletheia worriedly.

"It's six o'clock in the morning."

She looked back at him with a scared expression on her face. "Do you think it's them?"

Adam tried his best to soothe her as he climbed out of bed. "I don't know. Maybe it's your uncle...I'll go check."

He put his fingers to his lips reminding her to be quiet. He moved silently out of the room, and Aletheia followed him. She had to know if it was the police. Adam crept out to the front door. The knocking came again. He peeked out through the peephole and backed away quickly. Aletheia put her hand to her mouth to stifle a cry. They both backed far enough away from the door to whisper into each others' ears without being heard. She could feel Adam's breath as he whispered in her ear. "It's them. It's the detectives…they have an officer with them."

Another knock came then, louder and more insistent. They could hear Detective Reese's voice carry loudly through the door. "Adam, open up. The car's in the driveway – we know you're home. If you don't open the door we're going to have to come in."

A long moment of silence followed, and then some words were said on the other side of the door which Adam couldn't distinguish. There was a loud bang and the entire frame shook. Another followed shortly after, and then another. Adam knew what that meant, because he had been through it before. *They're kicking the door in. Glad I reinforced it, though I never thought it would be protecting me from the police. At least we have a minute or two before they get through.*

Aletheia's face was stark terror. She shrank away, looking at Adam pleadingly while shaking her head in denial. "No, no, no…I don't want to go. I don't want to go! Please…we can run. Let's just run. We can go out the back. I don't want to go to prison!"

Adam looked at her there, so small and afraid, and he made a decision. He wouldn't run, because he knew if they did then eventually they would get caught, and when they did it would be even worse for her. There was only one way; one way that she would be free of this forever. He would not let this happen to her. *I'll confess. I'll tell them I did it. She was asleep. She was innocent. She had no idea. I'll say I went out onto the porch and Meghan told me how she felt and tried to kiss me and I pushed her away. I'll say it was an accident. Maybe they'll go easy on me if they think it was an accident. I can't let them take her to jail. I won't!* He looked at Aletheia and smiled at her sadly and said, "I know how to fix all of this. You have to trust me…don't be afraid. I love you."

Aletheia looked confused as Adam kissed her gently on the forehead and started towards the door. She was about to ask him what he was doing when he peeked through the peephole one last time before he unlocked it. When he did, she saw him tense from the back and he cursed aloud.

The second Adam had put his eye to the peephole, the scene on his front step degenerated into madness. The first image he saw was the officer hurtling at the door foot first to kick it in, while Reese and Marsh stood back with their guns drawn. The look on Marsh's face went from concentration to blank as a large steel blade erupted from his throat. It was gone in an instant. The other two men started yelling and cursing so loud it carried through the steel door. Reese spun around, his back now to Adam's view, and brought his gun up to fire but before he could the blade slashed across and took his head clean from his body. The officer in the uniform had also turned away from the door by now and was trying to unholster his gun when suddenly his head jerked to one side and twisted too far and too fast to be of his own will. He too, crumpled to the ground with a thud. Adam's eyes searched the front step for the attacker – it had all happened so fast he hadn't seen him at all – but there was no sign of him.

Adam stumbled back from the door, away from the keyhole, and crashed backwards into his kitchen table, falling down over the first chair and knocking the table over sideways in the process. "What the hell?! What the…?!" He looked at Aletheia and she didn't recognize the man she loved. Adam wasn't afraid of much. He had seen some pretty horrible things in his life and not much fazed him. She had seen him scared a few times, but she had never seen him like this. His face was a mask of raw, abject terror. She went to the peephole herself, afraid of what she would see. Hesitantly looking through, at first she was confused by the emptiness in front of her. *Where did they go?* Her reaction changed drastically when she strained her eye to look down at the steps in front of the house. Although the view was distorted, she could plainly see three bodies lying in a heap there. And blood...quite a bit of blood. She backed away from the door as though it was on fire. Her hands were trembling.

"What happened out there? Oh my God...what just happened? Are they all dead?"

She turned to face Adam to see his reaction, but he just sat on the floor of the kitchen, mouth hanging half open, all pretense of speech gone from his lips. After a few moments he looked up at her, in complete shock, and managed to form words. "I can't believe that just happened. I know what I saw, but I don't know...what...I saw." Still dazed, he had enough presence of mind to add, "Get away from the door."

Now it was Aletheia's turn to calm him. She knelt down in front of him and took him by the shoulders. "What did you see?"

Adam looked at her, his eyes half-blank and vacant. He was clearly still seeing whatever happened on the front step in his mind. "I don't know. It was like something out of a horror movie. They were on the front step, trying to get in, and...this is crazy. Somebody with a sword killed them. All of them. He cut Reese's head off!"

Aletheia looked at him, her eyes wide with shock. "What?"

"He cut his head off...he cut his freaking head off!"

"Are you serious? Who? What did he look like?"

"I don't know. I didn't really see him. It all happened so

fast. They were trying to kick the door down and then…BAM…just like that. The blade and blood were flying and then Reese…" Adam looked down at himself, sitting on the floor, and seemed to get embarrassed for a moment. The embarrassment was enough to break him out of his shock and get him on his feet. He grabbed a nearby chair and pulled himself up from the floor. He headed towards the door, then hesitated and turned and bolted for the living room.

Aletheia stared after him, trying to make sense of what was happening. "What is it? Where are you going?"

He emerged from the living room holding his other pistol – a semi-automatic – in his hand. "I need to see who the hell is out there."

"Are you crazy?! You just said there's a freak with a sword out there cutting people's heads off! He just took out three armed policemen! Don't open the door!" Aletheia stepped between Adam and the doorway, trying to talk some sense into him. She had never seen him like this. He looked like he had completely lost touch with reality.

"Adam…I don't know what happened out there, but people with swords don't just show up out of nowhere and kill a bunch of policemen. That means there's someone out there who came to your house. Don't go out there! We need to call the police!"

The absurdity of the statement hit her as soon as it flew out of her mouth. *Call the police! So they can come and arrest me? Better than being skewered like a pig…*

Adam looked at her with a feverish expression on his face. He took a deep breath and tried to calm himself, then gently moved her aside. "Go lock yourself in the bedroom. Get the revolver out of the safe like I showed you when we loaded your prints into it. If you hear anything happen, call the police. Please...go."

Aletheia looked at him and saw that there was no reasoning with him about this, and said, "Wait. Don't open the door yet...hold on." She disappeared into the other room and reappeared a minute later with the revolver in hand. "We do it together. If they're still out there two guns are better than one."

Adam saw that she was determined, and nodded his head. "I'll go first. Stay behind me! If you have to use that, remember not to point it at me." He then walked to the door, slowly unlocked it, and opened it a crack. He peered out onto the front step and got a very dark look on his face. Opening the door some more, he walked out onto the cement, taking care of where he placed each step and looking everywhere at once in anticipation of an attack. Aletheia followed behind, having to do the same as she stepped out. Three bodies were heaped on the steps. There was no visible sign of anyone else in the front yard.

At first the images were so horrific that Aletheia backed up into the doorway again. The officer in the uniform lay twisted on the ground in front of the doorway. Reese's headless corpse lay halfway under the officer's body, while his head sat face-down in the grass a few feet off to the right. At the bottom of the stairs lay Detective Marsh. His torso was covered in blood and he had a large wound on his neck, and sticking straight up out of another wound was a sword. It was a samurai sword like the one Adam owned and trained with – a katana, he had called it. Looking over at Adam, Aletheia saw that his mouth was hanging open. He finally spoke as if he couldn't believe what he was seeing.

"No way. No, it can't be..." He looked around to see if any

of the gruesome scene was visible from the road. Luckily, the two police cars had driven up the dirt driveway almost all the way to the house, obscuring them from the street. Everything seemed to be safely hidden behind the large trees that lined the front of the yard, at least for the moment. Adam squatted down in front of Marsh's body and looked at the handle of the blade intently. "You've got to be kidding me." Looking back at Aletheia, holding the gun out in front of her like some kind of holy object to ward off evil, he said, "Come on...we need to get back in the house for a sec."

The two of them backed into the doorway, with Adam going in last and sweeping his gun across the area in front of him as he stepped backwards. When they got inside, he shut and locked the door and turned to run. Thinking quickly, he stopped and turned off the outside light first. "That should buy us a little more time, at least." He then turned and ran towards the garage. Aletheia followed him as he quickly unlocked the garage door and burst through, flipping the light on and running straight for the opposite wall. "No...no...how the hell did someone get in here? Dammit!"

Aletheia understood now what had him so panicked and perplexed. On the wall of his makeshift dojo, where he kept his training equipment, laid the rack for his two samurai swords. The smaller sword, in its sheath, lay nestled in the lower crooks on the wall mount. In the upper crooks rested the sheath of the larger blade. The sword was gone.

"Dammit! Okay, I don't understand what the hell is going on here. I need to think."

"Adam, I don't understand what's going on either, but there are three dead police officers on your front step. You're not *that* far from the road and it's almost light out. Someone's going to see soon. What are we going to do?"

Adam shook his head in denial. "I don't know. Okay, okay...ugh! That was the freakiest thing I ever saw! I mean, it's dark outside, but the front light was on, and I couldn't even see the guy! Whoever did it...maybe they ran away. Maybe someone's trying to frame me. It doesn't matter. First things first – if they were here to arrest you...or us – then the rest of the police at the station know they're here. Which means we're going to have more police showing up soon if they can't be reached."

Aletheia said, "What should we do? Should we call the police and just tell them what happened? I mean, there's a homicidal maniac running around out there!"

Adam thought for a second and said, "No. Lee...they were coming here to arrest you for murder. And now the cops are dead on my front steps with my katana. No...even if we had a chance before, there's no way we're getting out of this now."

Just like that, it happened. She had seen it once before. In crisis situations, sometimes Adam just flipped a switch in his head and all his emotions turned off. One minute, he was panicked and freaking out, and the next he was calm and his face was made from stone. He took a deep breath and said, "You need to tell them I did it. You need to say I did everything. I'll tell them I pushed Meghan off the porch while you were sleeping. When they came to arrest you, tell them I flipped out and you couldn't stop me. Tell them I killed them all and you're scared. Go hide in the bedroom and lock the door and call 911. It's the only way."

Aletheia looked at him as if he had gone completely mad.

"No, I will not do that! I'm not letting you take the blame for something you didn't do! I don't know what is going on – I feel like the whole world's gone mad – but I know I'm not letting you do that."

"Well, you don't have a choice. I'm going to confess, and that's that. They'll believe me."

"Adam, it doesn't even make sense. That lady said she saw another girl push Meghan. They won't believe you anyway."

"I'll say I dressed up in one of your dresses and wore a wig."

She looked at him incredulously. *He can be so stubborn!* "You do that and I'll confess too and say it was both of us."

Adam looked at her incredulously. "Why would you do that?"

"Why would YOU?"

He shook his head. "Lee, there's no other way out of this. We're both going to jail for life for this. At least this way, it'll just be me."

She looked at him, a glimmer of hope in her eyes. "We could run. I know you said we'd get caught but what do we have to lose at this point? If we get caught we're no worse off than we are now. There's no way anyone would believe us as it is. You think they're going to believe that your sword got stolen from your garage and then the person who did it killed three cops on your front step and left the sword there? Or maybe it got possessed and started chopping people down by itself? If we run, maybe we could make it!"

"Make it where?"

"I don't know. Anywhere that's not jail."

"This is so bad..." He looked at her then, this sweet girl

whose life was now ripped apart and she hadn't done a thing to deserve it. *How many times have I sworn I would protect her? I never thought this would be the way it would happen, but I guess this is the best I can do.*

"Okay. You're sure? You're sure you want to do this?"

She shrugged. "No, but what other choice do we have? I don't know what else to do. I just know I don't want to go to jail, and I'm not letting you go for me. We didn't even do anything wrong."

Adam nodded. "Okay then. Come on."

He didn't let it show on his face – didn't even let himself feel it – but he was nervous. It was one thing to grow up around crime and violence; it was another altogether to be a wanted cop-killer on the run. But as he always did, Adam let the emotions of the situation melt away. He felt the steel slide down over his face and his heart and decided right there that he would do what had to be done.

"We've got to get out of here – fast. Go to my closet in the bedroom and get my duffel bag and my backpack. Throw some food, water, and clothes in there. A good amount, that won't go bad. Keep it light. Hurry!"

Aletheia nodded and ran off, her heart beating a mile a minute. She did her best to keep herself calm as she grabbed the bags and started stuffing things in them.

11

Adam ran to the front door and outside. He grabbed his katana by the handle and grimaced as pulled it out of Marsh's body. He felt the sharp blade grate on bone as it came free from the man's flesh. Wiping it in disgust on Marsh's blazer, he threw the blade to the side and grabbed the man by the feet, and started dragging him around the house to the back. When he got there, he turned to look where he was stepping and saw the body of another uniformed officer lying on the ground in the well-lit area by his back door. Even in his emotionless state, he wasn't prepared for the sight and it startled him enough to make him drop one of Marsh's legs.

This just keeps getting worse. Picking his leg back up, he continued on until he had dragged him next to the other officer, well out of view of anyone from the street. Looking down at the officer's body, he saw several wounds like the ones the katana had inflicted on Marsh. *How the hell?* Not having time to figure it all out, Adam sprinted to the front yard and repeated the process with the other two bodies, doing his best to avoid looking at the bloodied stump atop Reese's shoulders as it dragged through the grass. After hiding both men, he returned to the front again and stared for a moment at Reese's head resting on the lawn, horrified. *Ick. You have got to be kidding me.* Adam walked over to the man's decapitated head and reached down, not wanting to look directly at what he was doing or even think about it. Using his peripheral vision, he squatted down and grabbed the head by the hair and picked it up. He then jogged as fast as he could into the backyard and deposited it by the bodies. Shaking off his revulsion, he sprinted back out to the front and went to retrieve the katana.

The sun was not yet above the horizon, but it had gotten close enough that it was not completely dark in the yard. Even with the abundance of trees that surrounded his home, the early morning light was enough for him to see his surroundings, albeit in shades of gray. He looked towards the spot where he had thrown the sword away but saw nothing but grass. Adam started pacing around the area, looking more intently for the blade, but found nothing. Running inside the front door, he flicked the outside light back on and ran back outside to the spot. Still nothing. He started frantically searching around the yard, but to no avail. After a minute or two he realized that they didn't have much time left and gave up and went inside.

As soon as the door closed behind him he turned the outside light off again and yelled for Aletheia. "Did you bring my katana inside the house?"

She emerged from the bedroom with both bags in hand and dropped them on the kitchen table. "No...why?"

Adam's face went ashen. "I just left it outside and now it's gone. We've got to get out of here. This is getting freakier by the minute." He ran to the bedroom and retrieved the revolver from where she had left it on the nightstand, along with a box of ammunition and his holsters. When he came out of the bedroom he was also holding a wad of cash.

"I've got about eight hundred dollars saved up for emergencies. Here…take half." He stuffed the rest in his pocket and packed the revolver and bullets in the backpack. He then ran into the garage. After a few minutes of rooting around he came out with a small, tightly rolled sleeping bag, a pup tent, and several more boxes of ammunition.

Aletheia looked at him as though he were insane. "What are you doing? We're running away – we're not bank robbers. If they catch us, I'm not shooting anybody to get away."

Adam looked at her as he packed the items into the duffel bag. "No…are you crazy? I wouldn't shoot a cop. Look…there's a killer out there. I still haven't figured it out – I don't know if someone is trying to frame us, or if we're the ones being targeted, or what the hell is going on…but whoever it is just killed four men. I'm not going anywhere without protection. Besides…I have a whole box of rubber pellet shotgun shells. The revolver can load them. They're nonlethal. Just in case." *In case I ever have to shoot a person to keep you safe. I won't kill anyone – I would never do that unless our lives were in danger – but would I hurt someone to keep you safe?* Adam knew the answer to the question before he even thought it.

Aletheia looked at him, confused. "Wait…four men?"

He put his head down. "Yeah…there was another cop out back, by the back door. Same as the others."

She looked shocked for a moment, but seemed to recover quickly. *At this point, nothing is a surprise anymore.* "Okay. Do we need anything else before we go?"

"No time. We need to get out of here."

Aletheia stopped Adam as he was about to head for the door. She held his hand tight, turning him towards her and taking his other hand in hers. "I'm scared. I'm not backing out – I don't think we have much choice – but I'm still scared. Thank you. Thank you for always protecting me."

Adam smiled at her – a sincere smile despite the insanity of the situation – and kissed her on the mouth. It was gentle, but quick. He looked her in the eyes as he spoke. "I love you. I will always do everything I can to protect you. Now come on...we have to go."

They ran out the front door and got into his car. Once they got in, he started the engine and drove slowly out of the driveway towards the road. Before they reached it, he stopped and looked back one last time, as did Aletheia.

Goodbye, normal life. It was nice while it lasted, he thought. With a quick, concerned glance at Aletheia, he pulled out of the driveway and headed down the street.

They made their way through the quieter, more rural area of the suburbs that Adam lived in. As they were driving, he said to Aletheia, "We can't take my car very far. They'll be looking for us. I'll try to stick to the really dead old back roads for as long as I can. We need to put some distance between us and my house." Looking down at the dashboard, Adam cursed.

"Of course...I knew I should have filled the tank last night. It's almost empty." Minutes later they pulled up to a gas station, and Adam nervously paid for the gas with his credit card. *Probably the last time I can use that,* he thought. *Only cash from here on out, especially once we start heading in the direction I want to go.*

Just as they finished fueling, Adam got back into the car and said to Aletheia, "We need to turn off our phones. They can track us using them." He was already shutting the power down on his as he spoke. When Aletheia dug hers out of her purse, he stopped her before she could power it off.

"No...wait. Is the GPS turned on?" She looked at the phone and then back at Adam.

"Yes – I always have it on."

Adam looked around the parking lot a moment, and then said, "Good. Put it on silent. Now give it to me – I have an idea." Aletheia handed him her phone and he jumped out of the car and casually walked over towards the trash can. As he approached it, he pretended to throw something away. Turning around to walk back to the car, Aletheia saw Adam very nonchalantly flip her phone into the bed of the pickup he was walking past. *Sorry, buddy.* He hopped back in the car and soon the Camaro's engine roared to life.

"That should buy us a little time, at least. If they try to track your phone by GPS, it'll lead the police to them and hopefully away from us. Anything to put some distance between us and buy us an extra hour or two."

They pulled out of the gas station and headed back in the direction they came – west. Aletheia looked at him. "Where are you going? Did we forget something at the house?"

"Nope. Just trying to throw them off in case they watch the surveillance footage from the gas station and see which way we pulled out. We need to go east – out in the boonies where the farm towns are. I figure maybe we can stay on the old, overgrown back roads through the woods for a while. There's a few of those roads that there's never anyone on. If we can stay on one for a half hour or so, we can get maybe twenty miles or more away. At least it's a start."

Alex took the keys to the rental from the man at the counter, grabbed his bag, and headed out of the airport. It worried him that he hadn't been able to get a hold of Aletheia all morning. Normally he wouldn't think anything of it, but given the circumstances every minute that went by caused him increasing anxiety. He knew there was a very real possibility that she was sitting in a jail cell right now, unable to take his call. He tried to talk himself out of his anxiety.

She might have called Adam to help her out. That didn't, however, explain why he had been unable to reach Adam. *Maybe they both were arrested...* It just didn't add up. Alex knew his niece well enough to know that if they had both been arrested, her one phone call would have been to him. *You could always call Janet,* he thought. He immediately dismissed the idea, knowing that to do so would only panic her. Better to just head out to Adam's house, which was where Aletheia had told him they were staying, and see if they were home.

As he pulled out of the parking garage in the sedan, he realized that they may have called their attorney. *Too early to call his office...not open yet. I could call him on his cell...no. Don't panic, Alex. Not yet.* His right hand went absentmindedly to his mustache, stroking it as he often did when he had a lot on his mind.

It was twenty minutes later, about halfway to Adam's house that his cell rang. He took the call, knowing his office would just keep bugging him if he didn't.

"Hey, Alex…we got a hot one right near you. I know you said you'd be in Seattle on personal business, but I wanted to know if you could jump on this one. You're the closest asset we have on the ground there."

His gravelly voice held more than a hint of annoyance when he answered. "Doubtful. I've got a family emergency I'm dealing with here. What is it?"

"Cop-killer. Maybe two. Bat-shit crazy. Killed three cops with a samurai sword and broke another one's neck. The other networks already have people on the scene."

Alex's throat caught when they said that there may be two. *What are the odds?* "What do you mean, maybe two?"

"Guy and his girlfriend. Wanted for another homicide."

Alex's hadn't even noticed that his knuckles had gone white as he gripped the wheel with all his strength. His jaw clenched. *No…*

"What's the location?"

Alex felt his chest tighten when he heard the address…Adam's address. "Sorry…can't do it. I'm going to be off for a few days. Like I said…family emergency. I need to go." He didn't even wait to hear the rest of what was said on the other end of the phone. Dropping it into the console, he rubbed his mustache roughly once, and then hit the accelerator hard.

The scene at Adam's house was pandemonium. Alex shut the door of the sedan and walked past the multiple cars and police vehicles towards the house. The entire front yard was taped off, and it continued around the left side of the house. He looked around for someone he knew but saw no familiar faces. He was soon stopped by an officer asking him to leave. A quick flash of his press pass and he was being directed to the backyard. Alex rounded the back corner of the house and saw another crime scene before him; a large area around the backyard was also taped off. There were multiple people on the scene, including a medical examiner and several plainclothes police officers. Alex walked up as far as they would let him and asked to see whoever had command. A man in jeans and a t-shirt came up, wearing a badge strung around his neck. He looked like he had been pulled out of bed to respond to the scene.

A short while later Alex walked back past the front yard and out to the edge of the property where he had parked his car. He had seen a lot of things in his life, but the thought of Aletheia in this situation had left him shaken. He was trying to add it up in his head. *Okay, what are the possibilities? Adam could have done this to protect her and they ran together. I can't imagine her going along with that, though. Adam could have done this on his own...could he have been the one who pushed Meghan? Maybe the eyewitness was wrong? After all, it was dark and pretty high up. I hate to think it – I don't get that feeling about him at all – but I have to consider it. Either way, he killed the policemen who came with the warrant. Would he have taken Aletheia hostage?* Alex's mouth twisted at the thought. He knew he had to be objective, but it just didn't fit with what he knew of Adam – not at all. *Keep an open mind, and be ready for anything.* That adage had kept him alive for many years, and had led him to answers where others had found none many times.

Stopping at the back of the car before he got in, Alex leaned against the trunk and took out his other cellphone. It was prepaid, and damn-near impossible to trace. He was dreading making the call. He felt like he had failed. He knew it would never be said – it would never even be thought by anyone but him – but he felt it anyway. *You had two jobs. You had two responsibilities. Two purposes for your entire life…and you may have failed at one.* Reluctantly, he pressed the contact info on the phone's screen.

"Yeah, it's Alex. I need to talk to him." He waited for a moment until he heard the voice he was waiting for on the other end of the line. "I'm here now. It's gone from bad to worse fast. She's gone – and in a lot of trouble. Apparently four police showed up at their door this morning and now all four of them are dead. She and the boyfriend are missing. I know, I know…don't worry. I'm on it. I'll do whatever has to be done. I know – believe me, if I need more backup, I'll call. Okay. I'll update you soon."

As he pressed the 'End Call' button in the screen, Alex retrieved the car keys from his front pocket and opened up the trunk. Unzipping his suitcase, he found the hard-sided case inside and entered the key combination. It sprung open and he reached inside the soft foam packing to pull out the large nickel-plated forty-five. Pulling out a few clips from the case, he methodically loaded them with a practiced hand, then inserted one into the pistol and pulled back the slide, chambering a round. Slipping it and the extra magazines into the shoulder holster he wore under his jacket, he closed everything back up and shut the trunk.

Inside the car, Alex looked up into the rearview mirror at himself. Many, many lines marked his face where once smooth skin had been. The black of his hair and mustache had long since retreated to allow the gray to advance. He felt old. *Not too old.*

Not too old to do this one thing. I'll find them and I'll do what needs to be done. The tires of the car kicked up rocks and grass as they pulled out of the dirt on the front of the property and headed down the road.

12

Adam and Aletheia watched as the rear end of the Camaro slowly sunk under the water. It had been Aletheia's idea – Adam had wanted to drive into the forest on the side of the road and cover the car with brush, but Aletheia had suggested they find a lake and drive it in. They had given themselves a ten minute time limit to find one; it was near seven o'clock and they knew they had to get rid of the car quickly. As luck would have it, they had come across a small reservoir a few minutes later with an access road leading to it. They had found what they hoped was the deepest part close to the edge – a grassy field led up to a ledge about six feet off the water. After getting their belongings and anything else they could salvage from the vehicle, Adam had put it in drive and gunned it, jumping out the door at the last moment and letting the car sail off the small ledge and out at least a few feet into the water. Apparently, they got very lucky, as the last bit of the black bumper slowly sunk below the surface of the water and disappeared. Even in the dark moment they were living in, Aletheia went over to Adam and hugged him, relishing the small victory. At least now they didn't have to spend every minute worrying that around the next bend would be a patrol car that would recognize them and give chase. The last hour had felt like ten.

Adam pulled away from her for a moment and said, "We should probably do this, too." He pulled his wallet out of his pocket and looked through it; taking one or two items out and then giving it one last look, he threw it as hard as he could out into the middle of the reservoir. Aletheia retrieved her wallet from her purse and did the same. Before she threw it, she looked at it long and hard. It was like letting go of who she was; admitting that her life was changed forever and she would never be the same again. She smiled sadly, pulled her arm back, and threw it as hard as she could.

"You throw like a girl." He had that dimpled smile, now. It was the first time in days she had seen a genuine smile on his face. She had missed it. He shrugged as though embarrassed and added, "Sorry...just trying to take the edge off." Picking up their bags they set off towards the woodline. They had decided to follow the course of the road, but keep deep inside the woodline, too far away from the road to be seen from it. Adam had driven this route before and he knew there were railroad tracks crossing a few miles up. If they could find them, they could follow them south to a train station and hopefully jump on a freight car and get far, far away from Seattle. It was the only way they knew to travel far and fast without either having to provide identification or risk getting recognized and arrested. Adam figured that they could try to find a train south and hopefully hop cars all the way to California. He wanted to make his way to L.A. and find his brother. Although it was a long shot, he was the only person he knew with the connections to get them new identities. If they could get some fake IDs they might be able to get into Mexico. They both knew there were a million ways the plan could fail and they could end up caught, but they had known that the moment they had decided to flee.

Gary wiped the grime from his forehead as he turned the wheel of the old pickup, swinging out of the parking lot of the feed store and into traffic. *I swear I get dirtier by eight o'clock than most people do all day. One more errand to run and then back to the farm.* He realized he had been whistling without knowing it, which always put him in the mood for some music. Turning on the radio, the corners of his mouth turned up in a smile when he heard one of his favorite country songs playing. Soon he found himself singing along, tapping his calloused hand to the steering wheel with the music as he gradually leaned harder on the accelerator. Before he knew it he was flying along, rocking his head from side to side and singing along out loud. He half looked up in his rearview mirror – out of habit more than anything – and was surprised to see blue and red lights flashing in it. The sight snapped him abruptly out of his private concert, and he quickly glanced down at his speedometer. *Fifteen over...dammit!* Letting out a deep, annoyed breath, Gary pulled the wheel to the right and slowed the pickup to a stop on the side of the road. He glanced up again in the rearview and side mirrors and was confused by what he saw.

A patrol car and another unmarked car, lights flashing, were pulling over behind him. To his left, a third patrol car screeched up beside him and jerked itself towards the side of the road, hooking around the front of his truck and boxing him in. Two officers jumped out of the vehicle, using their car for cover. Their weapons were drawn and aimed directly at him. He looked around, completely bewildered, and saw officers rush up to the right side of the truck with their guns trained on him as well. It seemed like there were a half a dozen voices yelling at him at once.

"Put your hands in the air and exit the vehicle!"

Gary had no idea what was going on, but he knew enough to put his hands in the air slowly and visibly. One of the officers rushed up to the truck and opened the door, his gun trained on Gary the entire time, and pulled him out and onto the ground. Gary's face smacked the pavement hard; he tasted blood as he felt the weight of the officer on top of him. They grabbed his arm roughly and he felt the cold steel of the cuffs close around his wrist just before they wrenched his arms down behind his back and cuffed the other wrist to match. As he strained his neck to look up the tiniest bit, he saw officers surrounding the bed of his truck. That was when he heard himself yelling – he hadn't even noticed he had been.

All he could say over and over again was, "What did I do? What did I do?"

Alex left the police station late in the afternoon with more questions than leads. Still, it was a useful visit. He had a chance to do some investigating both online and in person, although not as much as he would have liked. A large portion of his morning was spent consoling Janet, who was in a state of near-hysteria over what had happened. Combined with his visit to the station he now had a number of facts to go on. Most importantly, he had confirmed that Adam had killed the policemen. The murder weapon was found sticking in the ground near the bodies in the backyard, with his prints all over it. He knew that they – or he, if the worst had happened – had ditched Aletheia's cellphone in a move that he had to admit had been pretty smart. He also had Adam's cell number and a description of his vehicle. Lastly, he knew that he was armed. Not that it mattered. Apparently he was a dangerous young man even without a gun.

Four officers dead without any of them firing a single shot. With a katana...a damned katana. And one of them with his bare hands, apparently. Either a good protector for Aletheia, or a lunatic who may have already killed her too. Either way, a murderer. Either way, a very dangerous young man.

Of all the places he had visited that day, the visit to his friend Matt had been the most fruitful. In particular, one piece of information he had learned stood out in his mind.

So Adam has a brother who is in and out of jail. Years of investigation had blessed him with a strong sense of intuition. Usually when his gut told him to follow a lead, it led him straight to the truth. And now his gut was telling him that if Adam was in trouble and was going to contact anyone, it was going to be his brother.

A brother like that wouldn't turn him in to the police. Might not even judge him for killing four policemen. He's going to need a new identity, too. A brother like that probably knows all the right people to get him what he needs. Now all Alex had to do was a little research to find out who his brother was and where to find him.

L.A. Adam said he grew up in L.A. For what felt like the hundredth time that day, Alex pulled out his cell and made a call. *I'm going to kill my battery by dinner today,* he thought dryly.

He was onto something, and he knew it.

Adam kept his head down and his hood up to keep the wind out of his eyes and ears. It amazed him how even in the warm weather of early fall, the wind whipping by could sap the heat out of him, especially early in the morning. The rhythmic sounds of the train eased him into a trance. The sounds had been there in the background so much the past couple of days that he had stopped being consciously aware of them, but subconsciously they lulled him like a cast-iron lullaby. He looked over at Aletheia, still asleep in their sleeping bag. Her face was beautiful; smooth olive skin draped with dark brown curls. Her eyelids were gently shut in a serene sleep, hiding those beautiful green irises that had caught his attention the first time they had met.

The past couple of days had been exhausting, both physically and emotionally. Adam wanted to let her sleep as much as he could; the travel had been even tougher on her than him. The first day they had walked long and fast, always looking over their shoulder, always expecting to be caught at any moment. It had felt like a minor milestone when they had finally come across the first set of train tracks. Following them south had given them a second wind and a sense of purpose and direction, as though perhaps their plan might work. It had also brought with it a further sense of dread; they had both realized that this must be something that many fugitives had tried before, and if so, the police could be searching the tracks for them at any minute or waiting for them at the next freight station when they arrived. They hadn't seen any other options, though. The only other idea they had between them was to try and buy a bus ticket to California, but that had seemed far too risky. *Best to be invisible and stay as far from civilization as possible,* Adam had thought. At least until they had new identities.

They had learned a lot the past two days. Figuring out how to sneak into the rail yard had been easy. There had been only one security guard, and he had kept to his booth most of the time they were there. Deciding which types of car they wanted to try to ride in had been easy as well. The open cars were far too visible; pass through a town on one and everyone would see you plain as day. Many of the cars simply looked too dangerous to ride on. The closed box cars though, presented an ideal spot. They had just had to figure out how to get in one undetected. After a few hours of hiding out and observing, they had taken their opportunity and started to climb in one with an open door that was obstructed from the view of the security booth. That was when it had happened.

The man was behind them before they had even known he was there. The sound of his voice had startled them both so badly that visions of being arrested and going to jail had flashed through Adam's mind before his eyes had registered that it wasn't a security guard at all, but a young man in dirty work clothes. Both he and Aletheia had been relieved to see that it was a rail worker. Even still, Adam had been on guard the entire time; he wondered if the man had noticed his fist clenched at his side, ready to lash out at any moment. If he had, he hadn't shown it. Adam had considered whether or not he could do it; if he could attack an innocent person if it looked like things were going badly. Getting in fights growing up was all well and good, but Adam had never hurt someone who didn't deserve it, and he didn't want to. *I'll do what I have to in order to protect her,* he had thought. That thought – that single thought – had made Adam confident and afraid all at the same time.

Sitting in the box car watching the trees fly past in the early morning sun, Adam remembered that meeting. It had turned out to be a blessing.

Adam's fears had been quickly relieved when it had become apparent that the man not only meant them no harm, but was also a great help. He had made some small talk with them, nonchalantly asking about where they were going and what places they had been. Adam had been about to make up lies to both questions, when Aletheia had chimed in that they were new at this and weren't sure where they wanted to head first.

"Wherever the track takes us, I guess," she had told the man. Adam had looked at her, a smile on his face, realizing it had been a much less suspicious answer than the lie he had been going to make up. It had turned out to be the best possible answer they could have given, as the man had simply smiled at them and then given them a full rundown on how it all worked. Apparently, hopping freight trains happened all the time. He had told them he had met all kinds of people – homeless people, hikers, travelers, a few crazy people, and even one or two he thought for sure were criminals. He had told them about the "bull" – apparently that was what the security guard was called – and given them some tips on how to hop a ride, which cars were best, and a couple of other useful pieces of information. Adam had been shocked that the man talked about the whole thing as though he didn't mind, but he had just replied that while some of his colleagues would have chased them off or notified the bull, most of the workers knew about it and didn't mind at all. It didn't hurt anybody, and if anything went wrong they could always say they didn't see anything.

That first meeting had made their time at each stop on the way easier. They had managed to avoid detection for the most part, and the few workers who had noticed them had been either friendly or had ignored them as though they didn't exist, which sat just fine with Adam. In fact, he had preferred the latter. *Best to not talk to anyone if we can help it. I don't want to leave a trail for anyone to follow.*

13

Adam breathed in the fresh air flowing in the open door of the car and slowly closed his eyes. It didn't make any sense, but for some reason this all felt *right* to him. More right than his life at home had felt. In fact, as he sat there taking in the sunrise and breathing in fresh air, with miles of track flowing underneath him, Adam thought how odd it was that he felt more alive now than he could remember feeling in years. He knew that any sane person would note that it was stressful and tense, and held none of the comforts of home or modern life that he had become accustomed to. There was also the small inconvenience of a constant threat of life in prison at every turn. He wasn't sure if it was because he was crazy, or if it was just because he had always been different, but there was no denying that at least part of him felt better here.

Is it really a surprise? I know how I feel – how I've always felt. Walking around that campus; walking around that whole town. Everyone with their faces stuck in their phones, worrying about whether or not the barista got their coffee right or if they need to lose ten pounds or what kind of car they drive. If he was really being honest with himself, Adam had been disenchanted with both college life and suburban life for some time now. *It's funny,* he thought, *when I was growing up all I wanted was to get to that place. To be safe and secure and be around normal, healthy people. To have a quiet life.* Yet soon after he had gotten there Adam had realized there was something about that life that didn't feel like *life* to him. It felt...dulled. Humans were supposed to do more...be more. *There is more to life than lattes and brand names and getting a safe degree so you can spend your life working in some large, faceless corporation like a drone.*

The last thought really struck home for Adam. He hadn't realized it until then, but Adam hadn't been happy at school the last year. Realizing that fact made his brow furrow and the corners of his mouth droop, because he had always loved school. He had always loved learning for as long as he could remember. School this last year had made him very unhappy because he was running out of electives to take.

Electives – the classes he got to take because he wanted to; the subjects he got to learn about because they interested him. History, physics, philosophy, biology, mathematics, religion...Adam loved anything that had to do with learning about the world and the way it worked; anything that made him think deeply. What Adam really wanted was to figure it all out. How it all worked. *What is it all for? Why are we all here?*

That had all changed this year. This year he had to declare a major and had met with an academic counselor at the school to help him. It had been depressing to look over the employment statistics in each of the fields he was interested in. The pragmatic side of Adam – the survivor – wanted a career that offered more security and better income. *Something that makes sense. Something safe.* His counselor's advice had been to consider a degree in business or information technology. Adam had reluctantly chosen business. He had even taken an introductory class that had guest speakers and included a chance to work in a corporate office for a day. Adam's day had consisted of shadowing a director at a number of meetings and then working with several of her staff.

The meetings had been, quite literally, the most boring experience he could ever remember having. The only interesting thing about them, really, had been watching the behavior of the people around the conference table. There Adam had seen a broad range of human emotions on display: zeal, dedication, and selflessness, and also apathy, boredom, jealousy, competitiveness, manipulation, and bullying. You name it, it had been there. The rest of the day had been no better. Adam had met with three of the woman's staff members and they had each had him sit in a chair by their desk while they worked and complained about their jobs. From what he saw, their jobs amounted to handling emails and phone calls and then spending the rest of their time with him either gossiping about others in the office or complaining. They had all the trappings of success: they wore designer clothes and talked of recent vacations, and each had downed at least one four-dollar cappuccino in the time he was with them. The latter were part of a never-ending stream of caffeine and sugar boosts they used to get their exhausted bodies and souls through their day when what they truly needed was something to get their heart pumping fast, let them sleep easy at night, and give them a meaningful existence. The hardest part for Adam had been that they seemed oblivious – or at the very least resigned – to how obviously depressed they were. Each of them had mentioned at least once in the conversation hating their job or being unhappy.

It had been one of the worst days of Adam's life. It had felt worse than being beaten; worse than the day he was mugged and had the point of a knife held to his throat. It had been one of the worst days of his life because in looking at each of them, Adam had seen his own future. He had seen himself in ten or twenty years, just as miserable, just as unfulfilled. He had seen it and he had shrunk from it. That was not the life he wanted.

Adam snapped out of his reflection back into the present and considered how much better he felt now. He had spoken with Aletheia about it, but she had looked at him like he was crazy. She had echoed all his other feelings about the predicament they were in – that she was scared, and tired, and stressed out – but that had been where their similarities ended. Aletheia didn't seem to find any of this exciting in the least. Yet Adam also noticed that in the last two days she hadn't had any nightmares or scary visions like she had been having before. It had only been two days, but he couldn't help but wonder about it. He looked down at her face again. Even with the weight of the things that had happened to them in the last week on his shoulders, it all still felt...lighter...somehow. He felt lighter. Leaving that life behind for this one felt exhilarating. More than that, though, it felt meaningful. Giving up the life he had and going on the run to protect the woman he loved, now that – that was a life worth living. Adam inhaled the cool air deeply as it rushed by his face. *Yes,* he decided. For the first time in a long time, he felt alive.

The steering wheel rotated counter-clockwise in Alex's hand, the ridged plastic slipping through the skin on his palm as it returned to its normal position of its own accord. Alex glanced up into the rearview mirror and made a slight adjustment to it. It was the fifth time he had done it, more a reflection of his nerves than any need to improve its angle. The car's wheels kicked up dust as it accelerated off the turn; the dirt on the old county road was packed tight with repeated wear and dry from the recent sun. He reached up then and stroked his mustache fiercely, his brow wrought with worry over Aletheia.

Two days. Two days and the clock is ticking. I'm running out of time. It had been a long two days at that. Janet was an emotional wreck, sick with worry about her daughter. She had gone out on her own the each day, searching the Seattle area with pictures of her daughter and asking anyone who would listen if they had seen her or Adam. Alex had kept in constant contact with her all day each day, doing his best to help her stay sane as he barely clung to sanity himself. He felt bad about lying to her about his progress, but he knew it was the right thing to do. *Adam is too dangerous. I can't have Janet here with me.*

He had picked up on their trail earlier that day. A railway station, long forgotten by all except the rail crews who worked there, had held the answers he was seeking. He had been lucky to happen upon it; after an entire day of scouring every major bus station in Seattle and the eastern suburbs with no luck, he had decided that day to check the rail stations to see if anyone had seen them. He knew the police had all the roads covered. They knew Adam's vehicle and there was an APB out on it; if he tried to drive anywhere he would be caught as soon as an officer ran his plate, which happened often. When the bus lines turned up no leads, Alex had turned to a more desperate route. Fugitives – escaped convicts, in particular – sometimes used train-hopping as a way to get out of an area quickly undetected. It was one of the few ways a person could travel quickly in today's world while still remaining under the radar to the police. *But not to me.*

Before long he saw his destination up ahead of him. The railway station looked much like the last one, and the one before that, all the way back to the one where he had gotten the lead. He remembered how he felt walking into that one; going through the motions emotionlessly, trying to do the leg work that needed to be done to save Aletheia while not letting his fear get the best of him. He couldn't afford to panic; couldn't afford to fall apart or even to get too hopeful. So he had just focused on taking one step at a time and moving slowly and steadily towards finding his niece. He had started with the rail stations closest to Adam's house, and had gotten a hit right away. He had actually been surprised when he saw the flicker of recognition in the crewman's eye at the second station he visited. At first the man had denied seeing them, but when Alex told him the severity of the situation and what Adam had done, he had opened up like a can of tuna. *Thank goodness for that.* It had woken Alex up very quickly from his stoic demeanor. *Aletheia is alive. Or at least she was when they got into that box car, and that's something.*

It had been more than just that station, too. Alex had tracked them to two more that day; had found witnesses who remembered seeing two people who fit their description in and around the rail yard. The path was leading south, as Alex already found himself into Oregon as the day turned to evening. They had a good head start on him, to be sure. At least the private investigator he knew in Los Angeles had been able to take the case for him; he was establishing surveillance on the brother now. If Adam showed up there and tried to make contact with his brother, Alex would know it. He glanced down at the prepaid cellphone he carried. It had been morning since he had given an update. *I better call him again.* Reaching down he pulled up the contact – it was the only contact listed on that phone – and pressed 'Call.' As the phone rang on the other end, Alex thought, *Hang in there, pigtails. I'm coming.*

14

Aletheia looked down at the large truck stop and the glaring sign reading "Travel Center" just down the hill from them amidst other buildings. It was right next to the highway, which made her nervous – this was as close to real civilization as they had come so far – but they were both very hungry and didn't have many options left. Adam had said they were nearing the sprawl surrounding Los Angeles and had begun to get nervous about riding through the large train depots, eventually convincing Aletheia to finally abandon the train and venture into the outskirts of the community. They had watched from the obscurity of the train car as they had started to pass the town and had waited for the right moment, when the train was still moving slowly just after decelerating for a crossing, before leaping off.

Standing atop the hill, she looked over at Adam; he was already looking back at her. His face was grim and serious, and yet he had a sparkle in his eye like a child on Christmas.

"I hear they have showers at those places," he said.

A hot shower. The thought of it was too enticing to pass up, even if the hunger had not been enough. It had been almost a week since she had one. *At least we're clean enough,* she thought. Adam had been so happy when she had shown him she had managed to throw toothbrushes, toothpaste, and soap in the bags in their rush to leave, and it had turned out to be a lifesaver. As it was their clothes were starting to get filthy, and Adam was sporting a week's growth on his face. At least it had helped them escape detection, as they both looked the part of homeless travelers. She looked to Adam's short, blond hair and thought of her own curly locks, now short and bleached blond. Cutting both their hair short had been an easy decision – they had done it the second day out with Adam's pocket knife. The color change, though – that had been a stroke of genius on Adam's part. They had been low on food at one of the stops in southern Oregon, and had made the scary but necessary decision to leave the station and head towards the closest town to get some supplies. She had hoped they looked different enough to escape any notice, but in all honesty it was Adam whose appearance had changed the most due to his three days worth of stubble and short hair. Coming upon a small farm stand and general store on the side of the road in the middle of nowhere, Aletheia had waited in the woods while Adam ventured to it in order to get some food. Sitting in the brush, waiting to see if he would come out or if a sheriff's vehicle would come screaming up outside had been the longest fifteen minutes of her life. She had let out an audible sigh of relief when he had emerged from the store with a bag in his hands.

That one stop had turned out to be a good decision in so many ways. She and Adam had unloaded the bag right there in the woods into their packs, piles of easily carried food, water, and more soap. Adam had also managed to buy them sunglasses, fresh fruit from the farm stand, toilet paper, and his best find – three big bottles of hydrogen peroxide. The fruit they tore into right then and there with a voraciousness borne of days of hunger, subsisting on limited packaged food. It was some of the best fruit she remembered tasting. The other items, including the peroxide, they had packed up before heading back to the rail station. It had taken some time to catch another train south from there without being noticed, but all in all the stop had been well worth it.

Now standing atop the hill, looking down on the truck stop below, Aletheia felt they could at least walk in without being noticed too easily. Neither of them looked anything like they had just a week before. She was tired – the jump off the train and the walk back to the town, combined with the stress of their travels thus far had taken a toll on her. A hot shower sounded absolutely heavenly. Looking over at Adam again she saw he openly wore a smile now, and as he swept his gaze back to his left she knew why. His eyes rested not on the truck stop, but to what lay beyond. Miles of highway stretching away south of the town. They couldn't see the city yet from where they were, but there was one a mere ten miles south of them. *Santa Clarita*, Adam had said. The beginning of the sprawl, and only thirty miles more from Los Angeles. They had made it, at least this far. Grabbing his hand in hers, they descended the hill together as the evening sun set in the western sky.

Alex left the rail station, urgency pressing him faster now. He had made up some time on them, assuming he hadn't lost their trail. The man at the last station had remembered seeing a couple, but he had described them as both having blond hair. *They've either dyed it or I've lost them. No turning back now – it can't be a coincidence.* If it was them, he had gained a half a day on them – no small feat considering he had to stop to sleep and had to follow the roadways. They had been constrained by neither of those things. He had pushed himself as hard as he could, sleeping for only a few hours at a time in his front seat at whatever rest stops were on his route. He hadn't showered in days, resorting to buying fresh underwear and deodorant, and had eaten whatever he could buy and eat while he drove.

Old age must be catching up to me. I've never felt so tired. No matter...I'll find you, kiddo. I will. He hopped into the sedan and punched it as he left the station, speeding through back roads as fast as he safely could. It wasn't long before he met up with a larger road and turned onto it, quickly accelerating to and past the speed limit. As he did, he glanced up at a green sign on the right side of the road. *Los Angeles 48 miles. It can't be a coincidence.*

The hot water streamed down on Aletheia and washed over her body, rinsing away the aches and pains as it rinsed away the dirty soap suds. She shampooed and scrubbed her hair for the second time, breathing in the steamy air deeply as she gently massaged her fingers into her scalp, working out days of grime that had built up there. She could feel her muscles relaxing; feel the days upon days of stress melting away, if only for the next fifteen minutes.

Best seven dollars I have ever spent. The smell of the shampoo was floral and pretty – it reminded her of home and the life she had left behind. She hoped Adam was enjoying his shower as much as she was hers. He had been on edge as soon as they had gotten near the building, extremely aware of every single security camera in the areas they walked. She knew he was just being prudent, but she also knew he often had problems relaxing. She hoped he could let his guard down and enjoy his shower. He would really be missing out if he couldn't.

Drying off in the private stall they had provided, she took joy in the towels they had left for her. They were white and clean and fluffy. It was amazing how quickly she and Adam had adjusted to life on the road, and even more amazing how much it had already changed her appreciation of the smaller things in life. She stood upright and wiped the steam from the mirror in front of her and looked at herself. The blond hair definitely helped, but looking at herself now all cleaned up, she couldn't deny the fact that her face was her face. It would be recognizable if the person looking knew who they were looking for. She and Adam would have to find a way to fix that…somehow. Pulling on her clothes, she sighed deeply at how good they felt and smelled. It had definitely been more money well spent to use the truck stop's laundry before they showered.

She met with Adam outside the showers. He looked how she felt – relaxed and happy. A large smile spread across his face and he simply said, "Wow."

Aletheia laughed, leaned up, and kissed him. He grabbed her gently by the shoulders and said, "I am starving. Come on…let's go get something to eat."

She nodded and they started towards the exit, but before they did, she stopped him and said, "Wait. I have an idea."

As she started to drag him into the convenience store portion of the truck stop, Adam reminded her, "Don't forget to keep your face turned away from the cameras."

Aletheia nodded and quickly went to a rack she had spotted with non-prescription reading glasses on them. Picking out two of the weakest pair she could find, she paid for them in cash and they quickly left the building. Outside, she handed a pair to Adam and put hers on her face. Looking up at him, he had to admit it completed the disguise for her. At first glance, she looked like a totally different person.

"Brilliant," he said, as he put his on his face and smiled.

One parking lot over, they spotted an all-you-can-eat buffet. It looked like a little hole-in-the-wall, but at that moment any thoughts of pickiness were long since driven out of their heads by desperation. Besides, they had learned in the last week that small, little places were a good thing; for one, they were much less likely to have security cameras. Adam and Aletheia made their way to the buffet. The food was not what they would have found at a five-star restaurant, but after days of travel with growling stomachs it may as well have been a feast. They gorged themselves full, eating as much as they could without making themselves sick. It was the most content they had been since leaving Adam's house. When they finally left the buffet it was dark outside.

Adam and Aletheia walked deep into the night, wanting to get far away from the truck stop and closer to Santa Clarita. They stuck to the woodline as much as possible – not that there was much of one as it was mostly open land broken by stunted trees and brush – but at this time of night they had to stay closer to the highway for fear of losing it. That was a delay they could not afford. After a few hours they could see the lights of the city very clearly in the distance – Adam estimated they were only a couple of miles out. They were both tired and they knew they would need rest for the next day, and Adam pointed out that the city buses didn't run late enough to get them closer to Los Angeles at night. They walked along for a while longer trying to find a spot where they could set up camp, and eventually found a spot behind a small rise that was obscured from the highway. It was not long afterward that they had the pup tent set up and were falling asleep under the stars.

The next day they woke to the sound of the roadway in the distance, packed up their belongings, and started their trek again towards the city. Adam realized he had underestimated how far away they were in the night, but they still managed to make it to the city limits by late morning that day.

It felt strange to be in a city again. Although they hadn't been away from it long, Adam and Aletheia had already gotten used to the peaceful quiet of the woods. Even on the train, the only sounds had been that of the engine and the wheels on the rails. Here, in the city again, their ears were assaulted with a cacophony of noises. They passed more people in the first fifteen minutes than they had seen on the entire trip down to California. Unfortunately, with the people came the police. They passed officers in cars and on foot. Every officer they passed made their hearts race and their breath feel shallow. They did their best to walk determinedly and nonchalantly, as if they had someplace to be and nothing to be concerned about.

The bulk of their day was filled with bus rides, trying to navigate from Santa Clarita through several intervening cities to the outskirts of Los Angeles. Once they had gotten inside the gigantic city Adam had become more confident, knowing which bus routes to take to get them to the neighborhoods deep in the central parts of the city that he knew and remembered. It was many hours and transfers later before they found themselves across the street from a large apartment complex in a very seedy part of town. Aletheia caught herself looking around nervously and forced herself to stop. Adam had warned her against it – had coached her on how to act and hold herself. It was difficult though, as this was a more immediate danger that she felt than what she had known in the past week. She noticed her senses heightened as they leaned up against the entrance to an alleyway. It seemed as though every person that walked by was staring at them, looking them up and down to see if they were easy prey. Adam reminded her what he had told her multiple times on the way here.

"There's no way I'm leaving you out here on the street alone, so you're coming in with me. Let me do the talking…these aren't good people. Have you got the pistol hidden in a place you can get to it fast?"

Aletheia patted her jacket at the waist nervously. There was no way she thought she could use that thing on another person, but it made Adam feel much better to know she had it.

"Good. Don't show it or mention it unless I tell you to. Best not to let anyone know you have it. I'm not really sure how this is going to go, but even if it looks like it's going badly, just try to let me handle it. Okay?"

Aletheia cocked her head and gave him a look that made it very clear she wasn't going to answer the same question again. Adam smirked and said, "Sorry, I'm just nervous. I guess we don't have much choice. Here goes." With that he strode purposefully across the street and up to the apartment building.

Aletheia fell right in line behind him, keeping her focus on him and trying her best to ignore the people walking by. When they got into the building she was surprised to see some people camped out in the hallways. Not many, but a few. As they strode past a few of them tried to talk to them, but whatever they were offering or asking for was lost on Aletheia as she hurried to follow Adam up the multiple flights of steps.

15

Adam rapped on the door to the apartment. Aletheia stood behind him, trying to keep herself from checking over her shoulder for the tenth time. After what seemed like an eternity, she heard a sliding chain on the other side of the door. The door opened and in front of them stood a muscular young Asian man with spiked hair, wearing a white muscle shirt and sporting several colorful tattoos on his arms. The tips of his hair were dyed many different colors, like a rainbow of bristles on his head. He stood with the door only half open, his body inserted into the space between it and the door frame as if to block their view inside. There was something not quite right about the man – Aletheia couldn't place it exactly, but there was...something. Even just standing in the doorway he had an intense, nervous energy about him. She could hear other voices coming from the apartment, but she couldn't make out what they were saying. The man looked at them.

"What's up? What do you want?"

Adam replied, "I'm looking for James. You know where he

is?"

"James? I don't know nobody named James. Who are you?"

"I'm an old friend. He used to hang out here a lot."

The man looked Adam up and down and said, "Yeah, well like I said, I don't know no James. Maybe you got the wrong apartment."

Adam stood silent for a moment and then said, "Alright. I guess we do."

As he turned and motioned for them to leave, Aletheia heard a raspy female voice from inside the apartment yell to the man, "They looking for James? Tell them if they see him to bring us more of this good shit!" The woman's voice then erupted in a cackling laugh.

Adam must have heard her too, because before the man could close the door Adam had turned around and put his hand out to stop it from shutting. The man's face quickly contorted into anger.

"You better get your hands off this door before I bust your face!"

Adam kept his hand there, and then inserted his foot into the doorway as well when the man tried to shut it. It must have been effective, because the man seemed frustrated that the door would not budge.

"Look, I'm not looking for any trouble. I just really need to find James. It's an emergency."

Aletheia thought by the other man's body language and facial expression that he was about to attack Adam, but before he could the door opened up and a woman stood there. She was dressed in a large tee shirt that was too big for her. She didn't appear to have any pants on. Makeup in a myriad of colors was layered on her face, and bleach blond curls hung raggedly around it. She looked at the Asian man with wide eyes.

"Derek, quit being a jerk. You're getting paranoid again. They know James – they're just here to party a little is all. Quit acting like you own the place – it's my damned apartment." She turned to Adam and said, "Who are you? You're not cops, are you?"

Adam shook his head, "No, we're definitely not cops. Just friends of James."

The woman gave another look to Derek, who backed up into the apartment clear of the doorway, eyeing them suspiciously. She waved them inside and closed the door behind them. Once inside, Aletheia did her best to remain calm. She had been to enough college parties to realize they had just walked into a drug den. On a couch on the opposite wall sat two women sharing some sort of pipe. The glass coffee table in front of them was littered with bottles of beer, packs of cigarettes, and overflowing ashtrays. The apartment reeked of smoke. Aletheia stuck to Adam's back like glue.

The woman said to Adam, "Sorry about Derek. We may have to cut him off soon, he can't seem to handle his salts!" The last part she delivered at the top of her lungs, shouting directly at the man who answered the door.

He stared back at her defiantly and said, "We don't know them. They could be narcs. Or they could be working for...you know...*them*." He fidgeted nervously as he added the last part.

She just shook her head, "Oh yeah, that's right. I'm sure they're working for the aliens who are trying to steal your brain so they can use it to take over the Earth, right?"

He looked at her as though she had gone mad. He was

twitching. "You shouldn't talk in front of them. You don't know who they are. And they want to steal it *back*. I told you…it's not *my* brain."

Aletheia had to put her arm to her face to stop the laugh that was threatening to erupt from her mouth. Even as scared as she was, the words she had just heard uttered were too insane and too funny to ignore. Then it struck her how sad it was…this young man was clearly delusional. *Sad and frightening, actually*. The woman waved her hand at Derek dismissively.

"Like I said, don't mind him. He's getting paranoid lately – thinks some aliens abducted him and gave him a new brain and now they want it back or something. He's an idiot." She looked at Adam suspiciously. "You ain't a tweaker, are you? Can you handle yours? I don't need another one of him running around here."

"No, I'm not a tweaker. We're not here to party either. I'm looking for James. You know where I can find him?"

The woman looked at him, the smile gone from her face. "You said you're a friend of his, right? Cause we don't want no trouble around here."

Aletheia had moved up to Adam's left shoulder as the two had been talking, and from this distance she could see the woman's face up close. She realized what had looked odd about Derek. It was his eyes. This woman's eyes looked the same as his had; her pupils were so large that it made her irises look solid black. Adam looked like he was about to answer her, when a blur of movement to their right caught Aletheia's attention.

It all happened so fast she had barely had time to react. She felt a flurry of motion from Adam beside her, and the next thing she knew there was a smashing sound as Derek and Adam fell in a writhing mass onto the top of the coffee table. Derek was flailing wildly as they landed on the table, shattering it into a thousand pieces. She looked down and for the first time she noticed there was a knife in his hand. The girls on the couch, sprayed with glass shards, were screaming. Aletheia watched as Derek struggled to stab Adam with the knife, her breath catching in her throat and her stomach involuntarily tightening. Before she could yell for him to look out Adam had secured his grip on Derek's wrist with one hand while repeatedly bashing the man in the face with his other fist. He had managed to work his way on top of Derek and now had the man's arm twisted over his shoulder and was smashing it down into the remnants of the coffee table. Adam smashed his hand again and again while he straddled over him and knelt on his other arm, pinning it. Derek's hand finally lost its grip on the knife, and it dropped harmlessly to the dingy carpet with a thud. Throughout it all, Derek kept yelling that he knew why they were there and they couldn't 'have it back.'

Aletheia looked over to the woman who had answered the door. She stood, dumbfounded, her dilated pupils fixed on the scene of chaos in her living room. Glancing back over at Adam, Aletheia now saw that Derek was still fighting wildly and trying to bite Adam's face. Adam was doing his best to control him, but the man seemed possessed. The woman finally came to her senses then and started yelling and cursing at them all.

As the situation escalated, Aletheia suddenly remembered that she had a gun. *A lot of help I would have been. Didn't even remember I had it until now.* She looked to Adam, who had now twisted Derek so he was face-down on the floor and had his arms wrenched up behind his back, and asked, "Can I use it now?"

He gave a resigned look towards the drugged-out woman, who was becoming more and more belligerent by the second, and nodded. Aletheia pulled the revolver from her waist, pointed it at the woman, and screamed, "Shut up! Shut up! Shut up!"

The woman looked at her and then, almost as an afterthought, noticed the gun. The effect was instantaneous. She stopped yelling immediately, the girls on the couch following suit and halting their screaming to weep quietly in the background. The woman looked at her and put her hands out in front of her and said, "Hey, I told you. We don't want no trouble. Don't mind Derek...like I said, he's tweaking out on salts right now. We don't have no problem with you."

If Derek had noticed the gun from his position, he gave no indication of it. He didn't stop struggling or screaming at them; if anything, he was fighting harder to get free. Adam looked up at the woman as he struggled to control him.

"I know you don't, and we don't want any trouble with you either. You want us to leave? Then tell me where James is!"

The woman shrugged her shoulders and said, "How should I know? He comes around when he pleases."

Adam jerked his arms and re-established his grip on the wildly struggling man. "Just tell me where to find him. Where do you go when you want to meet up with him?"

The woman looked at them both and said, "Fine. It's your funeral. Just remember, I had nothing to do with it. Don't say nothing about me. I'm gonna get my phone – it's got the address in it. It's where him and his boys all hang out."

She made sure to keep her hands in plain sight as she retrieved her phone from a purse on the counter and looked through it. Aletheia kept the gun trained on the woman the entire time. After a few moments, the woman picked up a pen and wrote down the address on a scrap of paper. She slowly pushed it across the kitchen counter towards Aletheia. Aletheia cautiously walked up and grabbed it, and then looked towards Adam. He had managed to lock Derek down and was leaning forward trying to talk to him.

"Okay, Derek, listen up. You caught us...you were right. We were sent to collect it."

Derek halted his struggling for a moment and twisted his head up sideways to try and see Adam. "Really? I knew it! You can't have it back!"

As he started to struggle again, Adam raised his voice and tried to get his attention. "Wait! I said we *were*! We're not going to take it. Not yet."

Adam's words brought a second lull in Derek's struggling. "Why not?"

"Because I don't think it's ready to be collected. We need you to keep using this brain so we can keep collecting information through you. I think we will need about another year's worth. You've got one year. Unless you want me to take it today?"

Derek looked back up over his shoulder again, more calmly this time. "Uh...no. Another year? Seriously?"

"Yes. Now I'm going to let you up and we're going to leave...we're going to return to our ship. If you try to stop us, I'm going to take it today. You understand?"

Derek nodded his head wildly to ensure that Adam knew he understood. With a satisfied nod, Adam got up off the man and released his grip on his arms, moving back out of his range quickly but cautiously. He stood straight and looked at Aletheia and nodded. They backed out of the little apartment together.

As they were leaving, Adam reminded the woman, "Remember…we were never here. We were never here…and you didn't give us the address, right?"

The shell-shocked woman just nodded as they backed out the door. They turned and walked swiftly down the hall and all the way out of the building, glancing back over their shoulders the entire way. Aletheia tucked the revolver back into her waistband and picked up her pace to keep up with Adam. When they got outside, they moved quickly across the street and walked far and fast until they came to a place a few blocks away where they felt at least relatively safe.

Aletheia turned to Adam and grabbed him, frantically patting her hands all over his torso. "Are you okay? Did he get you?"

Adam shook his head. "No, I'm fine. I wasn't expecting that. That place has always been like that, but James used to be there all the time. Looks like he's moved on to bigger and better things. You okay? You did great back there."

"I'm fine," she replied. "You scared the hell out of me – I thought he was going to stab you." She noticed his shaking hands. "Are you sure you're alright?"

He looked down at his own hands and managed a weak laugh. "Yeah, I'm okay. It's just the adrenaline. It'll wear off."

She nodded and rubbed his hands in hers. "It's crazy to see a place like that…people like that. It's easy to forget they exist when you're not around it. That guy was scary – what the hell was wrong with him?"

"Bath salts. They make people crazy; aggressive, paranoid, delusional. He'll end up killing somebody or himself." He said it so matter-of-factly that Aletheia shuddered for a minute, not at the description of the drug's effects, but at Adam's numbness to it all. To her, it was a living nightmare. He gave her a small, apologetic smile as if he could tell what she was thinking. "Come on. We need to keep moving."

16

It was late at night by the time Adam and Aletheia reached the address on the paper. It had taken two bus rides and a lot of walking to get there, and they were tired. The adrenaline from their last encounter had worn off and left them both fatigued. It had been tempting to find a place to sleep and resume their search in the morning, but Adam and Aletheia both felt an urgency to continue. They knew they were likely only one step ahead of the police and needed to keep pressing on as fast as they could if they were ever going to make it into Mexico without getting caught.

A barren warehouse sat in a dead parking lot to their left. The small street in front of them curved up past the warehouse and then behind it. From the distance they were at they could already see the small house that sat at the address they were looking for. Adam checked for his gun and then started walking up the small street towards the house. As they got closer, Aletheia could see that there were numerous cars outside, as well as a few motorcycles. The number of people that must be inside the house gave her pause; she had to will her legs to keep stepping forward, one at a time. Adam was intent on the house, watching it carefully as they approached.

When they drew nearer, he whispered to her, "Don't forget: don't use my name. I don't want to tell them who I am unless I have to. The police might have already contacted somebody close to my brother to let them know if I try to reach him – they have informants and you can never tell who they are."

Aletheia nodded and soon Adam was opening up the small, dilapidated chain link gate and passing through it to walk up the narrow concrete walkway to the front door. When they got to the door, Adam paused a moment before knocking. A few moments went by and Adam knocked again, this time a little more insistently, and the door opened. A man stood there; he wore a black tee shirt with the sleeves ripped off and had a tattoo of a small snake wrapped around his upper arm. The hair on his head was blonde and was arranged in tight, straight corn rows running front to back on his scalp. He had a can of beer in his hand.

"What's up?"

Adam tilted his head towards the man and said, "I'm here for James. Is he around?"

"James? Not sure. Who's asking?"

"Just a friend of his. Name's Donald." Adam cringed as he said the name. He hated his middle name, but he thought it might spark James' memory if he heard it without also alerting anyone that his little brother Adam had shown up looking for him. Their mother had insisted on giving them their grandfathers' names for middle names, and both of them had hated them. He only hoped James would remember.

"Donald?" the man asked sarcastically. "What kind of name

is that? Is that British or something? You British?"

"No," Adam replied. "I grew up here. A few miles from here. You have any idea where I can find him? I really need to talk to him – it's urgent."

"Urgent, huh?" The man leaned over and spit on the side of the steps. "Let me see if anybody knows where he's at. Come on." He held the door open behind him as he walked in the house. Adam and Aletheia hesitantly followed him in. As soon as they got in the door she felt her stomach go tight with fear. The house was filled with people, both men and women. It looked like a party was happening, except that Aletheia got the sense that this wasn't a special occasion but the way these people spent every day of their lives. Several small groups of people in the house were gathered together doing various drugs. All of them looked pretty rough; some of them looked downright scary. All of them stared at her and Adam as the man with the cornrows led them by, deeper into the house. She stayed as close to Adam as she could and tried her best not to make eye contact with anyone.

They were led to a backroom where a large group of men and women were drinking and playing pool. The man in the cornrows walked past and stood by the pool table.

"Hey, these guys are looking for James. Anybody know where he's at?"

"James? I ain't seen him. Who wants to know?"

The man who asked the question looked up at them from his pool cue and stood up. He was a large man – not lean and fit like Adam but brawny and thick. The layers of fat on his arms and chest were clearly covering several layers of muscle as well. He wore a white tee shirt under a black nylon jacket. Tattoos of flames crept up his neck out of his shirt collar, and he had two more on the corners of his eyes. The hand he had wrapped around the pool cue looked like a small ham.

"Who are you?"

While Adam was answering him, Aletheia looked around the room and felt her chest tighten as she noticed all other activity in the room had slowed. Everyone was watching the interaction between Adam and the large man now. There was a tension in the air that was palpable. Even in the drug den she had still felt safe with Adam. Here she knew fear. There was no way he could protect her or himself if all these men turned on them, and from the sounds of the conversation, that was looking to be a very real possibility.

"Who told you to look for him here?"

Several of the men had closed in on Adam, creating a small circle around him as the large man shot him questions. To his credit, he looked like he was keeping his cool, but she wondered how much of it was an act. If she had picked up on the men's dangerous tone, Adam certainly had. She considered pulling out the gun again, but looking around at the number of people surrounding them and remembering Adam's words to her before they had gotten here she decided against it.

Adam had his hands in front of him now and was backing up, ever so slightly. It was useless, really, as there were as many people behind him as in front of him. The large man's questions had gotten more and more suspicious and belligerent, as Adam's backstory started to fall apart under scrutiny. Aletheia realized then that any initial assumptions she had made regarding these men's intelligence was a mistake. They may not have been educated, but they were cunning, especially the large one. They knew when they were being lied to. Adam was clearly in trouble. Panic welled up inside her. *This isn't worth it. We've got to get out of here.*

Before she knew what she was doing she had pulled the revolver from her waist band and brought it up to point at the men surrounding Adam, hoping he and she could back safely out of here as they did the last place and make a run for it.

"Hey! Back up! Get away from him!"

The gun in her hand stopped all activity in the room as it had before, but that was the extent of the similarities to the last time she had drawn it. While the men backed up a half a foot or so and showed it a healthy respect, they certainly didn't seem to fear it the way the bath salt lady had. That fact alone made Aletheia nervous.

Adam heard Aletheia's words and saw the reaction on faces and in postures around him. He knew what she had done before he even looked at her, and he couldn't be mad at her for it. It wasn't like he had the situation under control; to be honest, he had sensed the trouble brewing the moment the man with the corn rows had walked them into the back. It was odd that the man had even let them in. When he turned to look at Aletheia, though, his concern escalated quickly.

She stood there, holding the revolver out in front of her with steady hands. *That girl has more strength in her than I give her credit for.* Unfortunately, behind her and to her sides, others watched her carefully as they slowly reached behind their waists and in hidden places. Things were about to get very bad very quickly.

Dammit! I didn't want to have to do this. If the cops have gotten to anyone in this room right now we're screwed. Not much choice...better than being dead. Adam threw up his hands towards the people behind Aletheia and towards the large man, and yelled, "NO! Wait!"

He looked at the large man and said "Ricky, call them off, man! It's me...Adam Parker! James' little brother. Look at me...it's me!" Adam pulled the glasses off his face and pulled his newly blond hair out of the way.

The large man looked away from Aletheia at the sound of his name and turned to face Adam. He tilted his head and stared at him, and put his hand up towards the people around Aletheia. They immediately halted their slow-motion movements and waited to see what would happen.

"Ricky, it's me. Adam. You remember? James used to bring me around all the time. Your brother taught me to play pool."

If Adam had been expecting a happy reunion he didn't get it.

"Are you...?" The man looked more closely at his face. "It is you! Are you stupid or something? You trying to get yourself killed? What the hell are you doing, coming in here with all this Donald shit? I wouldn't have even recognized you. You realize what was about to happen to you and your lady friend?" He turned to Aletheia for a brief moment and waved his meaty hand dismissively at her. "Stop pointing that thing at me and put it down. I ain't gonna ask twice."

Aletheia looked to Adam, shaken and out of her element, and he nodded slowly for her to lower the revolver. She put it down and looked around her. People were staring at her with hard looks on their faces. She let go of the breath she hadn't been aware she was holding when several of them simply shook their heads in disdain and turned away. The room started to go back to normal, to some extent. Aletheia slowly inched her way closer to Adam, not feeling comfortable being separated from him anymore. Adam was talking with Ricky and several other men who had gathered around them.

"We're in trouble…the police…had to go underground. That's the deal with the blond hair and glasses."

"What kind of trouble?"

"The worst kind."

Adam stared hard at Ricky when he said the last part. A common understanding seemed to pass between them. Ricky was clearly still pissed off, but he seemed to be calming down the more they spoke.

"Okay…the cops are one thing. But why'd you come up in here like that? You could've just told us. We ain't gonna snitch you out."

"I know you wouldn't, but look at this place. I don't know more than a handful of these guys anymore. You remember what happened to James, when that little snitch Trey ratted him out?"

Ricky nodded his head, a dark look on his face. "Yeah, I remember. We took care of that. I don't tolerate that in my house."

Adam put his hands up. "That's all Ricky. That's why I didn't want to say who I was. No disrespect."

Aletheia watched the interaction intently. Each minute that Adam spent with these men, he slipped back more and more into their language, like picking up a bike after going years without riding. He was a little rusty, but he was remembering it all very quickly. Aletheia didn't like it at all. As she watched, Ricky yelled for someone to call James and tell him his little brother was there waiting for him.

A few minutes later, the word came back through the house that James was on his way. The twenty minutes that followed felt like an eternity to Aletheia. She hung to Adam's shoulder quietly the entire time, not wanting to interact with anyone there; partly out of the awkwardness of having just pulled a gun on all of them and partly because she was afraid she would inadvertently insult someone and end up beaten up or worse. Adam was doing his best to make small talk with the men in the gang that he knew; they wanted to know where he had been and what he had been doing all these years. That left Aletheia sitting in silent discomfort with her own thoughts. At that moment, her thoughts were dominated by an intense desire to leave this place and never return.

Some time later, Aletheia heard a small ruckus from the front of the house announcing someone had arrived. Adam must have heard it too because he stopped what he had been saying in mid-sentence, turned his head towards the sound, and got up expectantly from the stool he had been sitting on. A man entered the room. Aletheia recognized him immediately from the few pictures she had seen of him. He was a few years older than in the photos; more matured. His dark brown hair was short and he wore a very neatly groomed goatee. His eyes were the same deep brown as Adam's. He walked into the room and stopped a few feet from Adam. Aletheia could feel the awkwardness of the moment. She felt bad for both of them.

"What the hell is this?" he said, motioning to Adam's short blond hair. "You leave home and they turn you into Peter Pan or something?" A few of the people standing nearby laughed.

Adam just smiled sadly and said, "No. Just a disguise."

"Disguise, huh? Maybe next time you should dress up like Captain Hook. What? Don't look so surprised. Just because I didn't go to college doesn't mean I don't know my literature…" He stretched the last word out, pronouncing every syllable. "So what…you just disappear into thin air…you stop calling…you stop calling Mom…and today you decide to come walking back in here like the prodigal son returning? Why come back now?"

Adam just stared at his brother coldly. "We're here because we need your help. We're on the run from the police. We're in a lot of trouble. And you know why I left. You're the one who told me to, remember?"

James clenched his jaw as he spoke. "Oh, I see. You come back when you need my help. I told you to go to college and get a better life. Not to disappear off the face of the Earth and abandon your friends and your family!"

Adam didn't flinch as his brother spoke. Aletheia knew him well enough to know that beneath the stony exterior the words had hurt him, but he wasn't letting it show. "I did what I had to do, James. You really want to do this here in front of everybody?"

James looked around at the other people in the room, all transfixed on the reunion between the two brothers. He took a deep breath through gritted teeth and looked at Adam. He had been about to respond when someone ran into the room from the front of the house.

"Cops! Lots of 'em! They're coming!"

The room erupted into motion as people scrambled to either get out or hide whatever illegal items they had with them. Adam swore under his breath, and James seemed to understand why immediately. He looked around, shouting angrily as soon as the words were said.

"WHO DID IT!? WHO'S THE SNITCH!? WHOEVER DID THIS IS A DEAD MAN!"

There was no way James was going to get the answers he wanted in the mayhem that followed. As Adam and Aletheia turned to run, James grabbed him by the arm and said, "Blood is blood. I'll help you out. But you and me are still gonna talk."

He then looked around and grabbed two other people in the room – a man and a woman, both with blonde hair – and said to them, "You two...you're coming with me. Come on."

He then grabbed a young Hispanic kid who was frantically snatching drug paraphernalia off a table and said, "Ramone...take these two out the back way through the alleys. You do whatever you gotta do to get them out. If they get cuffed I'm gonna find you and hold you responsible. Got it?"

The kid froze in place, looking like a deer caught in headlights, and slowly nodded. He was clearly afraid of James. Satisfied, James turned to Adam and said, "I'm gonna help you get out of here, but they're probably gonna put a tail on me for the next twenty-four. Meet me in the skate park where we used to play when we were kids. Midnight two nights from now...go."

Ramone waved them on as the sound of sirens screaming up outside the front of the house rang through the walls. James looked back at them one last time through the crowd of people jostling to get out of the house. "GO!"

17

Adam leaned to the left on the park bench, whispering into Aletheia's ear. "I think it's almost twelve…" She looked at him and nodded, pulling her jacket tight against the early autumn wind. It was surprisingly cool, especially when the wind blew.

The last two nights had been rough. The first night they had fled the gang's hangout with Ramone. The boy had led them as fast as they could run out the back door and through a maze of alleyways that weaved through the neighborhood behind the house. They had just made it out of the house in time. The police had come crashing in as they fled; they saw the flashlights panning through the side yard just as they slipped into the alleys in the back. It had seemed like the alleyways went on forever, until they had lost all sense of direction and even Adam had no idea where they were. Ramone had finally leaned up against the opening of an alleyway, gasping for air, and told them they were safe. They walked the streets all night that first night, sticking to the poorly lit areas and keeping to alleyways. They had watched at least three patrol cars go by from the shadows, each one making them more and more anxious. They both knew the L.A.P.D. were aware they were in the city now, and probably had updated descriptions for both of them. Whoever had ratted them out at Ricky's would have seen their hair and glasses.

In the early hours of the morning, Adam had recognized a side street and after following it for a mile or so, gotten his bearings. They had continued to walk through the city, past the morning rush, past midday, always sticking to alleys and keeping themselves hidden from the police. Finally they had made their way to an old skate park. Exhausted as they were, Adam had actually smiled when he saw it, memories of simpler times in his childhood flooding back to him. The memories had proven useful as well as pleasant, as they had reminded Adam of an apartment building he and James used to play in nearby. He and Aletheia had gone inside and climbed the stairs to the top of the twelve story tenement. When they had reached the top, Adam led them up to the roof access door and out onto the roof. He had laughed as he noticed that the latch was still broken as it had been fifteen years before when he and his brother had frequented it as boys.

They had spent the next day and a half up there, eating, sleeping, and regaining their strength; each taking shifts to watch for anyone coming to the roof so the other could rest in peace. Luckily, they had made it through with no disturbances. At the end of the second night, after dark, they had ventured down onto the street again and into the skate park and settled down on a bench side by side to wait for James to arrive.

Sitting there waiting, Adam found himself worrying about his big brother and wishing he would show up soon – and not only because they needed the fake IDs that James could lead them to. He was pulled from his thoughts by Aletheia's voice.

"Adam? I just wanted to say something. I've been wanting to say it since we were at that house two nights ago."

Adam crooked his neck to look at her. "What is it?"

"I just wanted to thank you…for not being like that anymore. I can't imagine growing up like that. I'd like to think I would have loved you anyway, but I can't imagine living like that. I'm sorry – it sounds so insulting."

Adam chuckled quietly next to her. "That's not insulting. How could I blame you for that? Are you forgetting I left it all behind for a reason? I don't like it either."

She smiled at him and nestled her head on his shoulder. Aletheia wasn't really sure how long they sat there. Time itself had taken on a different meaning for her since going on the run. They were no longer held to specific hours or minutes; they no longer had any specific place to be by nine in the morning each day. Instead they measured their time by the rising and setting of the sun, the growling in their stomachs, or the way it felt as it passed. Times like this moment seemed to pass slowly. It felt far past midnight when they saw the shape approaching their bench in the dark.

Adam recognized the cocky strut of his brother's silhouette right away, and breathed a sigh of relief when he saw it. He wasn't sure if he had been more worried that James would be arrested and unable to come see them or that he would change his mind and simply not show up. The shadowed features of James' face came into view in the darkness as he approached. Aletheia was about to stand up when she felt Adam's hand press down on her lap, holding her on the bench.

"Wait," he whispered.

James kept walking and continued by them nonchalantly, heading over to a darkened area behind a large skate ramp about a hundred feet away. When he got there he continued walking away until he disappeared into the shadows. Adam sat still and gazed around, and Aletheia followed suit as she began to understand what was going on. She wasn't sure if she was impressed or appalled that the brothers seemed like they had done this before. Adam looked around the area, especially at the path James had come from. After a few minutes, Adam patted her leg and got up and started walking back along the path he and Aletheia had come in on, heading straight past the ramp and around a bend. It was only when they were on the other side that he casually ducked off the path and into the shadowy area behind the ramp, taking Aletheia with him.

Alex watched James enter the skate park from the alleyway on the other side of the street. The private investigator had done his job well; he had established surveillance and kept tabs on him for Alex without alerting him to his presence. The police on the other hand...

It had been a tough tail; James had seemed alert and aware he was being followed and had taken a very erratic path from his apartment to the park. He had lost the unmarked police car following him within the first mile through a series of double-backs and ditches down alleyways. Alex had simply hung back, tailing him from a distance. It was risky; if the man got too far ahead he might lose him, but it was a chance he had to take or risk being spotted. He had been happy James had been able to shake the police. The last thing he wanted was for them to be there if James led him to Adam; they would arrest Aletheia on the spot. Besides, once James had lost them he had relaxed a bit and taken a more straightforward path to his destination.

Alex waited for some time before moving swiftly and surely out of his darkened spot and across the street. He moved from shadow to shadow like a ghost, keeping his distance and waiting each time James disappeared up ahead. That was how he found himself in the shadows of two columns next to a paved path, watching James walk out of sight up ahead. Rather than moving to the next darkened area, he waited. *The man has a knack for doubling back at the worst moments.* After a moment or two, he was about to step out when he saw two figures emerge from the side of the path. It looked like they had gotten up off something – a bench – and they started walking in the direction James had gone. It was hard to tell from the distance in the dark, but from their relative sizes they looked like a man and a woman.

Adam and Aletheia entered the shadows of the overhanging ramp slowly, letting their eyes adjust yet again to the deeper level of darkness, and saw James standing there. They walked up to him, stopping about two feet away; any further away and they wouldn't have been able to see his facial expressions clearly. He spoke.

"Okay, little brother...I'm here. You couldn't have made it harder? What the hell did you do? They've been on me like white on rice for two days. Had to shake a tail just to get here tonight. Why is the whole damn city looking for you?"

Adam's shoulders slumped a bit. "Sorry, James. I didn't do what they said I did. They think I killed some cops up in Seattle."

James chuckled a bit. "Serious? What's some? How many

you gotta kill for L.A.P.D. to be on your ass like this?"

"Four."

James let out a low whistle. "Damn. Good riddance. I believe you, though...they practically got a SWAT team out looking for you. Had you staked out real good, apparently. I had no idea P.J. had turned, that little sneak. I never liked that guy."

"P.J.? Is that who told the cops we were there to see you?"

"Yeah. Skinny little bastard...stupid corn rows on his head."

Realization dawned on Adam's face. "Dammit...I knew it! I knew it was weird how easy he let us in there."

"He let you in? Figures. Well...don't worry about it. He'll be taken care of as soon as this all dies down. Stupid snitches never realize – the cops don't care about him. They ain't gonna protect him for long."

James' ominous tone made Aletheia's stomach tie in a knot. *Would they really...?*

"So let me guess: you need to get out of the country," said James.

"Yeah. We need some fake IDs. Can you help us get them?"

James pointed to Aletheia. "This your girlfriend?"

"Yes. This is Lee. Lee...James."

James reached forward and shook her hand. "Pleasure to meet you, Lee."

Even in the dark, James dimpled smile caught her attention. *Just like his brother.* He was charming, to be sure. She wasn't sure she liked it, though.

"Pleasure to meet you too, James."

He stood up straight again; he and Adam were almost the same height. "She seems nice. Why'd you drag her into this?"

Adam looked annoyed, from what Aletheia could see in the dark, but before he could answer she said, "He didn't. They think I killed someone too...a friend of mine."

James laughed out loud at that one. "Are you serious? You two are a regular Bonnie and Clyde. That's crazy."

He turned his attention back to Adam. "Like I said before, little brother...blood is blood. I'll help you out because I value family...unlike some people."

Adam stepped closer to his brother. "What did you expect me to do?"

"I don't know...call? Visit once in a damn while? Maybe call Mom. She worries about you all the time and wonders what the hell she did to deserve being abandoned."

When Adam answered his voice sounded different. Somber. Pained. "James...you told me to get out. You told me to get out and leave this life behind."

"Yeah...so?"

"You told me you didn't want me to end up like you. You told me to run as far and as fast as I could from all the people in my life who were trouble. That's why I moved."

"I didn't say for you to forget about your family."

Adam was silent for a long time. James sat patiently waiting for a response from him. In a sad voice, Adam finally said, "Look James...you're my brother and I love you. And I love Mom too. I do. But when you told me to do that, I realized something: that your advice included the two of you. You two were trouble in my life."

James took a step back. He started to say something twice, but each time fumbled over the words. He seemed speechless.

Adam continued and said, "I'm sorry, James. I'm just being

honest. You were in and out of jail. Mom was in and out of rehab…and jail. You joined a gang and were dealing drugs. Let me ask you something: if what I just described was two of my friends and not my family, and you were giving me the same advice you did, what would you tell me to do?"

It was James' turn to be silent for a long time. Finally, he looked at the ground and said in a low voice, "I would have told you to run as far and as fast from those two people as you could…" He looked up into his baby brother's face. "…and I would have told you to never look back."

He sounded so sad Aletheia could have hugged him right there. It was hard for her to watch – this moment between them – and at the same time she stood fascinated. Adam didn't have many close friends. She hadn't seen this side of him before, except with her. It made her love him more.

Adam looked back at James and said, "I'm sorry. I wasn't doing it to hurt you or Mom. I just had to do it. If I kept my ties to you I would've eventually ended up right back here. I didn't stop loving you. You're my brother."

Aletheia heard James' voice break for a brief moment, and as he spoke, he reached up and cupped Adam's cheek in his hand, smacking it like she would expect an older brother to. "You did the right thing, bro. You did the right thing. I just never realized when I gave you that advice that it would include me."

He opened his arms and grabbed Adam in a big bear hug. Adam wrapped his arms around James and returned it tenfold, squeezing him tight. In that moment – ten seconds, at most – none of the events of the past fifteen years existed. Adam and James were boys again. Best friends. Brothers.

When they broke apart James turned away for a moment

and wiped his sleeve on his face. When he turned back he said to Aletheia, "I'm sorry you got mixed up with this kid. I could have told you he's a dumbass. Been one his whole life." He laughed awkwardly, trying to shake off the last shred of emotion.

He looked back at Adam. "So let me get this straight: you actually manage to get out of this place, go away to college, stay clean, make good on your life...and end up back here a wanted cop killer on the run anyway."

Adam nodded. "Yeah...that pretty much sums it up."

James shook his head solemnly. "Man...that is messed up. Life is just...messed up."

The two were quiet for a moment before James broke the silence.

"Alright, I'll do what I can to help you two out..."

James didn't finish what he had been about to say. His sentence was cut short by a gravelly voice that came from the shadows behind Adam and Aletheia.

"Aletheia!"

She spun around and saw a man – she already knew who it was by the voice – step out from the shadows and into the dim moonlight. A dull shine reflected off the large handgun in his outstretched hand.

Before her brain registered the handgun he had pointed at Adam and James, Aletheia bolted for her uncle and hugged him.

"Uncle Alex! How did you get here?"

Alex managed to keep his gun trained on the two men while Aletheia hugged him.

"You two drop your weapons. Come on...I know you have them. Drop them."

Aletheia backed up a foot from her uncle. "Uncle...no. It's

Adam...and that's his brother, James." She looked at him confused.

"I know who they are, Lee. I've been following you two for nearly a week and I've been following James here for over a day now." He turned his attention to the two men again.

"Weapons. On the ground. Now. Don't make me ask again."

Adam whispered to James, "That's her uncle. He's not a cop. Just do what he says and we'll straighten this all out." James looked at his brother doubtfully but complied nonetheless. They both pulled out the semi-automatic pistols they had in their waistbands and placed them on the ground slowly. Adam looked at Alex and said, "Alex...it's me. Put the gun down."

Alex kept the gun trained on both of them and said to Adam, "Both of them. I know you have another. The revolver...on the ground."

"I don't have the revolver. Lee does."

Aletheia looked at her uncle and lifted up the bottom of her shirt to show him the pistol tucked in her waistband. He turned to look at her, his face confused. The expression passed quickly, and he said, "I wasn't sure if he had taken you hostage. Looks like he didn't." He still didn't move his own gun an inch; it pointed directly at Adam. "He's still dangerous, Lee. He killed four policemen. Even if he was protecting you...that's not right, Aletheia."

James interjected himself in the conversation. "He didn't kill them, man!" He looked to Adam and Adam gave him a sad but appreciative smile. Alex looked at Aletheia and she nodded her head.

"It's true. He didn't kill them. We don't know who did it,

but they did it right on his front step." Alex looked at his niece and then back to Adam and James. He lowered the forty-five slowly.

"So you two just decided to run then because it all looked so bad…"

Aletheia and Adam both nodded and she added, "Who would believe us?"

Alex took a deep breath and let it out, holstering his gun. He looked towards Adam. "Sorry…I had to know. I wasn't sure what happened. Whoever set you up set you up real…"

Alex's words died in his mouth as James was flung through the air backwards to smash into the wall behind him. He hit with such force that his head snapped back into the cement and he slumped down near the base of the wall in a heap, conscious but dazed. Adam screamed and lunged forward towards his brother to help him. His momentum stopped in midair and reversed as he too was flung twenty feet backward to slam hard into a steel pole near Alex and Aletheia.

"ADAM!"

Aletheia felt herself screaming before she even heard it. As she leapt to help her fallen boyfriend, Alex frantically reached for his pistol. Unholstering it, he swept it left and right over the area the two men had flown from, searching for the target. He saw none. Just then, James was lifted off the ground, his back dragging on the cement wall hard enough to make an audible scraping sound as he slid up it until his feet were a foot off the ground. He seemed to be struggling with something that wasn't there. He fought with the unseen attacker and for a brief moment made eye contact with Adam, who was lifting himself to his feet as fast as he could. He managed to choke out one word.

"Help…"

There was a loud, sickening crunch as James' head was smashed into the cement with enough force to send blood spraying out along the wall, its dark color a mere shadow among shadows like some late night graffiti artist's work on display. The sound was followed by a loud crack as what was left of James' head bent straight right at a ninety degree angle. His lifeless body dropped to the ground. It had all happened within the span of two to three seconds.

"JAMES!" Adam grimaced in pain, still reeling from being hurled into the metal pole, and lunged to his feet towards his brother. Before he made it two steps Alex had grabbed him with his free hand and was trying to pull him back, sweeping the pistol rapidly back and forth with his other hand. His eyes searched the shadows for something…anything to aim at. There was nothing.

"He's gone, Adam! You can't help him now. We have to run. NOW!"

Alex pulled furiously on Adam's arm, doing everything he could to drag him backwards while herding Aletheia back and doing his best to cover their retreat with the forty-five. It wasn't easy – the young man was much stronger than he looked.

Desperate, Alex yelled at him, "Adam! We have to get Aletheia out of here!"

The last words must have registered in Adam's brain, because he stopped fighting against Alex, reluctantly backing away from the scene of his brother's death. They backed out of the shadows and broke into a full run as soon as they hit the path. Adam wept as he ran, tears for a brother he hadn't seen in years but loved nonetheless. Aletheia had the presence of mind to pull out the revolver as she ran, looking back wildly for signs of pursuit. Alex's lungs burned; he wasn't a young man anymore and Adam was fast, even weeping as he ran. He did his best to turn and sweep the area behind them as often as he could and still keep up. They ran until they were out of the park, and then they ran some more. Once they were several blocks from the park, Alex called for them to stop and bent over, leaning on the wall of a building and gasping for breath. Aletheia did the same. Adam stood upright, his face pressed against the wall. He felt the cold, rough surface of the brick on his cheeks as his tears left his flesh and transferred to the wall, wetting it. *James…I'm so sorry.*

As soon as Alex could catch his breath enough to speak, he holstered his weapon and told Aletheia in jagged breaths to do the same. "We've got to get to my car and get out of this area. If I just saw what I think I saw, this is far worse than I ever imagined. Come on."

Aletheia wore a horrified expression.

"What was that?! WHAT THE HELL WAS THAT?!"

Alex just shook his head as he gasped and said, "We've got to get to my car. We can talk once we're driving. We need to go." He forced himself into a jog as fast as his legs would carry him. Aletheia peeled Adam away from the brick wall and he reluctantly followed, loping alongside them easily. They continued that way for what seemed like close to an hour, alternating walking and jogging depending on whether or not anyone was on the street to see. They kept to alleyways and darkened areas as they had the day prior, before Alex finally slowed to a walk. He led them to his sedan, still parked on the side of the road a block away from James' apartment. Looking around one last time, he unlocked the doors and they all climbed in. Adam and Aletheia both let their heads fall back on the headrests and closed their eyes for a moment. Alex allowed himself no such luxury. If they were dealing with what he feared they were, they had no time to rest now. He inserted the key in the ignition and the engine came to life. Slamming the car into drive, he punched the accelerator and tore away from the curb.

18

Aletheia gripped the dashboard as Alex sped through the darkened city, the car's tires squealing as he cornered hard on the tight streets. She did her best to keep herself upright as the forces pressed her relentlessly against the door and the seat. After several blocks, she remembered the number of squad cars she and Adam had seen in the city as they had walked through it.

"We have to slow down – if we get pulled over we're going to jail. Uncle!"

She watched as Alex looked in the rearview mirror again and then turned and looked back every few seconds. The expression on his face was beyond worry; he looked downright scared. He must have registered what she said though, because the car started to slow noticeably until they were driving through the city at a normal pace that wouldn't attract any notice. Glancing in the back seat, she saw Adam. Looking at his face nearly brought tears to her eyes.

He sat in a daze, rocking gently left and right on the seat as the car took each turn. When he looked up at her it was like he was staring through her at something he was seeing in his mind.

"His head...it just...there was nothing there..."

He seemed oblivious to what was going on around him. Aletheia couldn't see in the dark whether or not he was still crying, but his eyes glistened with wetness when the moonlight hit them. Her heart went out to him.

"Adam...I'm so sorry."

If he registered her words, it barely showed. She thought she saw the slightest hint of acknowledgement in his expression, but other than that he looked to be in shock. Realizing she couldn't do much to console or help him now from the front seat of the moving car, she decided to give him some time to process what he just experienced and turned her attention back to her uncle. She once again allowed herself to think about what she had just seen.

"What the hell happened to him back there? What *was* that?!

Alex let out an audible sigh and glanced at her out of the corner of his eye while he continued to navigate the car.

"I don't know...at least not for sure. I've seen a lot in my life, but I've never seen anything like that."

"Me either. That was like something from a horror movie!" Her eyes scanned her uncle's face, trying to read his expression. "Back there, you made it sound like you thought you knew what it might be. What do you think that was?"

He had a look on his face that she had seen before. It was the look he had gotten when she was growing up and he had to tell her something about the world that he knew would take away a small piece of her innocence. He had seen a lot of terrible things on his job, and although he tried not to share them with her there had been times she had pressed him. He had the same look now.

"Kiddo, there are things I can say and things I can't; at least not right now. We need to get to a secure location…"

Aletheia stared at her uncle hard. It was a testament to the fact that she had been pushed past her breaking point that she raised her voice to interrupt him.

"My best friend is dead. I've been having some of the creepiest nightmares I can imagine, had policemen decapitated through a door ten feet away from me, been on the run and wanted for murder, and watched a man – two men! – get flung through the air and one of them have his…" She lowered her voice to a whisper out of respect for Adam before continuing. "…his head crushed and neck snapped by something I couldn't even see! I don't understand what is going on or what I just saw, but if you know you need to tell me! I'm not a little girl anymore!"

The frustration in the last words, pointed at the man who had been kinder to her than anyone else in her young life made her recoil a bit as she let them out, but Aletheia held her gaze locked on her uncle. She was tired of wondering what was going on. She needed to know.

Alex looked at her several times as he tried to watch the road. Something she had just said had raised his attention to a new level – she could tell – but she didn't know what. He was silent for a while before he said, "I know you've been through hell the last two weeks. And I know you're not a little girl anymore. I can't tell you too much because I'm not one hundred percent sure what we are dealing with. I need to get us out of the city and make a call, because I need some answers too."

Seeing the determined look on her face, he added, "I guess it's not like your life is ever going to go back to normal now anyway. I'm sorry, Pigtails. I'll tell you what I can, for the moment."

She nodded, embarrassed now about her outburst but frustrated and nervous about how secretive he was being. It was very unlike him.

"There are things about the world you don't know. Things that almost no one knows, except a few." He stopped what he had been about to say and got a thoughtful look on his face. "Actually, that's not true. People know. They just don't let themselves believe."

He looked over to her as he spoke. "Aletheia, tell me something. What does an angel look like?"

She tilted her head, unsure of where he was going with the question. "What? I don't know...beautiful, big white feathery wings...glowing halo..."

The corners of his mouth turned up ever so slightly. "Right. What about a demon. What do they look like?"

"Umm...big? Ugly? Black skin...maybe red. Big bat wings. Fangs. Fire and brimstone, I guess. Why? You think I'm being haunted by a demon? Because Adam and I talked about that! Oh my God – is it true?" She looked frightened.

Alex tried to comfort her. "Hold on...let's not get ahead of ourselves. Why do you think it is that you *know* what they look like?"

She tried to shake off her fear at the way the conversation was headed and focus on the question. "I guess because everybody knows. From TV and movies, maybe? Or stories in the Bible?"

The two of them were interrupted by Adam's voice coming from the back seat.

"It's not just the Bible."

The two turned to face him, his face dimly visible in the darkened back seat. He was still dazed, but he was engaging in the conversation in a monotone voice as if half awake. Aletheia waited in silence to see if he would keep talking. After a long pause, he spoke again, his voice slow and robotic.

"Demons have always been described that way since ancient times. Angels too. Lots of different names – sometimes worshiped as gods – but always the same."

Aletheia turned to him, glad he was speaking, at least. "I thought angels were just in the Bible?"

Adam looked at her – actually made eye contact – and droned out a reply. "In the Bible, and Islamic and Jewish texts." He sighed. "And lots of gods from other ancient cultures...they're the same as angels. Marduk from Babylonia, Ishtar from Sumer, and lots of Greek gods – Nike, Eos, Morpheus. Beautiful...big feathery bird wings...light radiating from their heads..."

Alex had a smile on his face. "You like mythology, Adam?"

Adam nodded blankly. They had his attention, but he was barely hanging on to lucidity from the shock of what he had just seen. "Yeah. Mythology, religion, history..."

Alex nodded and then turned to Aletheia. "Your boyfriend knows more than most. That's good. That'll help this all make more sense. Maybe you're right, kiddo. Maybe the reason we all know what angels and demons are supposed to look like is because those ideas have been passed down through the centuries. But that doesn't explain where they came from in the first place." He glanced up in the rearview mirror.

"So tell me Adam, why do you think all those ancient cultures pictured angels, demons, and many other gods and mythological creatures the same way? Think about it: different civilizations in different places all over the world at different times, and yet they all came up with the same images and similar stories. What explanation would make sense to you?"

Adam thought about it a moment. The challenge of answering the question seemed to command enough of his brainpower to pull him out of his daze further. "That there's a common source way back in our history somewhere. Some kernel of truth that started it all and got retold and altered over time throughout the world. That would make sense to me."

Alex smiled at Adam; it was almost as though he was proud of him. He looked at him as though he had discovered gold. "The mind is an amazing thing. Free it from what it has been told to believe and let it loose on a problem, and it always seems to find the right answer."

"What does this have to do with what just happened back there?" asked Aletheia. She glanced at Adam. He seemed to frown for a moment, but otherwise he was now transfixed on Alex.

Alex replied, "Everything. It has everything to do with it."

"Are you saying that angels and demons exist?" she asked. "Is that what we just ran into back there?"

"No. There are no *angels*. There are no *demons*. Those – the way you know them – are just legends pieced together by ancient cultures from even older legends. Mythical creatures your ancestors believed in. But…they are mythical creatures that were pieced together from fragments of the truth that have been passed down for millennia."

Aletheia looked at him, trying to digest it all. "I don't understand."

"I am saying that these beings that started it all – the ones that are the basis of every myth, legend, and belief humans have ever had about angelic or demonic beings – they existed long ago in our past. And they are just the tip of the iceberg."

She looked deeply disturbed by the conversation. "How do you know this stuff?"

Alex took a deep breath. "Well, that's a little hard to explain, but I'll try." He turned to Aletheia. "Why do you think I chose to be an investigative reporter?"

Aletheia looked at him, confused. "I don't understand. What does that have to do with…"

Alex managed a smile and said, "Humor me, kiddo."

"I don't know…it seems like an exciting job."

"It is. But that's not why I'm one. I don't do this for any reason that has to do with money or career. I do this because it's my duty. I do this because I have a constant view of millions of things going on in the world: through the internet, other newsnets, a huge network of contacts. I have access to the police, the government, the military. Understand…even though I *work* for a newsnet, they are not who I *answer* to."

Aletheia was looking at him now like she wasn't even sure who he was anymore. "I don't understand. What does that mean? Who do you answer to?"

"I answer to someone whose duty it is to watch over all of mankind."

"Wait…what? Are you serious? What does that even mean? Why would a news reporter…?"

He interrupted her questions with one of his own. "Think about it, kiddo: if you were going to keep watch over the world, how would you do it?"

Aletheia's mind raced. The things her uncle was telling her were bordering on the insane. She wondered for a moment if he was losing his mind; if he had possibly come unhinged from the stress of her disappearance and what they had all just been through. But in looking at him and hearing him speak, he seemed as lucid and sharp-minded as ever.

Adam answered his question from the back seat with a question of his own, his voice low. "What am I keeping watch against?"

Alex's eyebrow rose. "You'd be keeping watch against the return of ancient enemies of mankind. Things we left behind so far back in our history that the only traces that exist of them are threads of truth woven through myth and religion."

Adam nodded slowly. "The news. I'd have...not just one...lots of news reporters all over the world. With contacts everywhere." His eyes were widening from their previous glazed appearance as he looked at Alex.

Aletheia's expression was similar to Adam's. "Wait...are you telling me that you track the news all over the world because you're real job is to watch for angels and demons coming back after thousands of years?"

"Look, if we're going to talk about this, let's call them by their proper names," said Alex. "Dy'ibalis. That's what they are called – the ones our stories about demons are based on."

Adam worked the word around on his tongue. *Dy'ibalis.* "What about the angelic beings?"

"They call themselves the Ankh, and the Ankh-el."

"Why the two names?" Adam asked.

"The 'E-L' on the end is a title given to the most powerful members of their race."

Aletheia looked at him, pale-faced. "Why do you keep talking about them in the present tense? I thought you said we left them far behind?"

"We did. The human race is…hidden…from the Dy'ibalis, at least. But eventually they will find us. That is what my duty is, or at least part of it. To watch for that day." He looked at Aletheia thoughtfully. "In any case, I've been watching my whole life, and until tonight, I've never seen anything that would make me think we've been found."

Aletheia looked frightened. "Right – so like I said – you think that was a demon – a *Dy'ibalis* – back there?"

His face looked very grim. "Possibly. I think it might have been. You didn't tell me about the nightmares."

It took her a moment to process the change in topic. It finally clicked to her what had caught her uncle's attention when she had lashed out at him earlier. *The man never misses a single detail.* "I'm sorry. I didn't want you to think I was crazy."

Alex shook his head. "No need to apologize, kiddo. I can understand why you didn't. But it's important you tell me now."

Aletheia spilled her story to her uncle, telling him everything she could recall about the nightmares she had been experiencing – all of them. He sat and listened quietly as he exited onto the highway and drove them out past the city limits and through neighboring cities. In the back seat, Adam listened quietly as well, his mind reliving his last painful memories of James. When she was done, she asked, "So does that mean it was a…Dy'ibalis…that was tormenting me?"

Alex nodded grimly. "I'm not sure, but that's what I think. Unless David Copperfield was in that park. There are a couple of other possibilities – like I said before, they are just the tip of the iceberg – but that seems to be the most likely."

"How do you know?" Adam asked.

He glanced up in the rearview mirror to look at Adam as he spoke. "Well, three things stand out to me. One, Dy'ibalis are able to turn invisible. They can supposedly remain unseen in broad daylight. Two, they're large and immensely strong. Those two things would explain what happened to the police officers at your house…and to your brother."

Adam felt punched in the gut at the thought of James being mangled by some invisible demon-thing.

"And three…" he looked at Aletheia. "…they can put images, sensations – sounds, tastes, feelings – into people's minds, whether that person is asleep or awake."

The look on Aletheia's face was pure dread. She looked stunned. "You mean…that *thing*…was in my head?"

"I don't know how it works, exactly. I know it's not like the stories of demons – they can't possess people. But they can send any images they want, along with any sensations they can imagine, into your mind."

Aletheia put her hand to her mouth in sudden realization. She looked at Adam in the back seat, overcome with emotion. "So that thing…that thing killed Meghan, didn't it?"

Alex thought about it and slowly nodded. "I hadn't thought of that, but yes…that would make sense. You said the nightmare you had that night was very realistic, right? That would explain why you even knew how she landed. It showed you."

"IT WAS IN MY ROOM!?"

Alex just breathed out hard and stroked his mustache furiously. From the back of the car she heard Adam mutter under his breath, "Holy shit…"

They rode along silently for a moment while Aletheia regained her composure. Adam finally broke the silence by asking, "Alex – how do you know all this stuff?"

"Like I said, Adam – I answer to someone whose duty it is to watch over humanity. He – and his people – taught me everything I needed to know."

Before they could continue their conversation, Aletheia blurted out, "Should we head to a church or something?" She looked absolutely terrified.

Alex shook his head gravely. "Like I said, this isn't about religion. They're not *from* the Bible. The Bible *talks* about them – includes the stories passed down about them by the Hebrew people – but the stories were convoluted by that point and the real truth is far older than that."

"So what am I going to do? Why is that thing haunting me?"

He was looking at the road up ahead as he answered her. "I don't know why, kiddo. That's one of the things that troubles me most. There are some things about all of this that just don't add up, like the eyewitness seeing a woman push your friend. As far as I know, Dy'ibalis can't change shape or anything like that – that part is myth. But I will tell you what we're going to do. We're going to pull over right up here and I'm going to make that call. And then I'm going to do everything I can to get you to him. That's what we're going to do."

Looking out the window, Adam and Aletheia realized they had been so engrossed in the conversation with Alex that they had driven all the way out into the desert. As they pulled over to the dusty shoulder on the side of the road, Adam sat back and tried to process everything he had heard. One question stood out in his mind.

"Alex…can he keep her safe?"

Alex smiled a genuine smile for the first time since they had been reunited with him – sad, but genuine. He nodded confidently. "Adam…" He turned to look at Aletheia as well before continuing. "…kiddo…as long as I can get you to him, you'll be in the safest place on Earth." The older man popped open the door and got out of the sedan, taking out his prepaid cellphone as he walked away from the car.

19

Aletheia turned to Adam as her uncle exited the car and walked a bit off in the distance. She looked at him, trying to gauge how he was handling his brother's death.

"Hey…are you sure you're okay? Do you want to talk about it?"

Adam looked at her, a pained expression on his face as though he was struggling with himself. After a moment he shook his head. "No…I can't talk about James right now." He looked at her sincerely. "I'll be ready to talk about it later. Thank you."

She smiled at him. "Of course. You're always there for me." She turned to glance at her uncle's shadow as he talked on the cellphone a short distance from the vehicle, and then spun back to face Adam. She looked overwhelmed. "This is crazy!"

Adam leaned forward in his seat. "I know. I always wondered about this stuff – maybe not the way he's explaining it – but I always wondered. How ancient do you think these things are? And who is he talking to?"

One look at Aletheia's face as he spoke told him that she

hadn't meant her comment the same way he had interpreted it. She glanced at her uncle again. "I meant...do you think he's lost it? He's always been solid as a rock...but this...this is too much. It can't be true."

Adam looked at her and thought about what Alex had said about people knowing but not letting themselves believe. "Lee, I know it all sounds crazy, but...think about what's been happening to you: the dreams, Meghan's death, what...what we just saw. Forget about everything the world has told you." He looked directly into her eyes. "Hey...forget about what you think your shrink would say, okay?"

He knows me so well. Her shoulders slumped as she relaxed and tried to let go.

Adam continued, "What do *you* think? What does your mind tell you is the most probable thing happening here?"

She nodded, a look of resignation in her eyes. "That I'm being haunted...or whatever it's called if it's not a demon doing it. That...that thing killed Meghan...and the police. I guess somewhere in me I know it's true. It was the first thing I thought when this all started – I just dismissed it. I told myself I was thinking crazy and it wasn't possible."

She slumped down in her seat and Adam gave her some mental space to process what his mind had already accepted. It hadn't been that far a leap for him. The oddest part to him was that he hadn't been tempted to fight against it. He was...eager. The world seemed more real to him when he thought of what he had just learned. He found himself envying Alex and the life he led. *Something that matters. Something worth fighting for.* Looking out the window he saw the older man continuing to talk on the phone. He had taken something out of his pocket and was writing on it. Curious, Adam reached over and depressed the button on the door panel slightly. The window didn't move. *Damn...he must have shut the car off completely.*

"Lee," he said quietly. "Reach over and turn the key. Don't start the car – I just want some air."

She complied, still deep in thought. Adam opened the window a quarter way – just enough to strain his ear to hear what Alex was saying. The man was turned away at the moment, and all Adam could hear was soft mumbling. After only a few seconds of waiting, Alex turned around and put the item he had been writing on back in his pocket. He didn't seem to see or notice Adam's window open. Adam could now hear pieces of his conversation.

"...completely isolated now...don't see how they can...go into hiding...in our world now...want answers...bring them in..."

The rest was jumbled as Alex again turned away. Soon he was walking back to the car. Adam closed the window when it seemed like the man wasn't looking. The door opened and Alex plopped into the driver's seat again. He seemed to pause when he reached to start the car and Adam saw the reflection of the man's eyes flicker in the rearview mirror.

Alex looked to them both as he pulled off the side of the road and rejoined the highway. "Okay...we're going to be okay. We're going to get you two out of here."

Aletheia shook herself out of her thoughts and smiled weakly at him. "Thank you, Uncle." She let out a deep sigh. "Sorry...it's just a lot to absorb all at once."

Alex nodded at her. "I know. Take your time with it. I remember when I was first...when I first found out. It took me near three weeks to come to terms with it."

"Where are we headed?" Adam asked from the back seat.

"Small, private airfield in western Arizona. There will be a plane waiting for us."

Aletheia's eyes widened in disbelief. "A plane? You mean like, a *private* plane?"

"Yes, kiddo…a private jet, actually."

"Who the hell do you work for?" Adam asked.

Alex swiveled his head towards them both. "I know you both have a lot of questions, and I'll answer whatever ones I can. But before I do that, it's my turn to ask. I need to know everything that has happened to you both since the nightmares started. I mean, any detail you can think of that is odd or different from your normal lives. And I need to know every detail of your friend Meghan's death and those policemen's deaths."

Adam looked to Aletheia and said, "You should tell it. This probably all started with the dreams." She took a deep breath and began to speak.

They had a long drive ahead of them and Aletheia was tired. She and Adam spent the next few hours recounting everything they could think of to her uncle. He listened to them both intently the way he always did, even when they were rehashing things they had already told him. Occasionally, Alex would ask them a clarifying question or two. She knew he was absorbing every bit.

It was the early hours of the morning when they finally finished relaying the details of their last day on the rooftop and their last meeting with James to him. Alex looked deep in thought and was silent for a few long moments before finally speaking.

"It doesn't make sense. Almost everything you've told me leads me to believe the Dy'ibalis have finally found us. I'm pretty sure it was responsible for Meghan's dreams as well. It's like it set this whole thing up."

Aletheia nodded in realization, but she disagreed with her uncle's claim that it didn't make sense. Everything that had happened to her the past two weeks – the insanity of it all – was finally *starting* to make sense. She looked at her uncle. "Why me?"

He shook his head. "That's why I said 'almost' everything you said is leading me to this. The details – they all make sense. Points right to a Dy'ibalis. But the behavior – the motive – that's not adding up at all."

"What do you mean?" Adam asked.

Alex looked at them both grimly. "You should both be dead. *Dead.* Without a doubt. And not just you; everyone in that building, everyone on that campus, everyone it could get its claws into within miles. By violence or by disease…" He paused at the shocked looks on their faces before nodding and continuing. "Yes…they like to use disease as a weapon. You should all be dead. And I should have been getting a call from my office to cover the story of a death toll that shook the entire Pacific Northwest. All this…subtlety, all this plotting…just to frame you for a crime? It just doesn't add up."

Aletheia interjected. "I thought that's what these things did? I thought they liked to torture people and tempt them?"

"No. Don't get me wrong, they are capable of it. They are a very intelligent race; intelligent enough to come up with a complex plan and execute it. But so much of this is…*off.* How would it know the laws or subtleties of our society enough to set you up like that? How long would it have had to be here undetected to learn that much?" He shook his head as if he were trying to clear cobwebs out of it. "Everything I've been taught is clear: when a Dy'ibalis tries to get in someone's head, it's not to play mind games. It's just a means to an end to eventually destroy its enemies."

He looked at them both. He looked tired. And old. Older than Aletheia had ever seen him in her life. "Understand this very clearly: they are not searching for mankind so they can torture us one at a time and drive us crazy. They're searching for us to destroy us – all of us. That is their goal: to destroy all of humanity."

Adam and Aletheia both wore expressions of surprise and horror on their faces. Adam's voice came from the back seat. "Are you serious?"

"Yes. As serious as it gets. I hate to say it – I'm so glad you both made it through – but it should have killed you both. I don't understand why it didn't. So you see, the bigger question isn't why it targeted you, kiddo…it's why *didn't* it?"

All three of them sat there in silence for a long time. It was Adam who finally spoke. "A while ago you said there were other possibilities. What are they?"

"I'm not sure. Maybe there are possibilities I'm missing. I can only think of two. One would be that someone or something else might want us to think it's a Dy'ibalis when it's not."

"I thought you said nobody knows about these things?"

"Only a few do…which makes that a very disturbing thought that I won't even entertain at this time. Even then, I can't imagine how they would be able to do what we saw done back in that skate park. If they could...well...if they could then we would have an even bigger problem on our hands."

Deep in thought, Adam eyed the back of Alex's head. "What's the second possibility?"

Alex's gravelly voice held notes of frustration and concern as he answered. "That it is exactly what it seems like, and is acting exactly the way it is supposed to. Which means it has a plan – a plan that leads to our destruction – and I don't understand it yet. I need time to think."

It was only an hour or so later when they pulled into the small airfield. The rest of the drive had been fairly quiet, each of them mulling the details around in their heads. Aletheia stared out the window at her surroundings, straining her eyes to see the details in the dark. The handful of lights illuminating the airfield did not provide much help. *Small is an understatement.* Resting just on the outskirts of the small town they had passed just off the highway, it consisted of little more than a single hangar and one strip which she guessed was used for both takeoff and landing.

As they pulled up in front of the building, she saw it. Parked on the runway was a small but very expensive-looking jet. Its sleek profile looked completely out of place in the old, outdated airfield. As they approached she could make out stairs coming down from the plane to the ground where two men in suits stood waiting for them. She heard Adam exclaim from the back seat.

"Whoa."

Alex stopped the car and got out hastily. He quickly set about emptying it out, including the trunk, of any items he had left there. He grabbed his suitcase and motioned for them to follow him, hurrying towards the plane as soon as they did. When he got there he said a few brief words to a third suited man who Aletheia hadn't noticed before, and before she and Adam could even close the distance the man was passing them and getting into the car they had left behind. Alex stopped and turned back towards them and waited for them at the foot of the stairs. As they rushed up to him, he waved them forward and said, "Come on." One of the men at the bottom of the stairs greeted him as he passed and then nodded to Adam and Aletheia as well as they climbed the stairs.

The interior cabin of the plane was dimly lit, allowing their eyes to adjust easily from the darkness outside. The furnishings were luxurious; the comfortable leather seats interspersed with small, built-in tables so that it almost felt like a small living room. Adam plopped his bags down on one of the seats and Aletheia followed suit, sinking into the soft leather and immediately feeling the weariness in her muscles. Adam looked around in awe.

Alex said, "Relax and enjoy the ride. I promise you'll get more answers very soon." He leaned forward and whispered to both of them. "These men are paid well to keep us safe, but they are *paid*. Bodyguards. Mercenaries. Understand? Best not to talk about the things we've been discussing until we get to our location. We should be safe here. Try to get some sleep."

Should? That doesn't make me feel any better. Aletheia looked at the two men in suits seated on the other side of the cabin. The man closest smiled to her and then resumed talking to the other one. *They seem nice enough. Mercenaries?* Trusting in her uncle, she gave up on attempting to understand what was happening. Instead she focused on trying to relax, leaning back into the comfortable leather, and closing her eyes. As she drifted off to sleep, she felt Adam's hand brush hers and then close over it, holding it tightly.

20

Aletheia slept well in the safety of the plane's cabin. The steady whine of the plane's engines combined with the comfort of the plush reclining seat provided her with the most relaxed environment she had slept in for some time. She finally woke to Alex gently shaking her shoulder. Opening her eyes, she groggily looked at him and saw that he was waking Adam as well.

"Come on you two…we're here."

It was a testament to their complete and utter exhaustion that they had slept through the entire plane ride, including the descent. The plane felt like it was already stopped, and sunlight shone brightly through the small windows.

"What time is it?" she asked.

Looking at his watch, Alex said, "Well…it's about two in the afternoon, local time."

Adam raised his head off his reclined seat beside her, squinting at the rays of sunshine that splashed across his eyes when he did so. "Local? Where are we?"

"New York. Come on…let's go. We're almost there now."

The two of them gathered their things while Alex spoke with one of the bodyguards. As Aletheia approached, she overheard the conversation. She kept quiet and watched the exchange while Adam rummaged through his backpack.

"He said he found it when he was doing one final sweep of your car. Apparently it was under the rear bumper," said the bodyguard.

Her uncle looked stunned. It was not something she was used to seeing. "Huh. That…I did not expect that. How did he find it there?"

"He said you missed something – your parking ticket from the airport. It was in the trunk. I guess when he took it out, he dropped it on the ground. When he knelt down to get it, he saw the tracker under the bumper. Pure luck that he found it."

Alex blew out a long whistle. "What did he do with it?"

"Took some pics and logged the specs, then destroyed it."

Alex thanked the man and then led Adam and Aletheia off the plane. When they got onto the tarmac, she asked her uncle about the conversation.

"Well, this just gets stranger by the minute. Kelvin – the man who took care of my rental car in Arizona – found a GPS tracker on it before he turned it in."

Aletheia's face screwed up in confusion. "Why would there be a GPS tracker on your car?" Her expression changed to panic as a sudden realization hit her. "Do you think the police were tracking you?"

Alex shook his head. "No, kiddo. They have no reason to. Even if they did and they knew I had found you, they would have either arrested us at that airfield or they would have been waiting for us when we got here. No...I think it was someone else."

"The Dy'ibalis thing?"

Alex looked at her, worry etched in his aged face. "If it did, then it had human help. Kelvin said it was just a regular GPS tracker – the kind you can buy online. So where would it have gotten it, and how did it know how to use it? It's not like it could have just waltzed into a store and bought one, and I doubt it has an Amazon account. No, I think it was someone else. But I have no idea who. All I know is, something's not right."

Alex's concern rubbed off on Aletheia, setting her mind to once again trying to figure out what was going on. Adam was beside them now, walking towards a black limousine up ahead. She looked around for the first time since getting out of the plane.

They were in another small airfield similar in size to the last one, with a single, shiny metallic hangar. The sky was bright and clear, only a handful of puffy white clouds drifting lazily across it. The area around them though, was a drastic change from the desert they had been in just a few hours ago. The field was surrounded on three sides by trees, their leaves blaring loudly in a bright palette of autumn colors. On the third side was a large swath of green grass with a paved road running through it.

"I thought you said we were in New York?"

"Upstate New York," Alex answered.

They were ushered into the limousine by more men in dark suits, each of them watching everything around them as though a threat might appear at any time. Alex quietly reminded both Aletheia and Adam to wait until they were in a more private place to continue their conversation from the night before. Had it not been for that, the ride in the limousine might have been enjoyable. Not being able to discuss the mind-blowing events of the last twenty-four hours though, made the ride seem like it lasted an eternity for Aletheia. Now that she had gotten some answers she wanted more. It nagged at her consciousness like an itch on her back that was just out of reach.

Trees turned to towns and towns turned to cities as they traveled along the highway towards their destination. Several times Adam peered out the window at a city they entered, hoping to see downtown New York. He had never been there in his life, but it was one of the cities he had always hoped to see. Even given the circumstances, he couldn't help but feel some excitement tingling in his fingers and toes. After the first few promising stretches of city came and went, he tried to sit back and relax. The traffic was starting to get thick, and they moved along at a snail's pace, taking a good ten minutes to even cross the bridge they were on. It was a long while before he noticed that the limousine had gotten noticeably darker inside. Looking out the tinted window, he found they were surrounded on both sides by tall buildings, one after another packed together tightly. Bringing his attention back down to eye level, he was shocked to notice that the other cars were driving mere inches from the limousine. *Damn. Very different city from Seattle. Or L.A.* He pointed it out to Aletheia, and soon the two of them were ogling out the limo's window like tourists on a vacation, their troubles temporarily forgotten.

They slowly wound their way through the avenues until the limousine finally came to a stop in front of a very tall glass building. Alex looked at both of them and smiled. The men in suits ushered them out of the limousine and a doorman greeted them at the large, oversized doors out front. As Alex came up and joined them, the doorman nodded to him and smiled.

"Good to see you again, Mr. Mann."

Alex smiled in return and ushered them into the palatial lobby.

"Aren't you supposed to tip him or something?" she asked.

Alex nodded. "Normally, yes. Here…no. It's all already taken care of…generously."

She accepted his answer and followed their escorts into the elevator, noticing the man pushed the button for the top floor as the stylized doors closed in front of her. She reached next to her and clasped Adam's hand tight, realizing more each second how nervous she was to meet this mysterious man her uncle worked for. Not for the first time in the last twenty-four hours, she glanced over at her uncle and wondered, *Who are you?*

The doors opened on the upper floor and they exited into a small, stylishly furnished room. It looked like an entry room; a short hallway punctuated by only one large door on the other side. At the doorway sat a man dressed as the others. *Bodyguard,* she thought. After some brief conversation, he tilted his head in a nod of acknowledgement to Alex and they were brought inside.

Of all the many things Aletheia had seen recently, none could have prepared her for this. She was awestruck as they entered the penthouse, wondering if that word was even sufficient to describe what she was seeing. It looked more like a modern version of a small palace perched atop this building, all contemporary design and earthy tones mixed with splashes of color. The ceilings were high, and the external walls they could see were solid glass, giving a breathtaking view of the

Manhattan skyline. Mixed in with the beautiful modern décor were pieces of art and artifacts mounted on the walls and in display cases on tables; ancient things that spoke of history and knowledge.

She looked to her right and saw Adam's face filled with wonder. He looked around and then briefly to her. "This is incredible." She saw his gaze dart rapidly among the things on the walls and in the cases and smiled. *This must be heaven for him. Good. He needs to be distracted right now.* Moving her gaze to her uncle, she saw him regarding both of them thoughtfully. He seemed to pause, probably to give them a moment to take it all in, before prompting them to follow him into an adjoining room. The men in suits stayed behind, remaining by the door.

The room they moved into was no less impressive, but had a more lived-in feel to it. Comfortable chairs and couches were arranged tastefully in the center of the room. The walls – all of them – were lined with bookcases filled top to bottom with books. At the opposite end of the room was a large, contemporary desk, and at the desk sat a woman. She was reading a book in one hand and seemed to be referencing a small tablet on the desk as she read, her fingers occasionally clacking the keys of the keyboard attached to it. When they entered she looked up at them.

Aletheia had seen many beautiful women in her life. Meghan had been beautiful, with gorgeous blue eyes, perfect tanned skin, and the face of a movie star framed by luxurious, shiny black hair. Aletheia had always admired her friend's looks. The woman seated at the desk before her, though, had a beauty that surpassed even Meghan's. Looking at her, Aletheia felt awestruck.

The woman was older than her, though not as old as her uncle. Aletheia placed her in her early forties. Her hair was up in a bun, with wisps of it hanging down as though she had put it up in a rush. It was the color of flax; pale yellow run through with streaks of burnished gold. Her skin glowed with a health that belied her age. More than that, she had a beauty that spoke of wisdom. If Meghan was the beauty of a woman's youth, this woman was the beauty of a woman's prime, ripe and mature. She looked directly at Aletheia. And then she smiled.

When she smiled at her, Aletheia felt all her cares fall away. She felt herself smiling back without even intending to, and her heart immediately filled with love for this woman. It seemed as though the sun shone brighter in the room than it had a moment before. As it did Aletheia realized what made this woman so beautiful. It wasn't her physical appearance; it was a *feeling* she radiated. It reminded her of the feeling she got when she looked at her mother. It was the beauty Aletheia saw when she looked at people she had loved for a long time and they became more and more beautiful to her. Except that she felt it when she looked at this woman for the first time.

She hadn't even realized how much she had been staring until Alex crossed the room and the woman stood from her work and embraced him in a tight hug. *She is so graceful she moves like a ballerina!* Her attention momentarily broken, she turned to Adam and saw the same happy, content feeling on his face as he looked at the woman. Alex turned to the two of them and introduced them to her.

"This is Adam, and this…this is Aletheia."

He looked to her and added, "Aletheia…Adam…this is

Sam."

"Hello, Adam. Hello, Aletheia." Sam moved across the room towards them, approaching Adam first. She shook his hand gently and smiled again, then moved on to Aletheia. She took her hand and held it rather than shaking it, and as she looked at her she tilted her head as if examining her. Aletheia stood transfixed.

"Alex tells me that the two of you have been through much." She looked at Adam, then back at Aletheia. "I am so very sorry for your losses."

Aletheia felt such empathy – such genuine feeling – in the woman's deep green eyes as she expressed the sentiment that she was taken aback. Feelings – about Meghan's death, about how terrifying this whole experience had been for her, about watching Adam lose his brother – that she had been suppressing the last week all floated up to the surface of her consciousness and threatened to pour out. Something about this woman made her want to open up to her and let it all out.

Sam must have noticed immediately, because she reached up and touched her cheek and said, "Perhaps now is not yet the time for us to speak of loss." Aletheia nearly trembled as she regained control of herself and smiled back at the woman as she continued. "We will have plenty of time for that later." She turned that smile towards Adam, and then to Alex. "I will be here for all of you, but as you know, this concerns him first and foremost. He is waiting for you in the pool." Turning back to Adam and Aletheia she added, "The answers you have been seeking lie with him."

Aletheia thought she saw a glint of humor in Alex's face when she mentioned the pool. He nodded and then embraced her in another hug. "It is good to see you again." She returned the sentiment with the same loving, motherly look she had given Aletheia and then sat back down behind the desk, watching them all thoughtfully as Alex led them out of the room.

21

They passed through several large rooms; each as beautifully appointed as the first two, and each holding more treasures from ages past. As eager as they all were, Alex let them take their time as he led them, with Adam in particular stopping repeatedly to look more closely at some item or another. Aletheia's head swam, trying to keep pace with all the things she was experiencing in such a short time. Glancing over at Adam she caught him looking at her as well, with the same expression on his face she must have worn.

"Do you know how much this place must be worth?" he said. "It's like a museum in here. Did she say they have a pool?"

Aletheia shared Adam's amazement, finding comfort in talking with the only other person in the room who seemed overwhelmed by what they were seeing. "I know! Can you believe how beautiful she was? She made me feel...I don't know how to explain it."

Adam got a weird look on his face and said, "Yeah. She made me feel...*safe*. I don't mean physically, so much...it's more like I feel like I could tell her anything." Aletheia reminded herself to talk more with him about it later, as they had just stopped outside two large double doors. Alex opened one of them, standing aside so they could enter. He had a smile on his face, and Aletheia noticed her uncle looked more relaxed than she had seen him since this whole ordeal began.

"Come on…he's in here."

The doors opened up into a large indoor pool area. It had the look and feel of an ancient bathhouse, with gray stone columns reaching up to the high ceiling and a large, rectangular pool in the middle. The outside perimeter of the room was more modern, the tinted glass walls matching the rest of the penthouse suite and giving a spectacular view of a different part of the city. The pool appeared to be empty.

Aletheia and Adam both looked to Alex. As though reading their minds, he chuckled and said, "He's in there – just wait. He likes to sit on the bottom of the pool sometimes. He says it helps him clear his head." His face lost its mirth for a moment and he added, "He's probably trying to reason through what's going on."

They stood and waited for a moment, and then Alex sat down on the raised stone edge of the pool and motioned for them to do the same. A full minute passed, and Adam looked to Alex but was surprised when he seemed unconcerned. Another minute passed, and then another. Adam was starting to become restless. Finally he blurted out, "Should we go help him? Is he even in there? It's been, like, five minutes!"

Alex smiled and nodded as he answered, "I know. I promise you, he is fine. Just be patient." Aletheia watched the exchange and Adam turned to her incredulously, looking for support. She considered speaking up, but instead just shrugged and went back to waiting, which at least seemed to make Adam calm down a bit. *Maybe this guy's sitting in his pool in scuba gear or something – who knows. I don't understand a single thing that's going on anymore anyway. Either Uncle Alex is crazy or he knows way more than I do. Besides, that Sam...I trust her.*

Several more minutes passed before the man finally came up from beneath the water. All three of their heads turned to watch as he broke the surface. He was light-skinned, with European features. His head was shaved clean and his face was handsome, with gentle but angular lines. His eyes were closed when he first appeared, and his expression spoke of serenity. Aletheia wondered if they should announce themselves, but didn't want to disturb the man in his current state. She was relieved when he opened his eyes, looked in their direction, and smiled. He then reached forward and ducked himself under the water, moving towards them.

Adam watched the man carefully. *Who can hold their breath for ten minutes?* As the man submerged and swam towards them, Adam noticed for the first time that the water was neither blue nor clear as he would have expected in a pool. Instead it was a rich, medium green; translucent but not transparent, it's opaque surface partially obscuring the view of the man gliding gracefully under it towards their side of the pool. A few seconds later, the man broke the surface and reappeared, rising up out of the pool until it was apparent he was standing and walking up a slope towards them.

As he emerged from the pool, Adam found himself wondering how old this man was. On the one hand, his face, build, and posture held a maturity that was immediately obvious. He certainly did not look young. Adam first guessed the man to be in his late forties – perhaps a little younger than Alex. And yet, looking at him standing there in his swim trunks, Adam could not believe it was possible he was that old. He had the physique of a twenty year-old Olympian. He was tall, but not overly so, with every inch of his frame layered in tight, compact muscle. It was not the bulky, brute build of a bodybuilder; rather, Adam had the sense that if he were to design a perfect human athlete it would look like the man in front of him.

He emerged from the pool and picked up a white towel resting on the stone nearby, drying himself as he approached them with a lithe grace. When he got close, Adam noticed his eyes were the same vibrant, clear blue that the sky had been when they had gotten off the plane. He reached over and shook Alex's hand, pulling him into a brief hug. Backing away, he rested his hand on Alex's shoulder. When he spoke, it was in a rich, gentle voice.

"Alex…it is good to see you. It's been too long since you've been here."

He then turned to face them. "You must be Adam. And Aletheia." There was a kindness expressed in his clear blue eyes as he looked to Aletheia in particular. "It's a pleasure to finally meet you. You can call me Nikolas. You both must have a lot of questions. Come – let's talk."

Aletheia found herself seated in another room with Adam and Alex. While still luxurious, this room had a more intimate, cozy feel to it. There was an unlit fireplace in the wall, with more artwork and artifacts surrounding it. They sat on several comfortable couches positioned around the fireplace. Nikolas had just rejoined them, now dressed in jeans and a loose white button-down shirt.

"So…there is much for us to talk about. Let's start with the two of you. Your uncle Alex has filled me in on what he could while he was extracting you two from the situation, but I am sure given the circumstances he didn't have time to tell me all the details."

Aletheia looked to Alex and Adam and found them both staring at her expectantly. *Looks like I get the short straw again.* For the second time in the last twenty-four hours, she retold their entire story, from the beginning of the dreams all the way to their arrival in New York. Unlike her uncle and the lawyer, Nikolas did not ask a single clarifying question. He simply listened to her story straight through until it was done. When she finally finished, he looked to Adam. Adam simply shook his head and said, "That's pretty much all of it. I can't think of anything else."

Nikolas' face was very grim. "Well, I agree with Alex's assessment. It certainly *sounds* like a Dy'ibalis. Even down to the details about the dreams your friend Meghan referred to in her journal. Dy'ibalis can only project what they can sense, experience, or feel into another's mind. Because they are a different kind of being than humans, they can't feel the same range of emotions humans feel. One of the emotions they don't seem to be able to project is love."

Aletheia thought back to reading her friend's journal in the police station. "That's why her journal said she didn't *feel* like she was in love with him…he just kept popping into her head and her dreams…" She looked over to Adam and saw the same look of understanding on his face that she felt on her own.

Nikolas nodded once in affirmation and looked to Alex before continuing.

"I also agree that there are pieces of this that don't add up. I am particularly concerned about the GPS that was found on your vehicle. We have had...false alarms...before. If I were sure, I would do my duty immediately. But I am not sure. We need to confirm this."

As Alex nodded in understanding, Adam – who had been sitting quietly to this point – spoke out. "I'm sorry, but I can't take it anymore. Who are you? I know your name is Nikolas, but who are you really?"

Aletheia held her breath, wondering if Adam had offended this mysterious and obviously powerful man. If he did, it didn't show on the man's face. He simply smiled as Adam again apologized for interrupting him.

"Of course. Your minds must be spinning with what you have been through in the last few days and weeks." He looked to Alex. "Have you discussed their options with them yet?" Alex shook his head, and Nikolas turned back to the two of them. He looked at them sadly. "I am a man of some means, but you two must understand that even I cannot get you out of the legal trouble you are in. I am afraid those lives you had before are broken. You can never go back to them."

Aletheia and Adam both nodded soberly and she replied, "We know. We were planning on escaping to Mexico and hopefully starting a new life there."

Nikolas smiled at them. "Well, if you would like to start a new life we can do significantly more for you than that. Do you like Europe?"

Aletheia sat stunned. She turned to Adam and saw a glint in

his eyes as well. "You could really do that?"

Nikolas nodded. "Yes, but understand something: you both have a choice to make. I will not send you out there, even in a new country with new identities as long as you are being threatened by whatever or whoever is threatening you. It is far too dangerous. You did an admirable job escaping from Seattle and yet you were still followed as far as California or even possibly Arizona. If you two decide that you would like to start a new life in Europe you will stay here until we have figured out what is behind this and ensured your safety. After that, I will help you."

Aletheia couldn't believe what she was hearing. It was the answer to all her prayers since the whole mess had started. It would be awful not seeing her mother or any of her old friends – the mere thought of her mother nearly brought her to tears – but she and Adam could be safe and happy again. They would make new friends, and perhaps Alex could find a way to act as a go-between for her and her mother, at least. Perhaps one day she could even see her again. *I miss her so much...*

More importantly, this man was offering to make all the nightmares and the horrible things that had been happening to her go away.

Before she could answer Adam chimed in beside her. "You said we had a choice to make. What's the other choice?"

Nikolas got up from the couch he was on and walked around to the back of it, facing them. "If you choose that path, then you must swear to never speak of what you have been told so far, and our conversation about the rest of the subject is over. The amount you know now is dangerous enough. I cannot tell you anything more. If you want to know the truth – about the things you have been experiencing, mankind's past, and the world you live in – then you can never have a normal life again. You will join Alex in our cause. If you choose that path, I will make sure you are educated and have everything you need. That is your choice."

Aletheia wanted badly to know what was happening to her. She wasn't sure that she could live with never knowing, but the thought of actually rebuilding the normal life that had been ripped away from her was far too appealing to resist. *Europe! I bet Nikolas could set us up so well there...* She looked to Adam, who seemed deep in thought. He looked up and his gaze met hers and she immediately knew they were in trouble.

"Adam...no. You want to stay and do this, don't you?"

"Lee...I just don't know. I know you – I know what you want. But me...I want to know the truth. I've been wanting to know it my whole life. Not to mention, I want to know what did that to James. Even what I've heard so far..." He stopped as he saw the stress and worry etched on her face and exhaled a deep breath. "I want you to be happy. If going back to that life is what you truly want, I'll go along. But before you decide, Lee...look around you. How many people in their lives get an opportunity to do something like this? Something that matters. We could help protect the *world*. Not to mention to know things that no one else does." He looked at her with an earnestness that both amazed and worried her. "I just want to do something that matters. *I* want to *matter*."

She looked at him, distraught by his last words. "You do matter! You matter to me." Her frustration with him faded quickly, though; she understood what he had meant. *He has never understood how much he matters.* Aletheia thought for a long time. The three men sat silently, giving her time to contemplate her choices. After a while, she looked up at Alex and said, "You've never been married, you travel all the time. I can't even imagine all the things you've seen. Do you regret it?"

Alex smiled at her; a sincere smile laced with sympathy for the choice she was facing. "Pigtails...you've already seen a lot of the worst parts of this life. But you haven't seen the *best* parts yet. No...I don't regret it. Not a single day of my life. I would do it all over again in a heartbeat...and I wouldn't take weeks to accept it this time either."

Aletheia turned to Adam and looked deep into her boyfriend's eyes. "I'm not sure if this is what I want. I mean, to get a life back...and Europe? I know just yesterday we were going to live poor in Mexico under false identities and not have a normal life anyway, but this...it's like getting that dream back and immediately losing it all over again."

Adam started to speak, undoubtedly to tell her he would follow her on whatever path she chose, but she cut him off. "No. I'm just talking out loud. I may not be sure if this is what I want, but I know that it's the right thing to do." She looked at Alex and Nikolas. "I choose this life. I choose truth."

All three men beamed at her, the two older men with pride and Adam with appreciation. He reached over and held her hand tight, mouthing the words 'Thank you,' as the two older men exchanged smiles between them. She interrupted their happy moment and added, "But...I am only doing this if Adam and I can do it together, as a team, always. And I want to see my uncle more often." She threw a nervous smile at her uncle then, and he beamed back.

Nikolas laughed. "Of course. That goes without saying..."

Before he could say more, Aletheia interrupted him again. "And...could you still send us to Europe sometime?" At that, the man laughed even harder.

"I am sure that can be arranged."

Adam cocked his head and looked at the man, as if he had thought of something that he hadn't before. When he spoke, his tone wasn't suspicious, but rather curious.

"Wait. This offer – both of these offers – sound great and all. They really do. Part of me wants to know where to sign up. But before I do, I need to understand something. I know Alex works for you, and I get that you are both involved in protecting, well...all of us from this craziness we're talking about. But that doesn't explain to me...why would you do all that? For us? Why would you help us create a whole new life, or offer to take us in and make all our problems go away? It feels like a magical fix for everything, and I've learned that those don't exist. If I'm going to trust you, I need to know why you're doing what you're doing. It can't be for no reason."

Nikolas looked at him, serious again. Alex moved from where he was to sit on the other side of Aletheia and put his hand on her shoulder. It felt strong, as though he was trying to steady her. Nikolas looked to Adam and said, "I am impressed more with you by the minute. There are not many people who impress me anymore. You are wise not to trust blindly when someone offers you such a generous gift. What are my motivations? What strings are attached?" He held his arms out wide, glancing at Adam. "Adam, I like you, and I care about what happens to you. The more you come to know me the more you will understand why. But beyond that, I will tell you plainly: you are not the reason I am offering to help the way I am. She is."

Nikolas gestured to Aletheia. She felt an involuntary shiver in her spine. The look on the man's face was still serious but also kindly. Adam was staring at him suspiciously. She finally managed to find the strength to ask, "Me? Why me?"

"Because, Aletheia…you are family."

Adam's mouth opened as a look of understanding spread across his face. Aletheia looked to her uncle for confirmation. When she did he smiled and nodded his head.

"It's true, kiddo. I know, because he's my family too."

She looked back to Nikolas. "So…are you like, another uncle or something?"

Nikolas shook his head. He was watching her reaction very carefully. That was when Aletheia heard her uncle's gravelly voice in her ear.

"He's your great-grandfather."

Adam's eyes went wide with shock; Aletheia thought hers must be even wider. She could feel her uncle's hand gripping her shoulder tightly, holding her there like an anchor to reality. She slowly turned to look at him and saw the confirmation in his eyes. Alex gave her shoulder one last gentle squeeze for support and then he slowly got up and walked over to stand next to Nikolas.

"You're…you're what?" Her gaze shifted towards her uncle. He and her mother had always told her that her great grandparents were all dead. He simply tilted his head forward and looked at her the way he had done when she was a child and he was waiting for her to figure something obvious out on her own.

"I've had two responsibilities my entire life, Pigtails. My two purposes for living. The one I told you about back in the car...and watching over you."

She looked at Nikolas. "But you're...you're not old enough! It doesn't make any sense!"

He chuckled. "I can assure you, Aletheia, I am more than old enough. As for my precise age...would you like to venture a guess as to how old I am?"

"I don't know...you look like you're forty or so, at most. Like you two could be brothers, or cousins or something." Adam was nodding in agreement from his side of the couch, watching Nikolas carefully.

"Now that, young woman, is very flattering of you to say."

Adam was watching Nikolas the way someone might watch a large, wild animal; with respect and reverence, but also caution. *This is no normal man. He may be a good man – maybe even very good – but not a normal one. What is he?* "Exactly how old *are* you?" he asked.

"It is hard to say exactly, as the years here do not pass the same way they did where I came from. But I have been here for well over six thousand years, and I lived another millennium before that."

Aletheia had been watching the exchange, her head spinning. As Nikolas said the last words, she looked at him and saw dark circles closing in around the edge of her vision. The last thing she remembered was Adam's hands catching her as she tipped over, and her own thoughts running through her head.

Seven thousand years? My great-grandfather is seven thousand years old?

22

We have drunk of the soma;
We have become immortal,
We have seen the light;
We have found the gods...
        -Rig Veda 8.48.3 c.1200 B.C.

Aletheia's vision came slowly into focus. Her uncle's face gradually became clearer, as did Adam's. She realized she was lying on her back, looking up at the high ceiling. Instinctively, she tried to sit up, but they both stopped her when she tried, encouraging her to take a moment. *Yes...maybe I do need a moment. Seven thousand years old...* Her head felt fuzzy; she tried to wait patiently for it to pass. *So many questions.* After a minute or two Alex said to her, "You okay, kiddo?"

"Yes, I'm okay. It felt like my brain was on overload for a minute there – my head was swimming. Everything just started to get dark."

"You passed out," said Alex. "It's okay...you've had a lot to take in the last twenty-four hours."

Adam looked at her, concern in his eyes. "You sure you're okay?"

"Yes. I'm starting to feel better already." She motioned for them to help her sit up, and they cautioned her to take it slowly as they did.

Alex's gravelly voice turned her attention towards him. "Maybe that's enough for one day. You look like you could use a good meal and some sleep."

"Actually, that sounds nice...but no. I want to hear more." She looked to Nikolas. "Some of the things you said...I need to understand."

Nikolas turned to Alex and said, "I wish we could give her more time to process this too, but she does not have the luxury you had. If we are dealing with a Dy'ibalis – or any of the other possibilities I can think of – we don't have weeks. We may not even have days."

Alex nodded and Aletheia said, "It's okay. Really...I can handle it. I just need a minute to adjust my thinking. It's a lot to accept all at once." She steadied herself and added, "Hi...Grandpa, I guess? It's nice to meet you."

Nikolas's smile stretched from ear to ear. He even chuckled. "It is very nice to finally meet you too, Aletheia."

"Keep going, please. I want to know more." She adjusted herself on the couch, trying to get more comfortable. Her head was still fuzzy.

"What is it that you would like to know?"

"How...how can you be that old? How are you not dead? I'm sorry – I don't mean that in a bad way. I just don't understand. Seven thousand years old? How is that possible?"

He nodded thoughtfully and said, "Well, I will do my best

to explain." He sat down on the couch across from them again, elbows resting comfortably on his knees as he leaned forward, and looked at her and Adam both as he began. "I will explain it to you the way it was taught to me, thousands of years ago, when I was a mortal."

Adam interrupted him immediately. "Wait…you're *immortal?*"

Nikolas nodded. "Yes."

Adam sank back into the couch with his hands on his head. "Holy crap. Okay…sorry, but that is insane. Go ahead…continue." He was staring at Nikolas at an angle, afraid to look directly at him.

Nikolas bowed his head once in acknowledgment and continued. "There are two realms of existence: the physical realm, and the spiritual. The physical is the world we live in." He put his arms out and gestured around him. "And everything in that world. Matter, energy, time, the laws of physics, our bodies…" He patted his arm for effect. "…all exist in this physical realm."

Aletheia listened carefully. Adam was nodding beside her.

"The spiritual realm – that is where our soul exists. The spiritual realm exists entirely outside space and time. The two are completely separate – they do not intersect or touch – except in one place. Can you guess where that is?"

Aletheia mulled over it in her mind, but before she could answer, Adam said quietly beside her, "In us."

Nikolas smiled at him. "Very good – in us – or to be more specific, in all living things."

His face took on a contemplative look. "In the last century alone, I have watched the human race make scientific advances I could never have foreseen. Humans can already clone entire organisms. I cannot imagine what else will be possible in the next six thousand years. But building cells or even organisms is only half of the equation of *life* – the physical half. To be *alive* also requires a spirit; a soul."

He extended the index finger of each of his hands and slowly brought them together in front of him until the points of his fingers touched. "The true definition of life is that for a length of time, a point in the spiritual realm connects with a point in the physical realm, like a bridge. When it does – when a soul connects with a physical body – it wakes it up. It makes it aware."

Aletheia struggled to keep up. It didn't help her confidence that when she looked over at Adam, he seemed to be comprehending all of it. He looked fascinated.

"The spiritual realm and the physical realm are very different. While the physical is bounded by time, the spiritual is eternal. While the physical is defined by movement and change, the spiritual is unchanging. That is the nature of our soul: it simply *is*. And *that* is why we must come here and exist in the physical realm for periods of time. That is why we are here."

"To change…" Adam had muttered it under his breath without even realizing he was speaking aloud. He looked up and saw Nikolas and Aletheia staring at him. "…to grow. We come here, because it's the only place we can grow." *He just explained the meaning of life to us in five minutes…*

"Correct again, Adam." He looked very pleased with him. "That is the reason we live: to spiritually grow. We come here many times, and as our soul grows with each life, an amazing thing happens. Not only does it grow stronger – more powerful –

but we become more aware of it. We learn listen to it. And in doing so, we learn to harness our own spiritual power. That process of growth and understanding is called Ascension."

Ascension. Adam thought back to all the workouts he had put himself through and wondered now which had made him stronger: the exercise or the meditation afterward.

"When a person is not in touch with their soul, or when their soul is young, it is at its weakest. It still has power, but only to affect itself. It can help the person find courage in times of fear, or heal them from emotional traumas that should have broken them. As a person starts to Ascend, their soul starts to grow strong enough to affect the body it is connected to – their own. At first it is only in very subtle ways; ways that might go unnoticed to the untrained eye. If you know what to look for, though, you can see the presence and power of even a weak soul. Have you ever wondered why it is that some people are born incredibly talented in certain areas? Why some people can say…learn to play the piano in a few months and already surpass others who have studied for years?"

"That's their soul?" Aletheia asked.

"Yes. Any time a person displays an innate talent for something – the arts, athletics, anything – it is the power of their soul being expressed through their own body. And as the soul grows stronger and they become more in tune with it, it can start to strengthen the body in more noticeable ways. It can help them reach their body's maximum potential. Olympic athletes performing at the peak of human ability. Poets writing pieces that touch millions of lives and go down in history as classics. The soul can also protect the body in times of crisis, enabling the person to do things in the moment that wouldn't normally seem possible. Like when a frightened mother lifts a three thousand pound car off her child and holds it up for over a minute, or when a person miraculously survives a fall from an airplane. Those are not accidents. They are the power of the person's soul shining through."

"That's...incredible. How long does it take to...Ascend that far?" Adam asked.

"That depends on the person and what they choose to do with their time here. Living a life of substance – a life that challenges you and has *meaning* – will make you Ascend further and faster than a life of shallowness or complacency. Experiencing things that force you to grow as a person will do the same, whether they are life-and-death situations or daily sacrifices that may go unnoticed by others. Saving someone's life would be an example, whether it is a fireman racing into a burning building or a housewife devoting her time and resources to save a starving child."

Adam felt validated. That was what he had always wanted. *A life of substance.*

"What I just described is not a very high level of Ascension – it is not that uncommon. While we certainly admire individuals who achieve these levels of greatness, they blend into society easily enough. But the higher we Ascend the more difficult it becomes, requiring greater and greater insight and growth with each step. Which means that the higher a person has Ascended, the rarer they are. As a person continues to Ascend beyond what is common, the effects become noticeable. They can start to exhibit powers and abilities that go beyond what can be scientifically explained: great strength or speed, or enhanced senses, for example. They can survive things that others could not. The way each person's soul manifests itself is unique, so the exact abilities they begin to exhibit depend on the individual. But the most telling clue that a person has Ascended to this level is that the person's unique abilities become obvious to others. Did you know there is a Japanese man alive today who can cut pellets fired from a gun in half in midair with a samurai sword? Scientists don't understand exactly how he does it, because the pellets are traveling faster than the human eye can track, but I understand it. I have visited with him – we have spoken at length. It is obvious to me that he is Ascending. He has just begun to scratch the surface of his abilities."

"Adam was taken aback. "You mean like, super heroes?" To his surprise, Nikolas did not laugh at his comparison.

"More or less, yes…that is how they would be viewed today. In days past they would simply have been called 'heroes'. They stand out in society. In the time I have been on this Earth, there have only been a few in the world at any given time. But that is not the only way they stand out. As the power of their soul expands, it starts to reach out beyond just their own body. While still too weak to affect the physical world, it starts to affect other souls around it. People who have Ascended to this point tend to have an effect on others. They make people feel uplifted, or happy, or safe, or any number of things."

Aletheia had a sudden realization. "Sam!"

Nikolas nodded and smiled. It was a distinctly different smile than he had worn thus far. "Yes, that is what you felt when you were in her presence. When it first begins to happen, it is not as strong or as noticeable as what you felt with Sam – but that is an example, nonetheless. As for her, she is Ascended significantly beyond that."

Aletheia and Adam exchanged looks at the last words. *This rabbit hole just keeps getting deeper…*

"As you can imagine, as Ascension continues, the effects continue to become more pronounced. The person is able to affect others' bodies as well, in subtle ways. They can strengthen others against injury or disease, or they can affect their minds – share thoughts and feelings with them."

Is that what the Dy'ibalis does?" Aletheia asked.

"That is a good question – it would seem to make sense – but no. I do not believe so, at least. A Dy'ibalis would need to be sufficiently Ascended to do so, and even among a race as long-lived as theirs, reaching that level of Ascension would be rare. I would not expect to see many of them demonstrate that ability. Yet all the stories I have heard and all the ones I have encountered have been able to send their thoughts and sensations to others, so the ability must originate elsewhere."

Adam looked confused. "Wait a minute…encountered?"

Nikolas looked at him and said, "Yes, I have encountered…and fought…many, though that was a long time ago. We will talk more of it later. For now, though, I am coming to the very long answer to your question. How is it that I am still alive? As you can imagine, continued Ascension beyond that which I have described to you results in abilities that would seem miraculous to the uninitiated. The ability of the soul to affect the person's own body becomes extraordinarily powerful. It starts to protect the body from diseases, injury, and even aging. As this happens, the aging process slows down. As the soul continues to grow, it eventually comes to a stop."

Aletheia looked to him and Adam and she understood. "The person becomes…immortal."

"Yes."

Adam was flabbergasted. "Holy…I can't believe it. So you're saying anyone can do this? I could become immortal?"

"With enough lifetimes and enough experiences…yes."

Adam looked astounded. "Wow…so…once you reach that level, that's it? You just live forever?"

Nikolas laughed. "No…that is certainly not it. As far as I know, we never stop growing. When a person reaches immortality, they are considered to have *Ascended*. Their growth is not ended, but they have reached a sort of…turning point in their existence. It completely changes the experience of living. Up until that point, time is of the essence. Even if a person lives a deep and meaningful life, they will most likely die of natural causes before they become Ascended. Achieving immortality is so incredibly rare it could take an individual soul thousands of lifetimes to get there. But after it is achieved, even if the individual were to live millions of years, it is only one life and one set of memories."

Adam had a thoughtful look on his face. "It sounds like the cycle of death and rebirth," said Adam. He turned to Aletheia. "The Hindus and Buddhists believe that the goal of life is to break free of the cycle."

"Yes," said Nikolas. "You have studied well. The concept of Samsara was born from the legends of these teachings, passed down through the ages."

Adam continued to question Nikolas eagerly. "So…if you're saying that we keep growing even after we reach immortality, what happens next?" Adam asked.

"Eventually, the power of the soul becomes so great that it is able to affect the physical world close by. The being can perform feats that would seem like miracles to others. Moving things without touching them, controlling the elements; for lack of a better term…magic. When one reaches this level they are known as *Divine*. Beyond even that, eventually the soul's power expands until it can affect huge areas…even entire worlds. That I know of, there are only a handful of beings in existence whose souls are this powerful, and they are millions of years old. They are known simply as *Primal*. These two types of beings, Divines and Primals, are often mistakenly worshiped as gods by those who are ignorant of Ascension."

Adam huffed. "What's the difference?" he asked sarcastically, overwhelmed and feeling very small and insignificant. *Any one of them sounds like they could crush me and every other person on Earth like a bug.*

"The difference is that they are not. They are simply beings who were once mortal and have grown beyond it. But they are not gods – there are no true gods that I know of, except The One."

Adam was shaking his head. It was so much to take in. "I don't understand – why hasn't anyone heard of this? If there were even a single immortal person in the world you would think it would be all over the news."

Nikolas nodded in agreement. "You are correct. To my knowledge, in the entire history of mankind, no human has yet fully Ascended. And I would be one of the first to know, because that is one of the many things we keep watch for. If it were to happen today it would be all over the news. At first, the person would receive attention for being in fantastic health for their age. Soon, they would become the world's oldest person and would still look young. After that, the news reporters and scientists would flock to them. The first time this happens in a species, it rocks the foundations of what they know and believe. When it first occurs, the individuals may even be heralded or worshiped as a god made flesh. But eventually, it happens again, and then again. And once it has happened even a handful of times and there are several living and breathing immortals integrated into a society, another change occurs. That species comes to accept it as a natural process. It changes the way that species sees and understands life at a very basic level, and it eventually becomes a goal for all members of society. At that point, the species as a whole is considered to be Ascended."

Aletheia looked to Adam who seemed to be deep in thought. She was confused. While she knew she understood most of it, her mind was flooded with terms and concepts that were so far from her everyday thoughts she knew she would need time to absorb it all. *Maybe a good meal and some sleep is a good idea.* Before she could let herself rest, though, she had to know one more thing.

"Nikolas…I mean, Grandpa?"

Nikolas laughed. "Yes?"

"I think I understand it, for the most part. But you…you talk about these things in a way that I feel like no one on Earth could ever know. Other species…processes that take millions of years. I don't understand how you know all these things. And you mentioned earlier that you came here from somewhere. Who are you…really? Where are you from?" *Who am I? Where am I from?*

23

What is your name?
I have seventy names,
Corresponding to the seventy nations of the world,
And all of them are based on the King of the kings
of kings;
My king calls me "Youth"
    -3 Enoch 3:1-2 c.300 B.C.

Nikolas looked to them and simply said, "I am a man."

The way he pronounced the word 'man' caught Adam's attention. He said it as though it were two syllables instead of one. *I didn't notice he had an accent before,* he thought. He didn't have time to mull over what type of accent it sounded like, though, as Nikolas continued to speak. The look on his face changed to one of amusement as though he had just thought of something funny.

"Have you ever heard of the game of telephone? It is an interesting phenomenon, the way words and stories change over many tellings. Many times, the final result is barely recognizable, with the exception of a few threads of the original story laced through it. Details change; even words or the ways the words are pronounced change until the meaning is assumed to be something completely different from the original message."

He got a faraway look in his eyes. "My given name – the name I was born to – is Enoki. I am also known, to those who know my title, as *Memattar-en*. It means 'The Keeper of the Watch.'" When I first arrived here, I did not take any pains to conceal myself. None of us did. It was a long time ago, and there was no need. Over the centuries, though, I realized the growing need for discretion and anonymity. I did my best to cover up any traces of my life that existed, but a few stories persisted. Over time, they grew; greatly exaggerated and confused, but about me nonetheless."

Nikolas – Enoki – took a deep breath and exhaled as he looked directly at both of them. He glanced at Alex and then continued to speak, his rich voice lowering as he did. "You may know some of those stories; likely not all of them, but perhaps a few. Depending on when and where the stories originated, I am called different names in them – variations of my true name or my title – as convoluted as the stories after many tellings. In Sumerian legends my name was pronounced 'Enki'. In other places at other times, 'Nechtan', 'Mithra' or 'Mithras', or 'Maitreya.' But the names from the stories you are most likely familiar with are Enoch and Metatron."

Aletheia looked at him confused, and at the same time sensing that something immense was being revealed to her. *Enoch...that's the only one I recognize. From the Bible. Does he actually mean...* She looked over to Adam for confirmation. His were so wide they looked as though they would pop out of his head.

"Holy…I mean…sorry. You're an angel?" he looked at him reverently, like he was considering falling to his knees on the spot.

Nikolas laughed. "Hardly. I am neither a pillar of fire nor as tall as the Earth." He turned briefly to show them his back. "And as you can see, the reports of my many wings and eyes are exaggerated. As to your question, no…I am not of the *Ankh-el*. I am as I said…a man."

There it is again, thought Adam. *Two syllables, like 'May-yen.' Wait a minute…I know he said he's not an angel but…*

"You said you lived a millennium before you came here. Did you mean to Earth? Where are you from? Did you come from Heaven?" asked Adam.

Nikolas laughed again, a deep, rich laugh. "No, Adam…certainly not. At least, no more than we all do. I – my people – came from another world. A world called Eyid-en."

"Eden?!" Adam exclaimed. "As in, the Garden of Eden?"

Nikolas nodded. "Yes. Like everything else, that story has changed much. Not so much in the last few thousand years, but before that – before the art of writing we taught to the people of Earth became widespread and stories were recorded. You must understand that every ancient story you have read – whether it be in religious texts or stories of ancient myths – was passed down orally for hundreds if not thousands of years before the art of writing allowed it to be recorded."

"Like the game of telephone," Aletheia muttered. "How much has it all changed? What *was* the real story?"

"Yes, like the game of telephone. As for Eyid-en, the details of our world and our exodus from it could take days to tell. It

will be quicker and easier to show you. We will do that soon."
Aletheia's eyebrows lifted. "But for now, I will tell you that we
were forced to leave Eyid-en because it was destroyed.
Destroyed by the Dy'ibalis."

"You weren't forced to leave by God? What about the
serpent and the apple and the Tree of Knowledge?" Aletheia
asked.

Nikolas shook his head. "I am not sure what is more grim –
the truth or that version of it. The things you just
mentioned...there is truth woven into them. As for why we left,
though...it was the destruction of Eyid-en by the Dy'ibalis and
their allies that drove us from our home. As I said, I will show
you soon. It is easier than explaining it."

"So you had to flee to Earth? How did you get here?" asked
Adam.

"The Ankh-el helped us flee. Not many of our people
escaped. We once had great nations; here on Earth we were
perhaps twenty thousand refugees...at most. We did our best to
find our place with the people here. They were so very much like
us...incredibly so. So much so that many of our youth who were
unwed fell in love and took them as husbands and wives over the
years...and bore children."

Aletheia shared an astounded look with Adam. Nikolas
noticed it and said, "Amazing, I know. I did not realize how
amazing it was until the technological advances of the last
century allowed me to understand genetics more fully. The Ankh
must have known our two peoples would be able to procreate,
or...no matter. In any case, it was harder for our elders. When
we arrived here, it took a long time before we were able to fully
communicate with the people of Earth. Much knowledge was

lost in that first generation."

Adam looked mesmerized listening to him speak. *The man has seen the entire rise of human civilization.*

He looked to both of them as he continued. "We were given explicit instructions by the Ankh-el who saved us. We were to rebuild a life here. We were not allowed to bring any weapons, tools, or books with us, but we were allowed to teach the people of Earth what we knew. Writing, metalsmithing, and many other crafts. When we left Eyid-en, we were more advanced than the people of Earth by several thousand years. It has only been in the past thousand years or so that you have surpassed our technology. The changes I have seen in that time have made me reconsider a great many things."

He paused for a long moment then, seemingly deep in thought, before continuing. "We were given other restrictions as well. Several of us were kings on Eyid-en. Here on Earth, we were forbidden to rule. We were forbidden to conquer. We were also forbidden to pose as gods."

Aletheia's face was scandalous. "Is that something that actually needed to be forbidden?"

Nikolas nodded. "Yes. You see, the Ankh had visited us for millennia on Eyid-en, as had many other beings, including the Dy'ibalis. They were so much more powerful than us – they knew so much more of the universe than we did, and some were Ascended even to the level of Primal – that we fell to our knees and worshiped them. It has taken me all my years to break those beliefs, for reasons which will be made clear to you as you learn and grow more. For now, I can tell you that the Ankh never fostered that belief. They never wanted to be worshiped as gods. Instead, they tried to teach us the difference, to help us Ascend to their level as a species, but for centuries our own ignorance prevented us from understanding. When they brought us here, I think they wanted to ensure we did not fall into that same relationship with the people of Earth."

Aletheia's head was spinning. "I guess that makes sense," she lied. "But why all the other rules?"

"The Ankh-el wanted to ensure that we did not disrupt the natural evolution of the people of Earth too severely. As it was, the knowledge we shared with them changed the course of human history, even though it took many centuries to become accepted and widespread. It also led to many misunderstandings about us...hence, the stories of old. Although we did not pose as gods, many times stories re-told about us from those early years continued and grew, only to be reiterated centuries later with one of us depicted as one. Even many of the stories we brought with us from Eyid-en eventually grew into religions."

Adam's mouth twisted into a curious smile. "Wait...so some of our ancient religions on Earth were based on stories from Eden and members of your race who never even made it to Earth?"

"Yes. Many of your ancient religions...and your current ones."

Adam looked at him cautiously, as though something had just dawned on him. "So...you're not human then, are you?" he asked.

Nikolas smiled a knowing smile. "No. I am not human."

Aletheia felt her mouth go dry. *He looks human...* "Then...what are you?"

"I told you. I am a man." He seemed to emphasize the strange way he pronounced the word this time, almost purposefully. "The question is, are you sure you know what it truly means to be human?"

Aletheia exhaled resignedly and said, "I used to think I did, but I guess now none of that matters anymore. Because all of this means I'm not one hundred percent human either, am I?"

Adam looked at her, stunned, as though the thought had not yet occurred to him.

Nikolas and Alex both smirked, and the immortal simply said, "I wouldn't go so far as to say that." He then turned to Alex. "Do you have something to write on?" Alex produced a small notebook and a pen and handed them to him. Sitting down between them, Nikolas turned to a blank page in the notebook and wrote a word on it. Even knowing he was her great-grandfather, Aletheia still felt strange with him sitting right next to her, his arm brushing against hers. *Not human.*

His handwriting was elegant and precise. *Ma-en.*

"Say it quickly."

"Ma-en. Man."

"Yes. That is what we call ourselves. Our name – the name for our race – is where the word 'man' in your language comes from. We taught the first people we encountered here on Earth – in Eastern Europe and Northwest Asia – to call us that, although it eventually became 'manu' in their language. They had a word for 'earth' in their language as well. 'Heum.'" The way Nikolas said the word sounded foreign, like he was trying to clear his throat. "Do you remember when I said many of our people coupled with the people of Earth and bore children?"

They both nodded as he continued. "Well, over the last several thousand years and hundreds of generations, our combined peoples have filled the Earth." He then looked at both of them and wrote the two words down in the notebook, with a hyphen between them.

Heum-Ma-en.

"Say it. Quickly." He was watching Aletheia intently.

"Heum-Ma-en. Hu-man. Human."

"I can see by the looks on your faces you finally understand."

Aletheia sat dumbfounded. Adam put his hands to his forehead, trying to absorb what he had just read. Before he could, Nikolas continued.

"You see, Adam…and Aletheia…all the people of the Earth today, all of humanity, is the result of that union. Over the last six thousand years, our bloodlines have combined fully. The pure-blooded people of the Earth that lived then are no more. Besides me and a few others, the Ma-en are no more either. All that is left are humans: the children of the people of the Earth and the Ma-en of Eyid-en."

The people of the Earth and the Men of Eden. It was as if a light bulb suddenly came on in Adam's mind. "I get it. I always wondered about that!" He turned to Aletheia excitedly. "In the story of the Garden of Eden it started with Adam and Eve and no others, but then when they left Eden, all of a sudden there were all these other people around…" He turned back to Nikolas and put his hands out in front of him as if to slow the whole process down. "So wait…you're telling me that we are all your descendants?"

"Yes, you are." He glanced at Aletheia. "Some more closely than others." Adam looked at her as if seeing her anew, but was surprised when Nikolas added, "You, Adam, should understand that better than anyone." He was smirking as he spoke.

Adam looked to Aletheia and Alex, confused, before turning back to Nikolas. "Why me?"

The immortal laughed. "Adam, do you know what your name means?"

"Yes, it means 'the first man.'"

Nikolas waved a hand back and forth. "No. That is what most people think it means today. Like most words, the meaning has changed over time. The peoples of Eastern Europe coined the term 'human'. The Hebrews had their own word for the children of Earth and Eyid-en. It was 'ben-adam', which was derived from their name for us: adam."

"Wait...what? I thought it was a proper name?"

"It is now, and has been for some time. But it was not always. Originally, it was their name for my people; to them, the first *men*."

Aletheia suddenly understood. "...that came out from Eden..."

Nikolas smiled at her. "Exactly." He sighed then, as if a tired from carrying a heavy burden. "And now you understand why we watch against the Dy'ibalis. That is why the Ankh-el showed me the things they did and named me the Keeper of that Watch. Because one day the Dy'ibalis will find us again, and when they do they will try to finish what they started six thousand years ago. The blood of Ma-en flows within all the people of this Earth, and they want to destroy it."

If Aletheia had been shocked before, she was floored now. She glanced over at Adam and saw his mouth hanging open. Nikolas smiled and looked at her kindly. Her mouth fumbled over the words that were trying to come out of it. After trying to formulate her thoughts into a coherent statement, she finally gave up and sat silent. They all sat silent for some time.

Finally, Aletheia managed to say, "I need time to absorb all this. I think I'm ready for that meal and some sleep." She looked to Adam and was relieved to see his excitement had been replaced by the look of a man who was completely overwhelmed. Alex and Nikolas nodded in understanding. It wasn't long before Aletheia and Adam were being seated at a large dining room table with a mouth-watering meal in front of them.

The smells of the food permeated Aletheia's senses, overriding everything else. Her attention was completely filled with the scents of roasted meat and vegetables sprinkled with fresh herbs and spices until there was no more room in her mind for thoughts or worries or cares. The aroma of fresh baked bread hit her nostrils next, causing her mouth to water and her stomach to growl angrily. The growling was made worse by the smell emanating from a large bowl of fruit salad that she guessed had been sprinkled with cinnamon and baking spices. It all made her once again conscious of the hunger that she had learned to numb herself to over the last two weeks.

She found herself seated between Sam and Adam; the woman was just as radiant as she had remembered from their first meeting. Aletheia could feel the peacefulness spreading outward from the woman whenever she looked at her, and it made her feel relaxed and content. She felt her worries and cares melting away, and as she did she found it easier to begin to accept the many things she had been forced to see and hear over the last two days. The extent of it all was still staggering, but somehow the longer she sat next to Sam she felt more able to handle it because she was filled with an understanding that even if her entire world turned upside down *everything would be okay*.

To her surprise, they held hands and Nikolas said a prayer of thanks over the meal before they ate. She had memories of her uncle doing the same when he visited during her childhood, but her mother had never really put much emphasis on spirituality in their life. She found herself embarrassed that she didn't register half of what was said, her mind now sifting through the array of stunning revelations it had witnessed in the last forty-eight hours. As she sat there, she felt Adam's hand clasping hers tightly. Glancing over at him out of the corner of her eye, his head declined and eyes closed, she thought he looked more peaceful too. As she closed her eyes again, her attention shifted to her other hand, held by Sam's. The woman's skin felt incredibly soft – like a newborn's. Where their hands touched, Aletheia started to feel refreshed; the aches and weariness in the muscles of her arm washed away by a light, airy sensation. The feeling traveled from her arm to her shoulder, and then through the rest of her body, leaving her feeling more relaxed and comfortable than she had in weeks. She glanced over at Sam in amazement, and when she did she was surprised to see the woman glancing back at her, smiling. Sam shut her eyes again, and Aletheia followed suit, reminding herself to ask the woman about it after she had eaten.

As soon as the prayer was done Aletheia felt like a sprinter at the starting line and the gun had gone off; she practically dove for the fresh bread, the sensation of hunger in her gut returning more strongly by the minute. The meal was a blur, all thoughts of proper etiquette lost on her as she ravenously partook of the food, which by her estimation was absolutely delicious. She left no time for speaking as she ate, content to enjoy the moment and the meal. Alex, Nikolas, and Sam were talking rapidly in low tones in what seemed to be a very in-depth conversation. Aletheia couldn't even muster the mental energy to listen in on what they were discussing. Every so often she would glance over at Adam; he was wolfing his food down even more vigorously than her, if that was possible. It was some time before she finally pushed her plate away, her stomach near bursting.

As though waking from a frenzy, she sheepishly looked to Sam and said, "I'm sorry. I was just *so* hungry. I apologize if I was impolite."

Sam laughed then, a melodious, heartfelt sound. "There is no apology needed. From what Alex has told us, you two have been through quite an ordeal. I would imagine you'd be famished…and exhausted."

Aletheia smiled and said, "My brain is on overload now, so I probably shouldn't even ask, but I have to know. Are you...my great-grandmother?" As soon as she asked the question she felt Adam stir beside her. Glancing over at him, she saw that he had stopped eating and was watching Sam.

"Yes, Aletheia. I am."

Sam looked at her for a moment as though trying to assess something about her, and then a satisfied look came across her face. She opened her arms and wrapped them around Aletheia, hugging her tight. If Aletheia had felt refreshed by her presence before, being hugged by her was simply amazing. The feeling it gave her brought her back in time, to memories that adulthood had long since faded for her. There, in Sam's embrace, she felt like a child again. Innocent. Safe. Like a babe in the arms of a mother.

Sam held her that way for a moment, then finally backed away and said, "It is so good to finally see you, Aletheia. We have watched you grow from afar, through pictures and videos and Alex's stories for many years."

Aletheia looked over at her uncle and saw that he and Nikolas had stopped their conversation. They were both smiling at her, obviously having overheard the conversation between her and Sam. She found herself feeling more open than she had in years. It was as though all the social norms that normally encouraged people to restrain their feelings had been lifted away for her, and with that freedom she felt great love and appreciation for her uncle bursting out of her. He returned her beaming smile with a knowing one of his own.

They spoke for a short while longer, but Alex, Nikolas, and Sam thankfully refrained from discussing any more serious topics out of respect for Aletheia and Adam and the limits of what they could hear in one day. Soon after dinner Sam was showing the two of them to a nicely appointed bedroom with a large, private bathroom attached to it. Having already said their goodnights to Alex and Nikolas, they thanked Sam again and she answered them both with another large hug. As it had at the table, her hug seemed to melt away all their weariness and fears.

"If you are ready, we will talk more tomorrow." With that Sam closed the door, leaving them alone in the room. After settling in for a moment, Adam looked to Aletheia and said, "I want a shower and then I want to sleep."

Aletheia chuckled as they walked into the bathroom, curious. As they looked inside her jaw dropped as she spotted the large whirlpool tub in the far corner of the room. "No. I want a bath."

Adam was nodding furiously, a large smile on his face. "I could get used to this." He laughed then, the first true joy she had seen in him since the horrors of the last two weeks had been inflicted on them.

"You look happy again," she said, a genuine smile spreading across her own face as well.

His smile turned to a smirk, and she knew he was going to say something sarcastic before the words even left his mouth. "What's not to be happy about? I just found out my girlfriend's family is rich and she's basically a princess."

Aletheia chuckled at the comments. His smile became less humorous and more sincere. "You are special, Aletheia. I always knew it, but now...it's even clearer to me now."

24

Aletheia woke to the morning sun rising through the large glass wall that filled one side of the room. She felt like she had slept for a week straight, the aches and pains that had haunted her muscles just a day before now seeming like a fading dream. The bath the night before had been the most relaxing experience she could remember, the powerful jets of the whirlpool tub kneading her sore, weary body relentlessly as her flesh soaked in the heat from the water. By the time she had slipped under the covers on the bed, her muscles had already felt like warmed butter. The mattress and sheets were absolutely luxurious, and she had melted into their soft, comfortable embrace the moment she had laid down in them.

Adam woke beside her, stretching forcefully as he yawned. He turned his head to look at her; the look on his face was blissful. They lay there, immersed in the moment for some time, talking and enjoying the comfort of their surroundings before finally getting up and joining the rest of Aletheia's family for breakfast. As they did, Aletheia noticed her stomach grumbling again despite the extremely generous meal she had filled it with the night before.

The morning meal was as delicious as the last had been. As they had at dinner, Sam, Nikolas, and Alex steered the conversation away from the more serious topics while they ate. Aletheia took her time eating, knowing that this wonderful lull couldn't last forever and would probably end with her last bite of breakfast. Predictably, moments after she put down her fork, Nikolas spoke.

"Aletheia, Adam...the two of you will stay here with Sam for the next couple of days. Your uncle and I are going to fly to Los Angeles to try and discover whatever is behind this. Hopefully we will be able to track it down."

Aletheia looked at her uncle worriedly. "What are you going to do if you find it? You saw what that thing did..." Her voice trailed off and she looked to Adam apologetically. Alex had a thoughtful look on his face. Nikolas' rich voice broke the ensuing silence.

"There is a protocol to be followed. We already enacted the first part of it last night. Our next duty is to investigate and confirm whether or not a Dy'ibalis has actually found its way to Earth. If, in the process of confirming that we are able to confront it, then my intention is to destroy it."

"How do you fight something like that?" asked Adam. "I know you're immortal, but you can't even see it. Not to mention the fact that the thing is ridiculously strong. I know – it hit me once and sent me flying. It felt like being hit by a truck."

Nikolas nodded gravely. "Whatever we are dealing with, it has already shown that it is dangerous. If it is a Dy'ibalis, then it is even more so. You have not yet seen half of their tricks. You are right to be respectful of its power. But I have fought and defeated them many times before. I do not fear them."

Adam's eyebrow lifted at Nikolas' comments. *Damn...my girlfriend's great-grandfather is a badass.*

Aletheia switched her attention to her uncle. "What about you? You said you've never encountered one before. Will you be safe?"

Alex looked determined, and Aletheia knew that meant he was at least concerned. He smiled nevertheless and said, "It's like I told you before, kiddo...I'll be in the safest place I can think of. Right next to him." He motioned to Nikolas. The immortal nodded to him and then responded to Aletheia.

"I would not risk my grandson's life any more than I would risk yours. If it were not absolutely necessary I would leave him here with you and go alone. But I am unfamiliar with that area of the city and the park, as well as Adam's home and your dormitory. I will need him there with me. He has been to all of those places and has witnessed whatever we are dealing with in action."

Aletheia perked up at the mention of hers and Adam's homes and asked, "You're going home, too?" Images of her mother flashed through her mind and sent pangs through her heart. She missed her dearly.

"Yes," said her uncle. "Those are the three places we know it has been, so we will begin there. While we're there, Lee, I'll talk with your mom. Let her know you're okay. We'll find a way for you to talk with her another time. In the meantime, you two need to stay here where you'll be safe."

"But...that thing has found me before. What if it tracks me here and you're both gone?"

Nikolas smiled at her and gestured to his wife. "Sam will be here with you. You will be as safe as you would be with me."

Sam leaned forward and placed her hand on Aletheia's shoulder. "My husband may be exaggerating a bit. I am no warrior, and he has been fighting battles for thousands of years. But I am not without my resources. He is barely older than me. I will not let any harm come to you." Her smile immediately alleviated the worst of Aletheia's fears.

Adam looked at Nikolas and asked, "You said there was a protocol, and you started it last night. What does that mean?"

"The first part of the protocol is to notify the others. We did that last night," said Nikolas.

"The others?" Adam asked. As soon as the words left his mouth, a look of realization came across his face as though he had just remembered something. "That's right...I meant to ask you last night, but I was so tired. You said that all that was left of the Ma-en were you and a few others. I am guessing Sam is one?" He looked to Sam and she nodded. Turning back to Nikolas he asked, "Who are the others?"

"There are two more like us. We are all that remains. Sam can tell you the details as well as anything else your minds have the appetite for once we are gone. Unfortunately, time is running short. The plane is already being prepared. If we are dealing with a Dy'ibalis, then we must act swiftly. It is time for us to be going."

Aletheia and Adam nodded in acceptance, knowing the severity of the task in front of the two men. A short time later, they all stood in the grand entrance to the penthouse to see Alex and Nikolas off. Aletheia hugged her uncle tightly, conflicted between trusting this man who had survived war zones and worrying that he was dealing with something far too powerful for him to handle. She then hugged Nikolas, and was surprised that it didn't feel strange at all. If anything, hugging him made her feel less fearful for them both. It made her feel…braver; like they were heading off on an adventure rather than a frightening, desperate search. Sam followed suit and hugged both men, sharing a long kiss with her husband that almost made Aletheia blush. *Grandma!* She said something to Nikolas in a language that Aletheia did not understand, and the two shared a deep look between them before he put his hand on Alex's shoulder and led him out of the room. As they stepped out the door into the hallway amidst several bodyguards, Aletheia raised her voice so they could hear her, reminding them to be safe.

As she turned back to Adam and Sam, the older woman saw the concerned look on Aletheia's face and said, "Do not fear, Aletheia. Your uncle is safer with him than he would be with anyone else. Come. Let's talk." She led the two of them out of the room and into the cozy one where they had first spoken with Nikolas. They made themselves comfortable on the sofas there.

Sam looked to the two of them. Aletheia was surprised when, rather than revealing more incredible secrets to them, she simply asked, "You have both been through so much. Would you like to talk about it?"

Aletheia paused, momentarily thrown off by the unanticipated question. After thinking about it a moment, she realized that she did want to talk about it. In truth, she hadn't had a chance to process all the things that had happened to her recently; everything had been so urgent moment to moment there hadn't been time. She looked over to Adam to see if he needed to talk first, but he just gestured for her to begin and sat back and listened. *Even around her, he still keeps his emotions tightly guarded.* And so she began the process of letting it all out.

They talked for the rest of the morning. The more she spoke with Sam, the more she was in her presence, the more open she felt. A torrent of her thoughts, fears, and emotions about everything that had happened poured out of her in a steady stream. The most painful of them were not about Meghan, or watching James die; they were her feelings about her mother. Having grown up an only child with a father who died when she was an infant, Aletheia's mother had been her whole world for most of her life. The thought of never seeing her again wrapped her heart in a casing of sadness.

It hurt to relive it all – hurt to *feel* it all – but as she did she found that the space left behind by all those feelings was now filled with a peaceful acceptance. She was healing, and she knew why. It went beyond the act of sharing the memories with someone; the effect Sam had on her was subtle but powerful. Aletheia had been through painful events before in her life, and in her experience the best you could hope for when you healed from them was a tender spot left on your soul that didn't hurt every day but was always there. It never felt fully healed. Sharing these feelings with Sam, being comforted by her as she let them all out, felt different. It felt like as she let all the bad feelings out they were replaced by a gentle balm on her soul. Somewhere in her she knew that while she would always remember the horrifying ordeal she had been through, she would eventually heal from it and be whole again. When they finally finished talking it was hours later. Aletheia felt drained, but she also felt less weighed down by the events of the last two weeks.

Adam stayed with them the entire time, watching and lending support and even making a few comments of his own, but he refrained from opening up about his feelings on it all. Sam made it clear that he was invited to share as much as he wanted with her, but did not press him. After Aletheia had gotten out all she needed to for the moment, Sam suggested they eat some lunch. The food was again delicious, and Aletheia found herself once more ravenously hungry, as though the process of letting out all those emotions had depleted her body of all its energy. When she finished, she sat back and closed her eyes. Sitting there, resting her mind and heart and soul, she realized she felt better than she had in a very long time.

After lunch they convened once again to the library. Sam seemed to sense that Adam was hesitant about opening up the way Aletheia had, so she instead asked them what they would like to talk about. Adam immediately started asking her more questions about the process of Ascension. After a short time, the conversation inevitably turned to his workouts and meditation. Sam listened empathetically as he described the stages of feelings he went through as he worked out, as well as how he felt when he finally released all his rage and sat down to meditate. She smiled at him, a deep understanding showing in her beautiful green eyes.

"Adam…listen to me. Those negative feelings you have inside you – shame, fear, anger – it is admirable that you have found a way to turn them into something positive. They have fueled your determination and driven you to be more than you could have been. But understand: they do not make you stronger. I know it feels like they do, but in truth they are holding you back. If you want to grow further and become the person you are capable of being, you are going to have to let them go. They are not where your true power lies. Now...the feeling you describe after you have worked through all of those emotions and let go of them...that is where you will find your strength. That moment when you feel like your true self, without all the pain...that is your soul. And it is infinitely more powerful than anger."

Adam paused for a moment, a look of deep introspection on his face as though he was working through something. "But...I don't think you understand. That...it's my armor. It's what makes me different from everyone else. It's how I protect myself." He looked at Sam almost pleadingly, as though she was asking him to stop breathing.

Sam's warm expression lessened his fear as she spoke. "Is it truly armor, Adam? Or is it a prison?" She gave him a moment to contemplate the thought before leaning forward and adding in a whisper, "Or is it a cocoon?"

Adam sat there with a staggered look on his face. Aletheia was surprised when she saw his eyes glistening. Sam gave him a long moment to consider her words and then said, "You know what lies inside that cocoon, Adam. You have felt it when you meditate. One day, it will break free and burst forth in all its splendor, and you will be reborn. Now, you can continue wearing your armor every day of your life, in which case you will one day die and break free of your cocoon in your next life. Or you can choose to do it now."

Adam looked perplexed. He sat silent for a long time. Sam seemed to sense that he was unable to move forward on his own, so she made a suggestion. "Why don't you tell me a little bit about these images you use to bring out your pain. What types of things are they?"

Aletheia watched in amazement as Adam did something completely out of character for him: he started to open up to this woman he had just met. Slowly…as if trying to force open a stuck gate that didn't want to budge, Adam shared a few examples from his past with Sam, describing the way they made him feel and how he used them in his workout to enrage himself. As he went on, he shared a few more, and a few more, until he was recalling events from his childhood that had been so buried he had never even shared them with Aletheia. The glistening in his eyes grew into pools below his deep brown irises, until eventually one filled to overflowing. A single tear spilled over the lower lid of his eye and ran slowly down his cheek. It was soon matched by one on his other cheek.

More tears followed as Adam continued to recount the painful experiences of his life to Sam, and more importantly, the deep emotional scars they had left him with that he carried around every day of his existence. As he continued he seemed to pick up momentum until it was as if a damn had broken inside him, his darkest emotions pouring out of him like a raging flood. Aletheia's heart went out to him as she listened to the horrific stories of a scared little boy, horribly abused by the people who were supposed to love and protect him, who had no one and nothing to cling to but his big brother. Her heart broke even more as his story went on and she realized what it had felt like to him to lose that brother not once, but twice. It wasn't until that moment that Aletheia realized Sam had accomplished what she had set out to do: she had found a way to get Adam to open up about everything they had been through the last few weeks.

It was a long time before he finally stopped, and Aletheia watched him compassionately as he sat there dazed, clearly astonished at what he had just done. He was silent for some time, and when he finally spoke he looked to Sam and said, "I'm sorry. I don't know why that all came out like that. I didn't mean to burden you with it. I must just be tired from all of this."

Aletheia almost chuckled to herself as she watched Adam seem oblivious to the effect Sam clearly had on him.

"You think that you sharing yourself with us is a burden?" the older woman asked him.

"I don't know." He turned to Aletheia. "I mean, that's why I never told you the worst of that stuff. I just don't think it's fair of me to put all that on you. Look at you now – that's exactly what I mean. You're looking at me all sad. It's not your fault – you didn't do those things to me. You shouldn't have to worry about it."

Aletheia looked at him incredulously. "Adam, it has nothing to do with whether or not I did those things. I am looking at you like this because I love you."

Adam had been about to debate her, but the look on his face changed as her comment hit home. Turning his attention back to Sam he said, "I guess I just feel like I carry around these scars on me, and I hate them. I hate that they were put on me. I didn't ask for them. I don't want to put them on her too."

Sam tilted her head and said, "Adam…there's not a lot you can do about the scars that were put on your body. You may not even be able to heal all the scars on your mind. But your soul belongs to you and you alone, and within it, you have all the power you could ever need to heal. You may not have asked for the scars on your soul, but you are the one keeping them there. Every time you wear them as armor you attach them more firmly to the fabric of who you are. You have the power to let them go.

But in order to do that, you have to be willing to. You have to know that the person you are underneath – the one who shines through when you meditate – is far more powerful than the one who wears the armor. You don't need those scars to not be afraid."

She sat back and looked at him, her body language and expression making it abundantly clear that the choice was up to him. After a long time, he finally nodded and said in a quiet voice. "Okay…I'll try. But I don't know how."

Sam smiled from ear to ear. "You've already started. You let it all out, and you didn't need to become enraged and go to such a dark place to do it. Look inside yourself. How do you feel?"

Adam got a quizzical look on his face, followed quickly by a flush of embarrassment. "I feel…good. I feel clean. It doesn't hurt anymore." He looked to Aletheia, an embarrassed smile starting to creep into the corners of his mouth.

"Good," said Sam. "Now live in that place. Don't be tempted to wrap yourself in that armor again."

He looked at her, confused. "But…what do I do if I'm…afraid? How do I protect myself like this? I feel…vulnerable."

She peered into his eyes. "Adam, you know the answer to that."

Understanding washed over him. "I need to find that place in me where I feel my true self. My soul."

She leaned back and stared at them both, a satisfied look on her face. Whatever she or Adam had been about to say next was cut short by her phone ringing. Seeing the number, Sam got a grim look on her face and answered.

Within seconds it became clear to Aletheia that she was talking with Nikolas. The call didn't last very long, and as she spoke Aletheia reached over and held Adam's hand while they waited. When she was finished, Sam hung up the phone and turned to them.

"They are heading to Seattle tonight. They didn't find any signs of a Dy'ibalis or anything else out of the ordinary at the skate park or in the area around it."

Aletheia breathed a sigh of relief as soon as her brain registered that the two men were safe. Looking out the window at the lights of the city at night she was awed by its beauty. It took her a moment to register how late it had gotten. Between her and Adam, they had spent the bulk of the day talking with Sam. Looking at Adam, she felt much better than she had the day before, and she could tell he did too. It had been a day well spent.

25

The next morning, after they dressed and ate breakfast, Adam and Aletheia joined Sam in the library where they had first met her. Aletheia felt markedly better than she had when they arrived a day and a half before, and from the look on his face, Adam did as well. Sam let them peruse the many books and ancient items there, taking time to answer their questions or to give them some history regarding one artifact or another. The cathartic experience they had with the woman the day before had stuck with Aletheia. For the first time in weeks her fears and worries were replaced by curiosity, perhaps even excitement.

After some time, Aletheia made her way to one of the large, plush chairs and sank into it, deep in thought. Adam sat down in the chair next to her, and Sam followed suit, gracefully lowering herself into one across from them. She looked to both of them and said, "I am sure the two of you have many more questions. What else would you like to know?"

Aletheia looked to Adam and shrugged, her body language stating clearly that she was open to anything. Adam must have had questions brewing in his own mind, because as soon as he saw that she was willing to let him take the lead he enthusiastically spoke.

"Okay, so I've been wanting to know since Nikolas mentioned it yesterday. Who are the two others? The other Ma-en?"

Sam nodded knowingly. "Ah yes. Well, when we first came here there were many of us, as Nikolas no doubt told you. We wondered if perhaps from that first group another immortal might rise...but it was not to be so."

She curled her legs up under her and adjusted the cushion to make herself more comfortable. Looking at her, Aletheia could have guessed she was a middle-aged model posing for a fashion shoot rather than a millennia-old immortal teaching them about the history of mankind.

"After the destruction of Eyid-en, the Ankh-el came to each of the four of us. One by one, they took us away and revealed to us many things. I learned more in those few hours than I have learned in any single century of my life. They also bestowed upon each of us a title. These titles are not rewards or honorifics; they each represent a sacred duty that we were individually given in addition to watching over our people. When we were returned from our time with the Ankh-el, the four of us spoke with each other about what we had been shown. We came to understand while much of it was the same, much was also unique to each of us; tailored to reveal what we needed to do to perform our individual duty. For example, Enoki – Nikolas – was shown many secrets about the Dy'ibalis, as well as prophecies about how they are tied to the future of our race. He was shown these things because he was entrusted with watching for the day when they find us again. While the rest of us assist him in that duty the same we all assist each other, ultimately the responsibility for protecting humanity from the Dy'ibalis or any other ancient enemy that should find us here rests on his shoulders. Hence, his title."

The Keeper of the Watch... thought Aletheia.

"There is Uturik. He now calls himself Turk, and lives in Egypt. His title is *Apellat-en*, or 'The Keeper of Truth.' He is responsible for keeping the history of the Ma-en and our time on Eyid-en, and to reveal it to humanity when they are ready to learn the truth of their origins."

"Are there any legends that were born from stories about him?" asked Adam.

"Yes. The ancient Sumerians called him 'Utu.' In days past he was also knows as 'Alaunis.' But you would most likely have heard of him through Greek and Roman legends, where they referred to him as Apollo."

Aletheia smiled broadly. *Apollo...at least I have heard of that one.*

"There is also Maneshta." The immortal continued. "Her title is the *Attanan-en*, which means 'The Keeper of Knowledge' or 'Intelligence,' depending how you interpret it. She has an amazing mind; she is one of the most intelligent people I have ever known. Her duty is to guide and ensure the scientific and technological advancement of mankind. She currently lives in Japan and has taken the name Tesha. Many legends have sprung up about her throughout human history. In Egypt she was called 'Neith' and 'Seshat.' The Armenians called her 'Nane,' and the Romans 'Minerva.' But again, the name you probably know her by best comes from the ancient Greeks, who called her Athena."

Adam looked surprised. "Athena...wow! But technological advancement? I'm kind of surprised by that."

"Why is that?" asked Sam.

"I don't know...it just seems like that would get in the way of Ascension or something. It seems like the more we learn through science, the less anybody believes in anything spiritual anymore."

Sam's eyebrow raised. "Are you so sure? What about you, Adam? You are a learned young man; you have said yourself that you love science, and yet you are also very curious about spirituality. Do the two have to be in opposition?"

Adam thought about it for a moment. "I guess *I* don't think they do, but it seems like most people do. Every time science disproves or explains something that used to be explained by religion, people think it proves that there is no God, or there is no life beyond this one. At least, that's the way it feels."

Sam nodded sadly. "Yes, some people see it that way. But the problem is not that science and belief cannot coexist. They *must* coexist. They are both essential to the growth and survival of mankind. Nikolas explained to you the two realms of existence and the ways in which they are different, correct?"

Seeing them both nod she continued. "We as living beings are the only places in the universe where the physical and the spiritual realms touch. We are made of *both*. If science is our way of learning about the physical realm, and belief is our way of learning about the spiritual realm, then the only way we can truly understand and master our existence as a whole is to use *both*. Where people run into difficulty is in trying to use one to answer questions that are best answered by the other."

Aletheia was relieved to see that Adam too looked

confused. She was barely following what the older woman was saying. Seeing that they were struggling, Sam sat upright and continued to explain. "Science exists *inside* of the physical realm, and is based only on what can be observed in that realm. But the spiritual realm exists completely outside of and separate from the physical. So how can science ever observe it or answer questions about it?"

"It can't," said Aletheia. *Okay, at least I understand that part...*

"It can't," confirmed Sam. "The only place we can observe the spiritual realm is in the only place it touches this world." She placed her hand gently on her own chest. "In here. When we want to find a spiritual truth, we must look inside ourselves for the answer. Think of it as the spiritual equivalent of our five senses. Our five senses allow us to observe the physical world around us. That act of observing is a powerful thing; all of science is based on it. In fact, science is just a systematic way of observing the world through our senses until we *know* or *understand* a physical phenomenon. To observe the spiritual world, though, we must look inside ourselves to where it touches us: our soul. When we do this, it is also a powerful thing. And if we do it in a systematic way, we learn to know or understand a spiritual phenomenon. That systematic way of looking inside ourselves to observe is called *belief*. So you see, science and belief are not in opposition to each other; they are twins. They represent the two ways that we learn about our world."

Aletheia was overwhelmed. Adam shook his head as though trying to shake away the confusion. He finally looked up and said to Sam, "I always thought I was a smart guy, but this is...really advanced. Can you give me an example or something?"

Sam nodded. "It is a lot to take in, I know. It took me a very long time to learn it...and even longer to *understand* it. I will give you an example. Science has shown us evidence of a Big Bang that created the physical universe. Some have taken this and leapt to the conclusion that it also means there is no God, because science has apparently explained the existence of the universe without one. But has it really? The question most of us really want to know the answer to is *why* the universe exists. Has science answered the question of *why*? Or has it just answered the question of *how*? Explaining the mechanism by which something happens – the *how* it works – is not the same as explaining *why* it happened. The question of *why* we exist – for what purpose – is a spiritual one. So you cannot answer it by observing with your physical senses, no matter how advanced the equipment you are using is. You must answer it by observing it in the only place you can: inside yourself."

She tilted her head then, watching each of them carefully as she continued. "So, when I ask you both if the Big Bang is the answer to the question of *why* the universe is here – why *any of us* are here – look into your own soul and tell me what it says."

Aletheia and Adam muttered their answers in a low voice, both focused inward as they spoke in unison.

"No," said Adam.

"No," echoed Aletheia. "There has to be more. There has to be a reason for it all."

As they focused their attention outward again, they saw Sam smiling at both of them. "Very good. Very, very good."

Aletheia dropped her head down, deep in thought. "That's amazing. When you look inside yourself, the answer is just

248

there." She looked up at Sam. "That was all so confusing until you just had me try that, and now it all seems so simple. How did we ever get it all mixed up in the first place?"

"Ah," said Sam. "That is the flip side of the coin. We get into trouble in the first place when we make the same mistake with belief – when we try to use belief to answer questions about the physical world. For example, nearly every religion that has ever existed on this planet has included a story regarding the creation of the Earth. Yet modern science paints an entirely different picture of that process, and we tend to trust it because the evidence is very reasonable and is based on what we can perceive through our senses. This has called into question the validity of all those creation stories. But does this mean every teaching in those religions – even the spiritual teachings – is invalidated? No. It just means that we were applying the wrong tool to the question. The reason science can – and will continue to – disprove the claims made by religion about physical phenomena is because *belief* is not the correct tool for answering questions about the *physical* world in the first place. It is not based on observing physical laws or evidence; it is instead based on the inherent understanding we have in our souls about the spiritual world. Do you understand?"

Adam huffed. "Yeah, I think I do. We're all idiots. It seems like we were born with everything we need to learn about our world and ourselves, and we screwed it all up."

Sam chuckled. "Do not be so hard on the human race, Adam. Systems of belief evolve in a species over time the same way scientific knowledge does. This process of trying to use one system to answer all questions is a natural part of that evolution. In humanity's past, they completely trusted belief – religion – to answer all questions for them. Now that science has disproved some of religion's answers, people have started to feel like belief has failed them. This causes them to trust it less – to look inside themselves less often for answers – and to trust science more. That trend will likely continue for some time, but a day will come when people start to realize that science is not giving them sufficient answers to their spiritual questions. When that happens they will feel like science has failed them. People will start to look inside themselves more for answers and the pendulum will swing back again."

"Will we ever break out of that cycle?" asked Adam.

"Yes," answered Sam. "Humans will break out of it when they finally learn how to apply the right tool to the right question."

Adam was nodding thoughtfully. "I need some time to think about that." His expression changed as though he suddenly remembered something. "Wait...before you explain it more, I don't want to forget to ask. You never told us about you. What is your real name, and what duty were you entrusted with?"

26

*Old mother, whence and who are you of folk born
long ago?*
                            Hymn to Demeter – Homer c.600 B.C.

Aletheia turned to Sam as well, eagerly awaiting her response. Sam's face lost its usual attentive look; her expression became distant as she spoke. "My name...my true name is Samarta, and my title is *Dwimater-en*. It means 'The Keeper of Spirit.' I am charged with ensuring the spiritual advancement of mankind."

"You mean, like Ascension?" asked Aletheia.

"Yes," said the immortal, seeming to come back to the present. "That is part of it. The other part, though, is advancing humanity's understanding of their spirituality as a whole. As I said, religion and belief – like science and technology – evolve over time. As people come to understand the physical world at deeper levels, their technology evolves. And as people come to understand the spiritual world at deeper levels – through

Ascension – their belief systems evolve as well."

She adjusted herself again, leaning back on the puffy cushions. "You must understand…much of what I now know I had to take on faith from the teachings of the Ankh-el before I understood it myself. On Eyid-en we worshiped many gods. At least, we thought they were gods. The Ankh were among them, along with several other ancient beings who visited us. Even the Dy'ibalis were considered dark gods to be feared and appeased."

"Did you still believe in them even after you came here?"

"For many years…yes. Of course we did. They had just destroyed our entire world. Who but the gods could do that?"

Aletheia found herself picturing the Earth being destroyed by supernatural beings. She shuddered, and also understood.

"Exactly," said Sam, seeing the younger woman's response. "The Ankh-el showed me the truth, and I was able to share it with the other *En* – the other Keepers. But most of our people continued to believe those beings were gods to the day they died, as did the early people of Earth they encountered and shared their stories with."

"So is that where some of our other myths and legends come from – the ones not including the four of you?" asked Adam.

"Yes, it is. As the years passed, though, I watched the spiritual evolution of mankind begin, just as the Ankh-el had foreseen. Beliefs about many gods started to be replaced by two distinct patterns of belief. One was a belief in individual spiritual growth and enlightenment, and another was a belief in a single god."

Adam's face lit up. "The five major religions today. Buddhism and Hinduism for the first one, and Judaism,

Christianity, and Islam for the second. Am I right?"

Sam's face glowed as she smiled at him. "Yes, Adam, you are right. You see, mankind is moving closer to a clearer understanding of their spirituality and the nature of the spiritual realm. It is a process that takes millennia of growth for a species, and humans are right in the middle of it."

Aletheia chimed in, a confused note in her voice. "I don't understand. If your job is to guide the human race and help us progress, why not just teach all of this to the world like you've done with us?"

Sam exhaled deeply. "If only it were that simple. The straightforward answer is that humanity is not ready, at least not the whole of it. Spiritual understanding is no different that scientific understanding in that one must master certain concepts before moving on to others. Each concept we learn acts as a building block for us to now explore something more advanced that we couldn't have understood without it."

Seeing the looks on their faces, Sam changed her approach. "Take computing and electricity, for example. If I were to take the diagram for a modern circuit board and show it to an educated person from the Middle Ages, do you think they would understand it?"

"No," answered Aletheia. "It would probably just look like gibberish."

"Exactly. No matter how much I tried to explain it to them, they were simply not raised in a society with the centuries of layered knowledge that would be needed to understand it. They would view it as gibberish, or magic...or at worst, witchcraft. But what if I showed it to an electrical engineer who lived fifty years ago?"

Adam smiled. "Yes, I get it. He would probably think it was brilliant, and you were a genius, but he could grasp it." He turned to Aletheia. "It's like math. You can't understand algebra without learning basic arithmetic first. And you can't understand calculus without algebra and trig, and so on. Show a calculus equation to a first grader and they'd be clueless."

"Yes!" exclaimed Sam. She seemed genuinely excited that he had understood, and even more so when Aletheia started nodding her head as Adam's example struck a chord in her. "Now...think about that concept and apply it to a species' spiritual growth. Mankind had to learn spiritual arithmetic before it could learn algebra. And it must finish learning algebra and trigonometry before it can move on to calculus...and beyond. Can the religions of the world today answer every question we have perfectly? No. Some of them still struggle vainly to answer questions about the physical world. Most of them are still based on stories and legends that have been distorted over time. But...they are right where humanity is supposed to be. They represented the next step in mankind's spiritual evolution from the beliefs in its ancestors, and they are the building blocks to the next step towards full understanding. They are not the final answer, because they are not meant to be."

Aletheia sat in awe. She had believed in God for most of her life, with the exception of her darkest days as a teen. She had never thought so deeply about her beliefs, though. Her mind was spinning as it worked through the implications of the conversation, challenged in ways it had never been in college.

"Sam...I still don't understand why we ended up with so many different religions. If most of them grew from the legends of your people, why didn't we end up with just one religion?"

"That, Aletheia, is an excellent question." Sam beamed with pride at her great-granddaughter. "It was no different on Eyid-en. Even though the same beings visited us over the millennia, different groups of our people revered one being over another, or theorized different relationships among them and created rules to appease them. All from the same observations. The people of Earth are no different."

"I get that…but doesn't that just mean that most of them are wrong? If there is one real truth behind them all, and they all say their version of the story is the truth, then most of them must be wrong. Which one is the right one? Or are they all wrong?" asked Aletheia.

Sam elegantly rose from her chair and motioned for Adam and Aletheia to follow her. "Come." She led them through various rooms to a large bedroom on a corner of the penthouse. It was a room that neither Adam nor Aletheia had seen before, and the large glass corner walls offered an unobstructed view of a large swath of the city. Aletheia gazed out upon a view that was breathtaking. The sky was clear and blue, with only a few streams of wispy clouds streaking across parts of it. Sam took both their hands, feelings of warmth and comfort passing through Aletheia's as the woman touched it, and led them to the corner of the room, a mere foot from the glass.

"Aletheia, do me a favor. Look that way." She positioned Aletheia on the North wall to look out across the city in that direction. "Now, Adam…you look this way." She angled him to look out the wall to the East.

"Now…you are both looking at Manhattan. Aletheia, tell me what it looks like."

Aletheia looked out on the city and started describing the

many buildings she saw. "There's a huge rectangular section of trees on the left side, like a huge park with a few ponds in it."

"What about the sky?"

There were no clouds in the sky to the North. "Umm…blue and clear?"

"Good," said Sam. "Adam, now you. Tell us what Manhattan looks like."

Adam described his view of the city as Aletheia had at first, but then started to call out things she hadn't. "There are two rivers – no, maybe it's one river with a long skinny island in the middle – and there's a huge bridge going across it." When Sam asked him about the sky, he described the long, wispy clouds stretching across it in the distance.

"Thank you," said Sam. "Now Aletheia. Adam says that Manhattan has a huge river with a long skinny island in the middle and a large bridge going over it, and clouds in the sky. Look in front of you. Judging by what you can see, is he right?"

Aletheia started to turn in Adam's direction, but Sam stopped her and turned her back in the direction she had been facing. Her touch was gentle but surprisingly strong. "Answer the question only according to what you can see."

Aletheia paused a moment and answered. "No. He's wrong."

Sam turned to Adam. "Adam…Aletheia says Manhattan has no clouds and a large park full of trees and ponds. Based on what you can see, is she right?"

Adam's tone conveyed that he was beginning to understand the reason for the exercise. "No. She's wrong. That is not what Manhattan looks like."

"Good. Now…" She reached out and gently took them each

by the hand, turning them to face her.

"You were both looking out at Manhattan. You both know exactly what you saw. And you both could plainly see that the other was wrong. After all, logic tells us that something can't both *be* and *not be*, right? Manhattan either has clouds or it doesn't. It either has trees or it doesn't. It either has ponds or it doesn't, right?"

Smiles were beginning to show on Adam and Aletheia's faces. Sam asked them a final question. "So...how can you both be right at the same time when what you said completely contradicts with the other?"

"We couldn't see the big picture," said Adam. Aletheia was nodding, a stunned expression on her face.

"Exactly. You both learn so quickly – I am truly enjoying this!" She seemed genuinely excited as she stepped forward and joined them at the glass, taking in the view beside them. "None of us are gods – even those of us who are Ascended. We all have a limited view. That view is shaped by our own personality quirks, our culture, our experiences, and our education. Asking two people about the nature of God is no different than asking two people what Manhattan looks like: it depends on their point of view. That is why there are multiple religions on Earth. Even when you take away a religion's claims about the physical world and focus only on its spiritual teachings, it still represents a single, limited view of the whole picture. And it attracts those individuals whose internal window matches its teachings. Those teachings resonate with the person because when they look inside themselves the picture they see matches what the teachings say. They *know* them to be true, through their belief. So you see, it is not a matter of who is right or wrong. They are all right, in their own way. They simply contradict each other because they can each only see one part of the big picture."

She looked to each of them and smiled, and they smiled back. They stood there, admiring the view of the sunlit sky for some time, Aletheia and Adam both thinking that the Ankh-el had picked their Keeper well.

It was late in the evening when Alex and Nikolas returned to the penthouse. Their news was disappointing, but it was not surprising due to the fact that they had called many hours earlier and let Sam know that they had not been able to find a single trace of a Dy'ibalis nor any other explanation for the events that had occurred. As they spoke to Sam, Aletheia, and Adam in the entry hall, Aletheia noted the grim looks on each of the men's faces. She also noted the way her uncle repeatedly glanced at Nikolas, as though some conversation had passed between the two of them that they were not sharing with the rest of the group. Looking over to Adam, she thought that he may not have noticed. He was still deep in thought regarding the many lessons Sam had given them both during the day. One glance at Sam, however, and it was obvious the older woman had noticed their behavior immediately.

Sam tilted her head at her husband to get a better look at his face and then glanced at her grandson. "What is it? Something is troubling you both; something beyond even this threat."

Alex mopped his mustache furiously, drawing a raised eyebrow from Sam. He stopped the gesture immediately, as if suddenly aware it had given away his mood. She turned her attention back to her husband. Nikolas seemed to set himself as he spoke. His expression and body language gave the appearance of someone trying to force themselves into a freezing pool of water.

"We are running out of time. If it is a Dy'ibalis, it is either alone or it is with a group. If it is a group, then an attack on Earth would seem to be imminent. If it is alone, then it is likely a scout or a traveler that somehow found its way to Earth. In any case, it is only a matter of time before it shares its discovery of humankind's presence on this planet with its brethren. I cannot allow things escalate to that point. I will have no choice soon but to alert the Ankh-el. Either way, we have to find whatever is doing this, confirm what it is, and destroy it."

Sam shook her head. "I know, Nikolas. We all know this. That is not what is bothering you."

He shook his head. "No. No, it is not." He glanced at Alex again, ever so briefly before continuing. "We visited every place that we could think of. Every place it made itself known. I even spoke out in Ma-en at each location. Made *myself* known. We found nothing."

He looked past Sam to Aletheia. "The only thing we know is, whatever it is we are dealing with, it is drawn to you. And I fear that the only way we will draw it out is with your help."

Alex hung his head down. Sam exhaled sharply, the only visible sign that she was upset.

"Are you two suggesting you use her as bait?" Adam blurted out.

Nikolas looked him in the eye. "Yes. I would never suggest such a thing unless the situation was truly desperate, and it is. I know I have told you what is at stake, but until you have lived it, you cannot fathom the depth of it. Against one, I can keep her safe. Against an army of them...there will be nowhere on Earth that is safe anymore. Not even with me. That is why I suggest it."

He looked to Aletheia. "I am sorry, child. You did not ask for this, and we have not had any time to prepare you for it. No one will force you. But I do implore you. I will do everything in my power to ensure that no harm comes to you."

Aletheia found herself reeling for a moment from the declaration, but surprised even herself by how quickly she was able to gather her senses. She stood straight and tall as she looked to each of them. As she locked eyes with her uncle, she asked him, "Is this what you think we should do too?"

Alex paused a moment and then nodded solemnly. "I'm sorry kiddo. You know where I stand. I love you like you were my own daughter. But this is so much bigger than just the five of us. The world is at stake. And we've had no luck getting whatever it is to come out and play. It either fears Nikolas, or it wants you. I don't see any other way except to try."

Aletheia nodded, secretly wishing her uncle had answered differently, but understanding how desperate he must be to have said what he did. She looked to Sam and the woman was watching her, sympathy etched in her beautiful face. As she looked at the woman she felt calmer, more serene.

"I do not like this," the older woman said. "But Nikolas knows more of these things than anyone on Earth. And I know the love he has for all of our children and grandchildren. If he is asking, it is because he sees no other way."

Aletheia turned last to Adam, who had a hard but sad look on his face. She worried for a moment that he had put his armor back up, but when he spoke she realized the hardness was simply his own efforts to rein in his overprotective instincts. "You are stronger and more capable than I have ever given you credit for, Lee. I know I can't protect you from everything. Whatever you choose, I'll support. But if you choose to go, I am coming with you, and there is no debate about that."

She smiled at the last statement, having already known what he would say. Turning back to Nikolas, she nodded her head and said, "Yes. Yes, of course I'll do it. My whole world's been turned upside down by what I've learned the last three days, but I learned it nonetheless. I can't 'un-know' what I know now. It has to be done."

She heard Alex exhale a deep breath as Adam reached over and gripped her hand. Nikolas nodded determinedly as he looked at her, and for a brief moment she saw something in his crystal blue eyes – a fire there – that drove home for her all the stories she had heard the last two days that painted him as a warrior of thousands of battles. The look washed away her fear and made her feel brave and strong; she imagined though that many enemies had seen that look and trembled. The immortal's rich voice broke the silence of the moment for them all.

"Tomorrow, we hunt."

27

Aletheia woke the next morning exhausted. Sleep had not come easily to her or Adam the night before. They had stayed up late into the night talking through their fears about the danger of the task ahead of them, even discussing the possibility of one or both of their deaths. It had been a difficult conversation for them both. The thought of dying together didn't frighten either of them nearly as much as the thought of only one of them being killed. The most difficult part had been discussing moving on in life and finding love again if that did happen. Aletheia was at peace with the idea; they were very young and she didn't feel like it was fair or at all realistic for her to expect Adam to live out his life alone. Adam, though, had struggled. It took some time and a lot of conversation before she realized why it was so hard for him to fathom. While Aletheia was surrounded by family, both old and newly found, Adam had no one in the world but her.

Even after they had stopped talking and closed their eyes in an attempt to get some rest, a buzzing anxiety had kept

Aletheia's brain alert and awake as her body fought to drift into restful sleep. She felt as though she had lain awake for hours. As she lay there in the morning, trying to bring herself awake, she looked over to Adam and immediately knew he had struggled as she did. Telltale dark circles hung below his eyes. He gave her an awkward smile and a kiss on the cheek before getting out of the bed.

Breakfast was quiet for Aletheia. She and Adam stayed silent, with the exception of some light conversation with Sam, as Alex and Nikolas discussed the plan for the day. Aletheia felt better sitting next to Sam as she always did. The woman looked at both her and Adam worriedly and asked, "You didn't sleep much, did you? You are both exhausted."

Aletheia shook her head and as she did Sam got up out of her chair and moved behind her and Adam, standing between them and leaning down as though about to speak into their ears. She put her hands on their shoulders and said in a low voice, "Close your eyes."

Aletheia complied and soon she felt a light, cool feeling wash over her shoulder, down through her body and up her neck. When the feeling swept through her head she immediately felt more alert and awake. Sam kept her hand there for a moment more, and when she took it away Aletheia opened her eyes and looked up at her in astonishment. "That's...incredible! How did you do that?"

Adam was looking at Sam in awe. The woman simply smiled and winked at Aletheia and then sat back down. "Finish your breakfast," she said.

Aletheia complied, absentmindedly putting her fork to her mouth as she let the experience settle in her mind. Glancing over at Adam he had a deeply contemplative look on his face. They finished their breakfast in silence.

It was barely twenty minutes later that they found themselves preparing to leave. Aletheia had been thrilled to find out that Sam and Nikolas had provided her and Adam with some new clothes to change into, even if they were utilitarian. Sam had chuckled and explained that these were for the business at hand, and that when they got back she would help them build a new wardrobe for themselves. Aletheia didn't mind them; the clothes were all dark but they fit reasonably well and were comfortable. She looked over to Adam and thought he looked good in the black cargo pants and jacket they had picked out for him.

Nikolas led them into the master bedroom. Were it a different time, Aletheia would have stopped and ogled the room. It had the feel of an island oasis, like those huts standing in the water she had always seen pictures of on the internet and dreamed of vacationing in. It was easily the most restful room she had ever seen, decorated in flowing whites and tranquil blues, and accented with gorgeous white lilies. They passed through it quickly though, to a small room attached to it. Nikolas led them up to a wall and stopped in front of a very old-looking painting hanging on it next to a large bookcase made of deep, rich brown wood. He reached up and swung the painting to the side; it opened like a door. Behind it was a metallic biometric reader shaped like a hand. Aletheia recognized it immediately as a larger version of the lock Adam had on his gun safes at home. Nikolas reached up with a muscular arm and placed his hand in the reader. Aletheia heard a scraping sound and watched as the bookcase next to them swung out to reveal a room inside.

Wow! A secret room!

Aletheia felt chills up her spine as she followed Nikolas and Alex inside. Glancing at Adam, she saw his face light up like a child seeing Disneyland for the first time. Turning her attention back to the room at hand, she immediately understood why.

The walls of the room were lined with racks, filled with equipment and a multitude of weapons of different types. It reminded her of the action movies Adam always asked her to watch with him when it had been his turn to choose. Predictably, he started admiring everything in the room seemingly at once, moving from item to item excitedly and turning to tell her what each of them was, from handguns to blades.

"This...is...the coolest thing I have ever seen in my entire life." He looked the happiest Aletheia had seen him in a long time.

Alex and Nikolas had been watching him with amused looks on their faces. Alex's voice brought Adam's attention back to the other people in the room. "It's like I told Aletheia...you haven't seen the best parts of this life yet." His gravelly voice took on a serious tone for a moment before moving back to an amused one. "This is dangerous work you have agreed to, Adam...and a massive responsibility. And yes...this part is pretty cool."

He and Nikolas shared a knowing look between them which was clearly about the younger man. Seeing it, Aletheia cocked her head at them, curious. "What is it?"

Nikolas chuckled and said to her as much as to Adam, "It doesn't matter how much time has passed or how much the world has changed...I always know when I see one."

Aletheia looked to her great-grandfather, confused.

"A warrior. You, Adam. You have the heart of a warrior. Were we on Eyid-en, I would have started your training a decade ago."

Aletheia looked at Adam and saw his cheeks go bright red. After the initial flush wore off, she noticed he was standing a little straighter and taller. He looked as though he had been knighted by the Queen of England. She heard Sam's voice by her shoulder and realized her great-grandmother had been watching the exchange as well.

"Men..." she said, and as Aletheia turned she saw the woman rolling her eyes and shaking her head in exasperation. "Leave it one to be excited about going into battle." With that, she smiled and lightly grasped Aletheia's arm once and left them all to their preparation.

Aletheia had meant to ask Sam before she left, but instead she turned and asked Nikolas, "She's not coming with us?"

Nikolas stopped fitting Adam for the armored vest he had been helping him put on to wear under his jacket. "No, she will not. She has her duty as I have mine. Should the worst happen and I fall, she will alert the Ankh-el."

Aletheia's heart sank at the thought of her great-grandfather being killed by the Dy'ibalis. Not only was she starting to grow fond of him, but he felt like the only thing standing between the rest of them and the terrifying creature. As he continued to help Adam, Nikolas motioned for Aletheia to come over. When she did, her uncle retrieved another vest from the wall and started to fit it to her as well.

"You okay, kiddo?" He tilted his body to the side to bring his blue-grey eyes down to her level. Aletheia nodded slowly, ot sure if she was being honest with herself. He met her gaze and said, "Everything's gonna be okay." Glancing at the numerous handguns on the wall, he asked her, "You ever have to use one of those?"

"No...well, yes. I mean, I've never had to *use* one, but Adam showed me how to use his."

Alex was nodding. "The revolver. Okay, well...let's see what we can do then."

"Wait," she said. "Can't I just keep using it? I'm not like Adam – I don't know a lot about guns. I'm kind of comfortable with that one, though. I carried it for the last two weeks."

Alex glanced back to Nikolas. Her great-grandfather said, "The most important traits for a weapon to have are that you are comfortable with it and you know how to use it. In this case though, it also needs to be powerful to have any hope of hurting a Dy'ibalis."

Adam chimed in and said, "It fires forty-five longs or four-ten shotgun shells."

Nikolas nodded his head in approval. "A good weapon. That will do just fine. Go and bring it back here."

Aletheia turned and ran to her and Adam's room and retrieved the revolver from her bag. She paused as she touched the cold steel of the weapon and felt the weight of it in her hand. It immediately brought her back to the desperate moments in Los Angeles when she had to wield it. She shuddered involuntarily and rushed back to the join the others. When she got there, Nikolas was placing a large handgun into the holster attached to the vest he was wearing.

"Is that a Desert Eagle fifty cal?" Adam asked enthusiastically.

267

"Yes." Nikolas answered as Adam's face lit up. He picked another large handgun off the rack and handed it to Adam. "Forty-five caliber ACP. This should fit your hand and it has plenty of power."

Adam nodded eagerly, holding the weapon in his hand to get a feel for its grip. He slipped the pistol into the holster on his own vest.

"Aletheia, come closer," said Nikolas.

She moved closer to the three men. Her uncle was loading bullets into a magazine as he listened to his grandfather address them all.

"Dy'ibalis are covered with hard, rough scales. I have seen arrows bounce off their hide, and I have seen men break blades on them. Good blades. I do not know if it is truly their skin that is that thick or if it is a type of body-fitting armor they wear. Their true appearance is so monstrous it is hard to tell the difference. In any case, I am not sure how effective modern weapons will be against them."

Aletheia felt her own eyes go wide as she sputtered out the words, "What if they don't work? How can we kill it with no weapons?"

Nikolas' rich voice took on a very serious tone. "The weapons are not meant to kill it. If it is a Dy'ibalis and we find it, you are not to attack it. You are to point it out to me. The weapons are solely for your protection. It has avoided detection by the people of Earth thus far, so I am assuming it will not engage us in plain view. Still, unless we are in the middle of nowhere, if you fire any of those weapons the sound alone will bring the authorities and create a whole new level of trouble for us that we do not want. Not to mention you risk hitting each other. The heat of battle can be very disorienting for the inexperienced. So please, do not use them unless you have to. As for killing it, I need no weapons for that."

He reached behind him and turned back around with several boxes of ammunition. "These are armor-piercing rounds. Again, I am unsure if they will pierce the creature, but they are our best chance."

He reached onto a shelf beside him and handed them each a tactical flashlight and a locking blade knife. Aletheia was shocked at the weight of the knife when he placed it in her hand, and she opened it up once to look at the blade. It was large and looked wickedly sharp. She started to try to close it, her hands nearly shaking for fear that she would cut herself, and Alex stopped her and showed her how to safely unlock the blade and close it up.

"I would not normally give you a weapon you did not know how to use. I do not want you to be a danger to yourself. But in this case, you must have something. Those knives have the hardest blades you can buy. They will pierce the roof of a car. Hopefully it will be enough. Better still, I hope you will not have to find out."

Aletheia slipped the knife into one of her jacket pockets and the flashlight in the other, and watched as Adam put his in the large cargo pockets on his thighs. Nikolas selected a few more boxes of ammunition from a shelf and handed them to each of them according to the gun they were carrying. He looked to each of them and Aletheia felt herself strengthened in those crystal blue eyes.

"Come. It is time."

Aletheia watched the cotton sea of clouds fall away beneath the view of her window as the jet climbed through the azure sky. Saying goodbye to Sam had been hard; in the few short days she had been with her, Aletheia had grown very close to the woman. The limousine ride into Connecticut had gone quickly at least; they had flown out of a different airfield than the one in upstate New York they had arrived at the first day. Aletheia had been surprised when she found out it was because the private jet had been in use by another member of their family – a cousin of Alex's. Her uncle had explained to her that because of the secrets they kept, family were now the only people they could fully trust. There were a handful of them, mostly grandchildren to Nikolas and Sam, and most of them news reporters.

The four of them now sat silent in the comfortable cabin, reserving their conversation for the moments when they had privacy from the bodyguards who accompanied them everywhere outside the penthouse. Nikolas had told them before they even left the building that they would first be heading to Arizona, to investigate the airfield where Alex had first loaded them onto the jet. Alex and Nikolas were still very concerned about the GPS device that had been found on Alex's vehicle. Both men felt it was the most likely way that whatever or whoever was stalking Aletheia had followed Alex to her. Because the airfield in Arizona was the last location it had broadcast from, it seemed like a good place to start looking for whoever had placed it on the car.

Sitting in the soft leather seat, Aletheia looked at her great-grandfather and it struck her what a lonely existence it must have been for him and Sam. To be constantly surrounded by bodyguards – hired men you couldn't really talk to about the things that mattered. To only have your spouse and a handful of children and grandchildren truly know who you were; your only true friends being the only other two people like you on Earth who happened to live half a world away. The worst part, she imagined, would be to have everyone you know or love eventually die before you. She found herself wondering how many of their own children Sam and Nikolas had watched grow old and die.

After some time she got up and moved to the empty seat next to her great-grandfather. He looked at her with his clear blue eyes and smiled. It was the first time she had noticed the many layered emotions in that smile. It was as if she could see the wisdom, sadness, peacefulness, and joy in it all at the same time. She smiled back at him and said, "I just realized that if this had all never happened I might have gone my whole life and never met you or Sam. I'm glad I got to meet you, Grandpa."

His face softened and his smile got so wide she thought it would split his cheeks in two. "I'm very glad we got to meet too, Aletheia. I am sorry I can't rebuild the life you had for you, but I hope we get to enjoy many years together in your new one. Did you know your great-grandmother and I have whole albums of pictures of you from the time you were born?"

Aletheia sat and talked with him as Nikolas recounted all the pictures they had seen. They talked that way long into the morning until she felt the plane start to descend noticeably. Nikolas looked out the window. He turned to his great-granddaughter, his face now grim and serious.

"Are you ready?"

Once again, looking at his face she found her resolve strengthened and her fear fading into the background. It was manageable.

"Yes. I'm ready."

"Good. When we land and get off the plane, stay close to me at all times. Do not wander too far, even if it appears safe. Understand?"

Aletheia nodded in acknowledgment. *I'm as ready as I'm ever going to be.*

28

Aletheia leaned back on the headrest and watched the slivers of sunlight disappear as the bodyguard closed the door to the plane. They had been at the airfield for four hours, searching the grounds, the hangar, and the small copse of nearby citrus trees beside it for signs of the Dy'ibalis. Nikolas had poured over the ground with a fine-toothed comb looking for tracks. Alex had led them all through the hangar itself, inspecting every scratch on every door as a detective would.

They had found nothing. Not a single sign of a Dy'ibalis, or anything else out of the ordinary for that matter. Nikolas had spoken aloud in Ma-en, attempting to call his ancient enemy out of hiding. When that had failed, he had even had Aletheia speak aloud and name herself. Still there had been no response but the empty whistle of the wind.

Alex had even searched the local news archives but had been unable to find any traces of activity in the nearby towns that would have suggested a Dy'ibalis in the area. Frustrated and their sense of urgency increasing by the hour, they had finally reboarded the plane.

Sitting in the seat next to Adam, Aletheia was surprised to feel a sense of disappointment. When they had first deboarded the plane she had felt nothing but fear and dread, knowing that the confrontation with her tormenter – whatever or whoever it was – was imminent. Now that it had passed and they had found nothing, she did not feel the sense of relief she would have thought she would. Sitting there, Aletheia realized that the never-ending sense of dread and impending doom had been far worse than the thought of actually confronting the thing she was afraid of.

Nikolas and Alex were discussing the group's next move as discreetly as they could, making sure to not say anything in front of the hired men that would raise too many questions. Aletheia and Adam changed seats and crowded closer to the two older men in order to take part in the conversation. When they did, Alex leaned towards them and motioned for them to do the same.

"We are trying to decide where to go next. We have a flight plan scheduled to head to Los Angeles again. We are hoping that by having you with us, we will have more luck. But we are concerned beyond that because it is too dangerous to take you to Seattle. There is still a manhunt going on for both of you and the chances of you being spotted are too risky."

Aletheia nodded in understanding. Beside her, Adam glanced back to check on the closest of the bodyguards before turning back around to speak to Aletheia and the two older men in a low voice.

"Is there any place else you can think of that it could have gone?"

"Well," said Nikolas. "As I said before it appears to be

drawn to Aletheia. It followed her from her dormitory to your house. It then followed her – apparently by following Alex – to Los Angeles."

Aletheia looked confused. "It followed Uncle Alex?"

"I believe so, yes," said Nikolas. "When I was first told your story, I assumed it had simply followed you; that it had some method of finding you wherever you were. It made sense: it had reappeared at Adam's house once you were there, and it had done the same in Los Angeles. But when I found out about the GPS tracker on Alex's car, I began to suspect that it had perhaps lost your trail during your escape from Seattle. My suspicions grew when you confirmed that you had not had any nightmares since leaving Adam's house. In truth, it sounds like it made no contact with you at all until that night at the park."

"When Uncle Alex showed up..." said Aletheia, understanding dawning on her face.

"Yes," said Nikolas. "Which is troubling in its own regard. If my theory is correct, then it somehow knew you were related and at least suspected that Alex would find you."

"That is why we checked here," said Alex. "I still don't understand how it would have gotten its hands on a human-made GPS system, much less known how to use one. But if that is how it was tracking you at that point – through me – then this is the last place it knew you were. If it could have found its way to Manhattan, I would think it would ha..."

Alex got a peculiar look on his face, and then turned to Nikolas. "We know it didn't make it all the way to Manhattan, but who is to say it didn't track us to Monticello? We just assumed it lost our trail here."

Nikolas nodded gravely. "Yes...that is an excellent point.

Check the news around Monticello."

Alex immediately took a tablet out of his bag, opened it up, and started searching. Aletheia and Adam exchanged confused looks.

"The village of Monticello is in upstate New York," said Nikolas. "The private airfield you landed in when you first arrived is close to the village. If Alex's hunch is correct, then that is where it would have lost your trail, not here. It may have even shown up there to investigate."

Aletheia took a deep breath and exhaled, and found herself hoping that the hunch was a good one. She felt conflicted inside when she realized that part of her was eager to find whatever was stalking her and end it all once and for all. The lead Alex had just proposed wasn't a strong one, but it was as good as any they had. They sat and watched as Alex searched through news databases. It was quite some time before he finally stopped his typing, his mouth hanging slightly open as he read the screen. When Aletheia started to ask her uncle what he had found, he just gestured with his index finger, asking them all for a moment under his breath. He began typing furiously and then pausing, bursts of keystrokes punctuated by moments of silence where his eyes darted across the screen quickly reading text they could not see. After a few moments, he turned the screen towards Nikolas and the immortal's blue eyes scanned it rapidly, a look of satisfaction appearing on his face. Alex immediately got up and disappeared into the cockpit, while Nikolas spun the tablet around so they could read what her uncle had found.

Three windows were open on the tablet's screen. The first was a news story from Monticello about a suspected cougar in the area. The story went on to state that mountain lions were very rare in that area of the Catskills, but were suspected because several local owners' dogs were found mauled by a large predator of some sort. All of them had been found in the last three days.

The second was a Twitter search for the word 'nightmare' near Monticello, New York. Listed below were multiple tweets over the previous three days posted by various users. Aletheia noted two or three of them were complaining of terrifying, lucid nightmares.

The third window was another news story, this one a breaking story only a few hours old about an accident that had occurred in the hangar at the airfield they had landed at. Apparently, a mechanic working on a plane had been horribly injured when a power tool had 'gone crazy on him.' The man, named Jonathan Stills, was currently in stable condition at a nearby hospital. What struck Aletheia about the story was that the man was quoted as saying 'it was as if the thing had a mind of its own.'

She looked up from the screen and over to Adam, who had finished reading already. His face was grim as he nodded to her and then met Nikolas' gaze.

"So...when you said we would join the cause with Alex, is this the kind of stuff we would be looking for?" he asked.

"Yes," said the immortal. "We are always searching for patterns like these. Now that you know the types of things a Dy'ibalis can do and what it is capable of, I am sure you can figure out most of what to look for. As for the dogs, it is not surprising. The Dy'ibalis' ability to make itself undetectable is actually even more impressive than just remaining unseen. When they choose to go undetected, they can also mask their scent, their sound, and the heat they generate."

Adam's eyes were wide. "Really? Heat? As in, they could be invisible even to nightvision goggles?"

"Of that I am unsure, but I would guess that the answer is yes. As for their body heat though, it is far more profound than that. Dy'ibalis naturally exude heat; to get close to one is to feel like you are standing next to an oven. And they reek strongly of sulfur. These two traits, along with any sounds they might make, would be quite a giveaway and would negate any advantage they had achieved by being able to render themselves invisible. Unluckily for their enemies, they have mastered ways of masking all of their sensory signatures, at least to most creatures. Which is why they would hate dogs. On Eyid-en we had many creatures that, like dogs, had additional ways of sensing the world around them beyond even their sharp senses of hearing and smell. They would typically react to the Dy'ibalis hostilely, and the Dy'ibalis in turn would always kill them first if they wanted to remain undetected."

Aletheia's heart sank at the thought of innocent dogs being slaughtered by one of those monsters. She had always loved animals and felt an empathy for them that most people didn't seem to understand. Adam just whistled and leaned back, no doubt deep in thought about how to fight something with so many advantages. Their thoughts were interrupted by Alex, returning from the cockpit.

"Buckle up. We're on our way to New York."

The ride to New York went by quickly, each of them resting their minds and bodies as much as their adrenaline would allow. Before she knew it, Aletheia was stepping off the plane onto the familiar tarmac. She couldn't help but think back longingly to the first time they had landed here, the autumn sun dazzling in the blue sky and leaves of rainbow colors filling the forest of trees surrounding the airfield. *Funny how a simple thing like the time of day can make all the difference.* She looked around at her surroundings, the darkness of nighttime barely held at bay by the floodlights on their area of the tarmac. Nikolas had been the first to depart the plane; Aletheia stuck to his shoulder, never letting herself get more than a foot from the man.

Once they were all off the plane, Nikolas ordered the bodyguards with them to re-board and close the door. When the last of them had gone back inside, Nikolas surveyed the area intently for a moment, and then turned to Aletheia and the others. The tarmac was silent; the engines of the jet had long since died down and turned off completely, and when the door had finally closed the silence was profound. Aletheia was suddenly and keenly aware that they were completely alone out in the middle of the tarmac, a small circle of muted light from the floodlights the only thing fending off total darkness. Beyond the areas of the floodlights she saw strips of ground lights marking the edges of the runway, and beyond that, nothing. Nikolas's rich voice spoke in a hushed tone.

"I think our search has ended. Something is here...I can feel it. Ready your weapons, but remember: use them only as a last resort. If you see anything, tell me. And remember: if you do need to use your weapons, your first priority is to not hit one another. Do you understand?"

"Yes," said Aletheia and Adam in unison. They both pulled the pistols they had been given out from the holsters inside their jackets and took a deep breath. Nikolas looked into each of their eyes one last time; the affect was instantaneous. Aletheia felt braver, stronger, more fearless. She still understood intellectually that whatever they were about to encounter was dangerous, but her emotion had shifted from fear and near-panic to courage and determination. *I'm tired of being afraid. Let's just end this once and for all.*

The immortal turned and started forward and they followed closely, mercilessly approaching the edge of the light. As they reached it, Aletheia watched her surroundings get dimmer until they were all bathed in shadow. Even the mild transition from the dim light into the darkness of night was enough of a change to force her eyes to adjust, and she struggled to see anything for the first several steps out of the protective circle of light. As her eyes adjusted, Aletheia saw the hangar grow larger in her field of vision. The building was cloaked in deep shadows, with areas and recesses disappearing into complete darkness. Even in Nikolas' presence, she felt a chill run up her spine.

Nikolas turned on his flashlight, and Aletheia quickly followed his lead as did the others. They made their way to the small door on the right side of the front of the building. When they reached it, Nikolas nodded to Alex and the old reporter moved up and took a small black case from his jacket pocket. Aletheia watched in surprise as he took out several keys, working them until he found one that not only fit the door, but coaxed a gentle click from the lock. *I guess there are still a few things I don't know about my uncle,* she thought. He eased the door open slowly and Nikolas moved past him to enter first, surveying the room and ushering everyone inside. Once they were inside with the door closed, Nikolas turned on the lights.

From a vantage point in the deep shadows of the trees fifty

yards from the hangar, a pair of eyes watched the small group enter the building.

They stood in a small office space, filled with cubicles. Alex was scanning the walls and the door frame, and after a few moments Aletheia heard him confirm to Nikolas that there were no alarms. Her eyes quickly adjusting to the light and glad for its sense of safety, Aletheia turned off her flashlight and put it back in her pocket as soon as she saw the others doing the same. They began to move through the office space slowly, going from area to area and turning on lights as soon as they stepped into a darkened space. As they walked along Nikolas began to speak aloud every few minutes in language that sounded both eloquent and ancient. In the moments of silence that stretched between his words, he seemed to be listening for something.

Adam was moving along beside the Ma-en as he led them down a small hallway. He almost laughed to himself at the irony as he realized he had been tip-toeing as quietly as he possibly could as Nikolas spoke out in a completely normal tone of voice beside him. The immortal nodded for him to check the doors to their left and told him to turn on the lights inside them as they went. At the first door, Adam adjusted his grip on the pistol in his hand until it was just right. Reaching down with his left hand, he closed it around the cold steel knob and slowly turned it counter-clockwise until he heard the latch release. He pushed the door open at the doorknob, leading with his gun hand. The light from the hallway he was in slashed into the room and began to spread, illuminating the lower half of the far wall. Adam reached across with his left hand and felt for the switch, and feeling the smooth, squared plastic in his fingers, flipped it up.

Light filled the room immediately. Adam looked straight ahead and saw a man standing directly across from him, pointing a gun squarely at him. *Shit!* He instinctively ducked and rolled out of the room. Clutching his pistol to his chest, his brain spinning through a million scenarios in the split second it took. He pictured himself being shot in the chest, in the face, in the head. He pictured himself shooting the man in those same places.

The second he had reacted, the others had as well. Aletheia nearly jumped out of her skin and watched as her uncle moved quickly to the opposite side of the doorway Adam was standing at, his pistol ready. Nikolas moved more quickly than Aletheia could have imagined; one moment he had been by her side and the next he was bursting through the doorway before Alex had even moved or she even had the chance to gasp. Her first instinct was to flee, but instead she gripped her gun and started to step over to Adam to help when she heard her great-grandfather's voice tell them it was clear.

Aletheia hesitantly peered into the room after Nikolas, gripping the revolver tightly. Inside she saw a large restroom and changing area. On the far wall, directly opposite the door, was a large mirror. Adam and Alex had now stepped into the doorway as well and were peering into the room. If he had been facing her, she was sure she would have seen Adam blushing furiously.

"Sorry," he said apologetically to the others. "Shoot. I thought...damn. Sorry. I guess I'm just a little jumpy."

Nikolas was already walking back out of the room into the hallway to stand next to Aletheia. He had a look of sincere sympathy on his face. "It's okay, Adam. You did well to react; I would rather you did when you shouldn't than you didn't when you should. You are doing well." They all fell into place and continued forward down the hall. Before long they had cleared every room in the small area, filling the entire area with light.

At the end of the hall stood a door, larger than the others. They moved up to it and Nikolas didn't hesitate as he reached down and turned the handle, opening the door. With the exception of a small section of concrete floor that was illuminated by the light spilling out of the hallway they were in, what lay beyond was pitch blackness. Nikolas was peering into it intently. As Aletheia strained her eyes to see into it, she got a sense that the darkness in front of her was vast and deep.

29

Nikolas reached around the frame on the other side of the door, searching for the switch. Light intermittently flickered in the room beyond, at first giving them only flashes of what lay there before finally remaining on. Aletheia knew immediately why the darkness had seemed so vast. Beyond them lay the hangar bay. As she stepped though the doorway after Nikolas, she was struck by the silence. It was as if they had stepped into a vacuum, with only the quiet hum of the fluorescent lights high above to fill it. Those lights cast a dull, dead light onto everything in the bay, a sharp contrast to the vibrant, natural light of the daytime sun. Two planes filled the hangar; both modern-looking, small, single propeller models. The cement floor was clean and free of debris and along the high walls hung many posters and pegboards.

Aletheia remained close to Nikolas and kept her eyes trained carefully on her surroundings, only occasionally looking over to glance at Adam. Up ahead there was a large mechanical section of the bay; a steel cage filled with assorted tools and equipment, much of it hanging from the cage walls. Nikolas led them up to it and they walked through it carefully. He was inspecting the area methodically, and his attention to the area jogged Aletheia's memory. The news story of the mechanic who was hurt badly by the power tool he was using resurfaced in Aletheia's mind. She found herself looking at each of the devices she saw with horror and suspicion, imagining the many ways each could eviscerate her were it to suddenly gain a malicious mind of its own.

It happened so fast her mind didn't immediately have time to register what was going on. Aletheia heard a loud sound and before she could turn around to see what it was, something heavy struck her in the shoulder. She leapt forward away from the blow more out of instinct than anything else and heard an even louder metallic clang resound in the spot where she just had been. Time slowed down as she felt her heart leap in her chest and accelerate immediately to twice the rate it had been a mere second before. A mix of fear and adrenaline ripped through her body as she spun around in a panic, her brain deciding in that split second that it would rather face whatever had struck her than be ripped to pieces by it from behind. When she turned it took her mind a moment to catch up to what it was seeing.

Her uncle was stooping down to pick up a very long metal bar off the floor. He looked up at her as he leaned it back against the side of a toolbox with the other pieces like it. He was looking around the area to see if the noise had attracted attention, as were Nikolas and Adam. "Sorry, kiddo...you brushed it when you walked by it and I couldn't catch it in time. You okay?"

Aletheia rubbed her shoulder where the bar had hit her, realizing that it hadn't actually hurt so much as frightened her.

She now understood exactly how Adam had felt after the mirror incident. "Yeah, I'm fine. I'm sorry. I guess I need to get better at this."

Nikolas shook his head. "No, this is good. We are not trying to stay hidden. We are trying to get its attention, if it is nearby."

Aletheia appreciated his kindness, and when she looked over at Adam she saw empathy etched on his face. He smiled and shrugged at her, the most humor he could muster at the moment, but it was enough to take away her embarrassment. *At least I'm not the only one who sucks at this.*

Nikolas and Alex continued to inspect the tool area very closely, apparently looking not only for her tormentor but also for any clues they could find that might indicate its identity. After some time Nikolas motioned for the group to continue on. They spent the next half hour making a complete circuit of the hangar. Finding nothing, Nikolas looked to them all and said, "There is...something...here. If it is not inside, then we must search the woods. Come."

Walking through the empty, lonely aircraft hangar had been unnerving enough for Aletheia; the thought of venturing out into the deep, dark woods was terrifying. She looked at Nikolas and he returned her look, seeming to pick up on her fear. His gaze didn't take away her fear completely, but it made her strong enough to overcome it. She looked to Adam who had a scared but determined look on his face. *If he can do this, so can I.*

As they stepped outside, Aletheia once again had to let her eyes adjust to the darkness. They had left through a door on the back of the building and had stepped out into an unlit section, darker than dark. She felt in her pocket for her flashlight and quickly turned it on, the small circle of light temporarily illuminating whatever section of darkness she pointed it at. Nikolas checked with each of them to make sure they were ready, and then led them along the wall on a search of the perimeter of the building. As they moved along, Nikolas specifically searched the ground, moving slowly around the building until he had brought them all the way around the side. Watching him, Aletheia thought about all the ages he had lived through and realized he must have had centuries of experience as a tracker, gained from days gone by when that was an important skill and knowing how to work a smartphone was not. She followed along with Nikolas as he walked them around the back and sides of the building over and over again, making larger and larger arcs and gradually moving further from the building each time until they were deep in the woodline.

As they entered the wood, Aletheia grew more tense. The deeper they went the more pitch black it became. All light from the moon was blocked out by the canopy of leaves above them. The only things left she could see were the small circles of light dancing along a few feet head of them where they pointed their flashlights. Twigs cracked and snapped around them in the wood; sometimes off in the distance and other times so close they made her jump. Every time she heard a noise, Aletheia swung the circle of light from her flashlight in the direction she had heard it, only to swing it back when she heard another noise from where it had just been. It was a terrifying choice she was forced to make over and over; surrounded by a sea of darkness and having to decide which six-foot area to light up at any given moment.

They searched the woods for what felt like hours to

Aletheia, until she knew that it must be well past midnight. Even Nikolas seemed to be showing signs of frustration. He finally called them to a halt, suggesting they make their way back to the hangar and regroup. The walk back through the woods took a short while, but Nikolas led them straight and true, bringing them out of the woods directly across from the door they had come out of. He seemed perplexed as they re-entered the building. They walked out into the hangar and stood by the mechanical bay, Nikolas deep in thought. Alex was pacing back and forth a small distance away from the rest of them, as if trying to sort through what their next steps could be in his head. After a few moments, he turned to face them all and looked up.

"We could head into town; find a place for the night. In the morning we could interview the guy in the hospital who was attacked, maybe the people who lost their dogs, search the areas around those homes."

Nikolas was nodding; the conflicted look on his ageless face the only sign of his reluctance. "Yes, those would be good courses of action. But that does not settle me. Danger is imminent. I can *feel* it. I am not usually wrong about these things." He turned away from them for a moment; chin in hand, deep in thought.

Aletheia looked back to her uncle and saw him take a deep breath as he scrubbed his mustache, deep in thoughts of his own. He started to exhale in frustration as a large metal bar, like the one that Aletheia had knocked down earlier but at least two inches thick, lifted away from where it was leaning against the wall and whipped towards him in a wide arc. It smashed into him with tremendous force, sending him hurling through the air to crash into the wall behind him. His body crumpled to the ground.

Time slowed down as her eyes caught movement where the bar had come from. She watched as a figure shimmered into being, holding the bar in its hand. *Not a hand...* Aletheia's mind froze, shocked at what she was seeing. Standing at the edge of the mechanical bay, not twenty feet away from her, was a creature the likes of which she had never seen. She had seen similar ones, perhaps – in horror movies mostly – but they did not do it justice. Aletheia's heart froze in her chest as the creature rested its gaze upon her.

It was tall, nearly twice her height, with lanky, grotesque muscles. Its body looked like it was covered in shiny black scales, striped though with irregular crevices of red that glowed as though they were rivulets of heated metal or bloody cracks in burned flesh. Its hands ended in long, spindly, powerful-looking claws that matched those on the creature's feet. Its face looked less like a face than a war mask; a gruesome, menacing visage that did not change despite the timbrous, guttural growl that was emanating from it. The putrid reek of sulfur filled Aletheia's nostrils. As quickly as it had appeared, the creature shimmered back out of existence; its disappearance accompanied by a warping akin to the shimmering waves of heat that come off the desert sands in the height of midday. As the initial shock of the moment wore off, time seemed to speed back up for Aletheia.

"UNCLE ALEX!"

Before she could react, before she could even think to move, Nikolas was by her. He moved with startling speed; Aletheia's mind fought to match his human-looking appearance with the quickness of his movement but could not. Nikolas reached the point where the creature had been just after it shimmered out of sight. The immortal grabbed the metal bar, apparently before the creature could drop it, and twirled it around with blurring speed. A deafening gong resounded through the hangar as the bar struck home on its unseen target. The blow must have sent the creature flying through the air, because Aletheia and Adam jerked instinctively as a large, invisible mass of *nothing* ripped clean through the other side of the cage and into the wall on the far side of the hangar, smashing a large gaping hole into the drywall. Nikolas threw the now useless bar to the ground with a clang, its length bent well over forty-five degrees from the force of the blow. He did not let up; he was at the place where the creature had hit the wall in a second, but it must have recovered quickly and moved because he stalked around for a moment in frustration, finding nothing.

After a moment of trying to locate the creature and failing, Alex's collapsed form caught Nikolas' attention. The immortal ran over and dropped down beside him, tending to the man as his eyes scoured the hangar for signs of the creature. He shouted to Adam and Aletheia in a clear commanding voice.

"Come near to me! Quickly!"

Aletheia felt Adam leap forward next to her to comply, but he abruptly stopped when she didn't move. He looked back at her, pleading. Somewhere deep inside her mind registered what he was saying but for some reason it was as though she were in a soundproof glass ball and he on the outside. She sat frozen, her mind unable to unlock itself from the shock it had just experienced. She stared at Adam helplessly from behind her mental glass as he was hurled into shelves of tools in the mechanical bay.

Aletheia was jarred from her shock by a series of loud, booming cracks erupting from where Nikolas crouched over

Alex. The immortal had one hand laid upon her uncle and in the other his pistol was barking like thunder, raining bullets into the area where Adam had been. Sparks sprayed off *something* between her and Adam, exploding in the air as Nikolas was now shouting to her over the deafening gunfire.

"Aletheia! Run to me! Alex is bleeding out!"

She looked to her left and saw Adam struggle to get to his feet only to be thrown up against the racks again and held there. Images of him suffering James' fate flashed in her mind and a new emotion rose up inside her: rage. White hot rage boiled through her as she realized that the thing that had done this to her uncle, to her best friend, to her *life*, was somewhere right in front of her hiding like a coward from the one man who could fight it. She started to raise the revolver to fire but instead noticed several cans of spray paint on the top of a toolbox to her left. Dropping her gun onto the toolbox, she snatched them in her hands as she leapt towards the spot in front of Adam. She held out both cans and depressed the buttons, filling the air with aerosolized paint. Most of it fell in a harmless mist, but soon she saw the large, terrifying shape of the creature appear out of thin air, outlined in white.

Let's see you hide now, you son of a bitch.

Aletheia screamed as Adam battled as though he was trying to keep something away from his throat. He seemed to be locked in a stalemate with it, but she knew how it would end. Not daring to use the gun with Adam in the line of fire, Aletheia fumbled frantically for the knife in her pocket. Grabbing the blade and pulling it open, she felt the solid click as it locked into place. Her adrenaline surged as she rushed forward, raising it up and bringing it down on the thing's back with all her might.

The knife clanged hard into the creature's scales and turned aside with such force that Aletheia lost her grip on it and it fell to the ground. Before she even realized she had lost her weapon, she watched the white outline twist in front of her and then was hammered down to the ground by a thunderous blow. Aletheia fought to stay conscious; she couldn't breathe. Her mind screamed at her legs and arms to move – to roll out of the way – but her body refused to respond. Through her dimmed vision she saw the telltale white spray patterns looming over her and knew that her time on Earth was at an end. She cringed, her eyes half-shut as she waited for the blow that would end her life.

Instead what she heard was a roar of rage as Adam collided with the creature's outline. She felt him struggling with it over her for a moment, and then he was crashing into a toolbox. At the same moment, she heard a curse from behind her. Nikolas' form flew over her in a blur, striking the creature and sending it flying for the second time, this time into the near side of the cage. With the creature's outline now visible, the immortal closed in instantaneously. Aletheia stared in awe at what she watched through her still-distorted vision.

The immortal moved impossibly fast. As she watched the powerful creature lunge at him, arms like tree limbs flailing, Aletheia was mesmerized with Nikolas' movements. She remembered thinking how graceful he and Sam had both been in their daily activities, but that had been nothing compared to the spectacle before her. Nikolas moved in and out of the creature's blows with a speed and grace no human could ever attain; landing blows of his own seemingly at will which shook the entire cage as they landed. It was like watching a beautiful, terrifying dance. For all the terror it had inflicted on so many people, the creature was being utterly decimated by the immortal. Within seconds, it burst past Nikolas with all its might and tried to run, lunging straight at Aletheia. Adrenaline flooded every cell in her body, but before she could even scream Nikolas had somehow managed to trip the creature up so that it fell right before her face. The immortal was standing over its head. A loud crack like the sound of a boulder breaking echoed through the hangar as he struck down on the back of the creature's neck. A moment later, it stopped moving.

Adam hauled Aletheia to her feet and she threw her arms around him in a desperate hug. As she looked over his shoulder to the outline of the creature, a flurry of emotions rushed through her all at once. Her adrenaline surging, part of her was still enraged and felt a grim satisfaction when she watched it die. Another part of her shuddered and felt a wave of relief; a finality that struck her as she realized that this *thing*, this horrible, vile thing that had terrorized her and ruined her entire life was finally no more. Another part of her still eyed the immortal in both awe and fear. It was one thing to *hear* about the amazing things a person was truly capable of doing; it was another to witness someone moving with speed and power that was clearly *inhuman*. It had been beautiful and terrifying at the same time.

She didn't have time to embrace Adam for long, because seconds after the creature stopped moving, Nikolas stepped off of it and pulled Adam and Aletheia towards the area where Alex was.

"Quickly. Move away from it."

Aletheia had been about to ask why when she looked back and saw the outline of the creature start to glow a furious red, then progress through orange, yellow, and white, glowing brighter and brighter every second until the whole creature was blazing with a bluish-white light so bright that she had to shield her eyes. A loud, sustained, *whooshing* sound filled her ears as the creature immolated itself in an intense display. When it ended, there was no sign of the creature any longer. Where it had been lying, a large pit in the hangar floor was filled with glowing orange and red embers and molten cement.

"Holy crap!" said Adam. "What the hell was that?"

"When they die their body heat increases to an incredible level and they incinerate themselves," said Nikolas. "It would not do well to be near one when it happens. I cannot imagine what temperature they reach in those few seconds. Are the two of you okay?"

Adam nodded absentmindedly as Aletheia answered, "Yes. I'm okay." She looked over at where her uncle lay. His heart broke when she saw him there, but she was still in too much shock to cry.

"Alex!" She rushed over to his side, followed by the two men. She looked up to Nikolas. "Is he...?"

Nikolas smiled sadly. "No, he is not dead. But it was very, very close. I am sorry if I put the two of you in danger. He was bleeding very badly internally, and I only had moments to stop it and save his life."

Adam gaped at Nikolas. "You...stopped the bleeding? How?"

Nikolas just raised an eyebrow at both of them. Understanding dawned on their faces. His face took on a more humble look. "I cannot help him heal fully from this. His internal injuries are...significant." He leaned down and stroked Alex's gray hair, a look of pain and sadness crossed his face as he considered his grandson. "But we will take him home to Sam, and he will recover."

"Shouldn't we get him to a hospital?" asked Adam.

"If we were not so close to the city I would say yes. But I can keep him stable until we get to Sam, and in her care he will heal even faster than he would in the best hospital." Nikolas looked back to the mechanical area and took a deep breath. He had an unreadable look on his face. He walked over and sat down on the floor cross-legged and considered the pit of melted slag. After staring at it for several seconds, He shook his head.

"We are found. Six thousand years, and the day has finally come. We have had so many false alarms over the millennia that I held out hope this would be one too. Our only hope now is that it was alone, and we stopped it before it could find a way to call its brethren to Earth. I must alert the Ankh-el immediately."

"So that was a Dy'ibalis then," said Adam.

Nikolas replied with a simple, "Yes."

Aletheia stood there in Adam's arms, trying to absorb the immensity of what the immortal had just said. She opened her mouth to speak, but instead opted to remain silent, sensing that it was not a moment for words. Soon, Nikolas rose to his feet and walked over to stand next to Alex. The immortal reached down and gently lifted his grandson's unconscious body as if the man weighed nothing.

"Come. We must go. I will have the men stay and clear what they can of this before morning. As for that..." He motioned to the hardening pit in the middle of the destroyed tool area. "...chemical accident. Yes. One of my mechanics. I will pay for a new, state-of-the-art mechanical bay for them, plus perhaps a large contribution to the airfield to keep it quiet."

Aletheia pulled away from Adam for a moment and walked over to the spot where the Dy'ibalis had been. She stared at it for a few moments in silence. *It's finally over. Freakier than I ever could have imagined...but over.* Taking a deep breath, she turned and started back towards Adam and Nikolas when something reflective on the floor caught her eye. Reaching down, she picked it up. It was hard and glossy black, and was shaped like a guitar pick. She ran her fingers over it; it felt incredibly smooth in her hand. *It looks like a scale.* As she approached the two men, she held it up and looked to Nikolas. "Is this...from that thing?"

Nikolas looked at it in wonder. A smile spread across his face. "It is. I have seen them before, on Eyid-en. Many thought they held mystical powers. We did not have the technology then to analyze it the way humans do now. Keep it. I know someone who will be very interested in it."

Aletheia looked again at the scale, her feelings towards it a mixture of pride, revulsion, and curiosity. Not wanting to overthink it, she put it in her jacket pocket and followed Nikolas and Adam out of the hangar to the jet outside.

30

It was over an hour before the limousine arrived at the airfield. The three of them had waited inside the plane's cabin, Nikolas tending to Alex and staying in physical contact with him the entire time. Alex had looked terrible to Aletheia and had not regained consciousness, but his breathing was deep and steady and he seemed as though he was sleeping. Nikolas had given his men orders the moment they had gotten on the plane, instructing them to clean up all traces of a struggle in the hangar until only the damage to the floor and walls remained. His men had gone to work on it the moment he had stopped speaking. The immortal had then called Sam and told her what had happened.

The car ride back was solemn. Nikolas seemed lost in thought for the majority of it, as was Adam. Aletheia leaned on Adam, her head resting on his shoulder, and watched Nikolas as he held Alex in his lap. She had started to grow closer to her great-grandfather over the last two days, but the events of the night had caused her to take a momentary step back. While she trusted him and understood that he loved her, the memory of watching him destroy the Dy'ibalis with his bare hands had disturbed her in a way she had not expected. It had reminded her of the biologists she had always admired who managed to form bonds with lions or gorillas. It must have been a wonderful feeling to be with those beautiful animals; to love and be loved by them. But in the back of their minds they must have known that the creature they loved could casually tear them to pieces.

Watching him there in the limousine, though – watching the care with which he tended to Alex – Aletheia felt a surge of empathy and affection for him that overrode her trepidation from the previous night. He looked decidedly human, she thought, even if she knew it wasn't true.

She thought back to her experiences the last several weeks – the worry and dread she had felt at every turn – and wondered what it must have been like for him to feel that for six thousand years. She tried not to think about what would come next now that humanity had been found, instead choosing to hold out hope that this one Dy'ibalis had been a rogue and that the threat was ended. After what she had just been through, the alternative was too much to consider.

It was early morning when they arrived back at the penthouse. Rather than dropping them off out in front of the tall glass skyscraper, the limousine pulled around the building and drove down into an underground parking garage beneath it where Nikolas spirited Alex to the elevators. When they got inside, Aletheia watched as he opened a panel underneath the buttons and punched in a code on the keypad. The top floor button lit up. After they passed the tenth floor without stopping at any others, Aletheia realized what the code had been for.

When they arrived at the top Nikolas led them out and straight into the penthouse, barely stopping to nod to the bodyguards seated outside the door. Once inside he called for Sam and carried Alex to the room he had been sleeping in. Aletheia followed him, not wanting to get in the way but also wanting to make sure her uncle was going to be okay.

When she entered the room she was surprised to see that the previous furniture had been moved and a hospital bed was in the corner next to the window surrounded by numerous pieces of medical equipment. Sam entered the room seconds after they did, swept to the side of the bed as Nikolas laid Alex down on it, and then raised the head of the bed so he was laying at an incline. Sam took Alex's hand in hers and placed her other hand on his chest and closed her eyes. Aletheia sat there silently, as did they all, afraid to move or speak for fear of disrupting what seemed to be a hallowed moment. The minutes passed like hours, until Aletheia thought she would burst. Her breath caught when her uncle opened his mouth and drew a breath through it rather than his nose. His eyelids fluttered for a moment before stopping and then creeping open. He turned his head slowly and looked at Sam. The corners of his mouth twitched. He turned his head the other way and saw Nikolas there, and this time he managed to get the corners of his mouth to inch upward.

It was a few moments before he could speak, but as Aletheia watched in amazement he seemed to grow stronger every minute he was in contact with Sam. Eventually he was able to pick his head up to look at her and say, "Pigtails..." Unable to contain herself any longer, Aletheia rushed to the bedside next to Sam and leaned over, gently hugging him as tears rolled down her cheeks. He managed to raise his arm feebly and hug her back. When she pulled away she saw that he had managed a weak smile for her.

He turned to Nikolas, his voice rough, and asked, "Did you get it?"

Nikolas nodded. "*We* did," he said, correcting him. "Your hunch was right. We encountered it in the hangar. You were the first one it struck, and then it appeared for a moment before vanishing again. Aletheia and Adam and I were able to defeat it."

"So...it was one. A Dy'ibalis. They finally found us."

Nikolas' face was solemn. "It would appear so. But we destroyed it, and that may be our salvation. So long as it did not have a chance to contact its kind before we did. Do not worry over it, Alex. I will contact the Ankh-el and all will be well. For now, you need to rest." Nikolas then did something that surprised Aletheia: he leaned forward and placed a kiss on his grandson's forehead. He was frowning.

"I am sorry, Alex. It is my fault you were harmed. I let my guard down – let you get too far from me – that is when it struck you."

Alex almost laughed at Nikolas' comment, but the condition of his throat made it come out as a harsh, croaking sound.

"I'm the one who walked away. I knew the rules. Let my guard down once we had checked everything; got too confident. Besides, what kind of person would I be if I blamed an old man for that?"

Aletheia found herself laughing despite her tears. *Still the same sense of humor.* She knew then that her uncle would be okay.

I've flown more miles this week than I've flown in the last ten years, thought Aletheia as she stared out the window of the jet. Below them – far below – churned the deep green waves of the Atlantic Ocean.

The visit had been too short-lived for Aletheia's liking, but Nikolas had been adamant about leaving immediately to alert the Ankh-el of what they had discovered. She wished she had more time with her uncle, and with Sam, but her great-grandfather had told her and Adam that he wanted them to accompany him. Aletheia had been scared by the proposition, wondering if he meant for them to meet the Ankh-el, but he had clarified that he would be contacting them alone. There was something else important he wanted to show her and Adam. Knowing she would have all the time in the world to visit with Alex and Sam when they got back, she had agreed to go along.

A glance at her watch brought Aletheia back to the present. *Four hours in, six to go. I can't believe we're going to the Ukraine. What could possibly be there?* She looked to her left and saw Adam peering out the window past her. His face looked excited. When he noticed her watching him he smiled.

"I've never been overseas. This is amazing."

Looking at him, she decided that maybe it was amazing after all. "Yes, it is." She turned to gaze again out the window and caught Nikolas regarding both of them. She cocked her head at him, curious.

"What is it?"

Nikolas beamed at her. "I was just thinking about how very proud of you I am, Aletheia. You did exceptionally well last night. I am ashamed to admit, you did better than I thought you would. I did not have you pegged for a warrior. That was quick thinking on your part to use the spray paint – very clever."

Aletheia blushed at the compliment and shook her head as she replied, her voice humble. "It just came to me. I didn't have time to think about it – I just reacted. It's not the way it looks in the movies, you know?" She looked at Nikolas for confirmation that he understood. "I was terrified, and I couldn't think straight, and there were moments where I couldn't even move. I was so scared. I don't know how anyone actually comes up with anything clever in those moments; I just reacted."

"Yes," said Nikolas. "Even in those moments when our brains do not function because they are stunned by what is happening, our soul will guide us and tell us what to do. You listened to yours." He moved his gaze to take both of them in and smiled again. "You both did exceptionally well. I am very proud."

Adam half-smiled but looked disappointed, turning his head to Aletheia as he spoke. "Lee was amazing. I just wish I could have been of more help. I feel like I didn't do much except get thrown around." He shook his head and then looked over to where the bodyguards usually sat, conscious of his choice of words. Seeing the empty seats, he remembered that the larger jet they were on had a separate cabin for the men. He turned back to Aletheia and Nikolas.

"I know it sounds ridiculous. I get that those things are super powerful. It was stupid of me to think I could stop it, but when it was about to hurt Lee I felt this…certainty…inside of me that I would not let it harm her. I don't know how to explain it, but it gave me confidence. It made me feel…invincible. But then when I tried to stop the thing, it just threw me aside like a rag doll. If you hadn't been there she'd be dead." He looked over at Aletheia. "I'm sorry. If I can't protect you, what good am I?"

Aletheia looked at him as though he had gone insane. "Adam, you saved my life! That thing would have killed me."

Nikolas put his hand on the younger man's shoulder and said, "Adam, your worth is defined by more than your ability to protect those you love. That is not the only reason you matter." He took his hand off his shoulder and sat back in his seat, his ice blue eyes resting on him as he spoke. "Have I ever told you that it was our people who taught the people of Earth how to break and ride horses, and how to fight from horseback?"

Adam looked confused for a moment, not understanding why the immortal was changing the topic. He shook his head tentatively. "No...not yet."

"On Eyid-en we used to have an animal called an *ekh-wa*. They were very similar to the horses here on Earth, and over the millennia our people developed a relationship with them. We trained them, rode them, and used them as mounts in battle. When we first came to Earth, we saw the similarities between the wild horses of the steppes of Eastern Europe and the ekh-wa. It did not take us long to train them in the same way. When the people of Earth saw us riding them, they were fascinated, so we taught them how."

Adam did his best to let go of the self-pity he had been expressing earlier. In truth, the story had caught his attention, appealing to the parts of his mind that were fascinated whenever Nikolas spoke of these things. The immortal continued.

"Adam, I have watched men ride into battle against the Dy'ibalis. I have done it myself. And I have watched one rip a half-ton ekh-wa in half." He leaned forward, intent on the younger man. "Just grabbed it – shoulder and rump..." Nikolas reached his hands out to the sides to demonstrate. "…and ripped it in two." The look on his face softened. "Last night I watched you struggle with one. I watched you manage to keep its claws from your own neck. I watched you hit it and knock it back a solid two feet. And I watched as you held it back from harming the woman you love for two or three seconds. That may not seem like much to you Adam, but I can tell you this: no average person could have done that."

He leaned back, a satisfied look on his face as Adam pondered silently the ramifications of what Nikolas had just explained to him. *No average person…*

"That feeling you described – that *certainty* you felt rise up inside you – that was your soul. That is what it feels like when it strengthens you. It doesn't *hope* it can do something. It just *knows*. You must learn to let go of your doubts about yourself. They are not part of you. They were put there by others. The real you – the one you felt awaken last night – is much more than you think you are."

Adam sat back, stunned. He had been so busy thinking he hadn't been able to contribute much – that Aletheia and Nikolas had been the true heroes and he had not carried his weight – that he hadn't truly thought about the few seconds he had bought them both. As he considered the thought more, he was surprised to find himself smiling. *I mattered.*

31

The rapid, dull chopping of the helicopter's blades through the air drowned out most other sound as Aletheia sat looking out the window at the bouquet of colors below. Nikolas had informed them both that they would be traveling into the Carpathian Mountains in western Ukraine. The morning sun behind them splashed across the tops of the trees below, bringing sections of them blazing to life in vibrant displays of red, orange, and yellow. She leaned back and closed her eyes, taking comfort in the rhythm of the beating blades. She was still tired; her body not yet adjusted to staying awake the entire night before or the significant time change between New York and Ukraine. Luckily, she had slept most of the ten hour flight, even through the refueling stop they had made in Spain. The remainder of her weariness was temporarily offset by the thrill she felt about her surroundings. She glanced over at Adam peering out the window.

I hate to admit it, but he was right. Never in my life did I think I'd have adventures like this. The choice was worth it.

Aletheia and Adam had both been shocked to find men waiting for them at the airport. Nikolas and the other immortals apparently had a small army of hired men and contacts all over the globe. It wasn't until Aletheia thought about how long he had been on Earth that it all came into perspective for her. Apparently, one could amass an impressive base of power and wealth over six thousand years. Nikolas had wasted no time once they had landed, moving them towards their objective at a steady but rapid pace. They had been back in the air in the helicopter within thirty minutes of landing.

The ride in the helicopter had been long but exhilarating. The further from the city they flew, the more beautiful it became. They passed over stunning vistas and mountainous lands that looked completely untouched by modern society, holding only a handful of small villages and homesteads. Soon Aletheia felt her stomach lift as the helicopter began to descend towards a particular mountain ahead of them. As they drew closer, Nikolas gestured to both of them, not bothering to raise his voice over the beat of the engines. He was pointing to something up ahead of them.

Aletheia craned her neck to get a clear view out the side window. Nestled into the side of the mountain, surrounded by a forest of vibrant autumn trees, was a castle. Aletheia felt her eyes open wider, all weariness temporarily washed out of them as she took in the rapidly approaching sight. *That is beautiful.*

The castle looked as though it had been built right into the mountain, shaped to fill in a crook on its side where a huge plateau had blossomed into a grassy field. Its grey stone towers and walls looked more like a natural extension of the mountain's crags than a man-made structure jutting up from the ground. As the helicopter began to land on the field in front of the structure, she could see that it was indeed connected to the side of the mountain. She looked over to Adam and he looked back, giddy.

Several men came out to greet them; rough-looking men with automatic rifles. Aletheia was taken aback by their appearance, but one look at Nikolas told her the men were supposed to be there. Once the engines shut down Aletheia exited the helicopter with Adam, following her great-grandfather up towards the castle. The men declined their heads quickly towards the immortal in recognition and without a glance at Aletheia turned towards the helicopter, scanning the area around them. Nikolas motioned for her and Adam to follow as he led them across the field and up massive stone stairs to the front of the structure. Aletheia had to lean her head back far to take it all in, so large was the building now that they were up close to it.

A man greeted Nikolas at the top of the stairs, falling into step beside him. Aletheia thought he looked close to her age, with slightly darker coloring. She guessed he was of mixed descent, possibly Middle Eastern. He had a thick head of black hair and wire-rimmed glasses seated on his face. He nodded towards them before he turned away to talk with Nikolas. Aletheia got the impression that he was giving the immortal updates as they walked. He led them to the heavy wooden double doors that marked the main entrance to the castle.

They must be twelve feet tall, she thought. The man pulled one of the doors open for them and held it as they entered. When they got inside, Nikolas turned to them both, raising his hand and sweeping it across the view in front of them.

"Welcome to *Dom'anderas.* The 'Second Home.'"

The inside of the castle was palatial; the entry way was grand, with vaulted ceilings rising up ten times the height of a man and two large, sweeping staircases curving up to the center of the second level like mirror images of each other. The walls were filled with paintings and collections of ancient things that put even the one in the penthouse to shame. Suits of armor, weaponry, and tools were displayed randomly throughout the entry hall, giving it the feel of an upscale museum. Aletheia was surprised to find technology blended in with history as well. There were several modern devices in view and music was playing in the background through an integrated sound system; the men and women who kept this place clean for Nikolas must have been playing the music for themselves. Considering the size, the area was immaculate.

"Is this…yours?" Aletheia asked, her eyes wide.

"We share it," answered Nikolas. "It belongs to the four of us."

Adam looked astounded. "This place is incredible!" He managed to tear his gaze away from his surroundings long enough to turn it towards Nikolas. "Why is it called the 'Second Home?'"

"Because," said Nikolas. "You are standing on the spot where our feet first touched the Earth."

Aletheia watched as Adam reflexively looked down to the rich, aged hardwood floors at his feet. She caught herself doing the same. "So this is where you…landed?"

Nikolas laughed. "Landed? Not exactly, but the spirit of your question is correct. Yes, this is where we first arrived in this world."

As she stood there, immersed in the significance of the

moment, it occurred to Aletheia that the Middle Eastern man was still standing silently next to them. She looked to him, concerned that he had overheard the conversation, and he smiled and extended his hand.

"Hi, I'm Abdul."

Aletheia looked at the immortal for direction as she took the man's hand and introduced herself. Adam followed suit. Nikolas put his hand on the man's shoulder and said, "Abdul is Turk's grandson. He watches over this place when none of us are here." He turned to the younger man, his face taking on a serious tone. "Has Tesha made contact with you as well?"

Abdul's face went dark. "Yes. She stands ready, as does my grandfather."

"Good," said Nikolas. "Sam stands ready as well. Hopefully it will not come to that. We will see what guidance they have to give. I must go and make contact. While I am gone, there is no use in the three of you sitting and worrying what will come. I will find you when it is done. Should the answers they give be dire, we will all know soon enough. Show Aletheia and Adam around a bit while I am gone, and do not worry over things that have not yet come to be."

Abdul nodded. "Of course, Nikolas." He looked shaken, but quickly put on a smile when he turned to Adam and Aletheia.

The immortal turned back to Adam and Aletheia. "I should not be gone long – hours, at most. When I return, there is something important you need to see." With that, he turned and strode away into the castle.

The time with Abdul was more enjoyable than Aletheia thought it would be. Nikolas' ominous words had placed a dark mood in her mind before he left, and it looked like it had done the same for Adam. But soon Adam and Aletheia found themselves conversing and laughing with Abdul as he showed them around the castle. As wonderful as Nikolas, Sam, and Alex had been, it was nice to talk to someone their own age. Abdul was humble and funny, and had several interesting anecdotes to share about his father and the things he had seen. It was enough to let Aletheia forget about the immensity of the situation they were all dealing with. Abdul seemed appreciative of the reprieve too.

It was close to noon before Nikolas found the three of them in a sitting room, eating by a large window. Abdul had been answering the questions they had about the Ukraine and the Carpathian mountains. When the immortal entered the room, the conversation died as the three of them watched him approach the table they were seated at. Aletheia had expected him to look somber, or even shaken, but instead the immortal looked incredibly relaxed and happy; almost serene. He exhaled deeply.

"I am sorry, the aftereffects are quite powerful. No matter how many times I am in their presence, it does not lessen. No matter. The news is good. They have delved into the Earth – do not ask me, for I do not know how they do it – and they have found no signs that the Dy'ibalis traveled here by any means they can detect, nor did they find signs that the one we defeated contacted its brethren."

Aletheia breathed a sigh of relief, stress releasing from her pores at his words. Around the table she heard similar sounds of relief coming from the two men.

"That is the good news," he continued. "However, there is much work to be done. We must ensure that it was alone. We will redouble our efforts to find any signs of activity on Earth. We must also uncover the mystery surrounding the tracking device. The Ankh-el are very concerned by the possibility of a human aiding the Dy'ibalis. Lastly, and most importantly, we must find out how it got here. That is paramount."

He turned to look directly at Abdul. "It is safe? It has not been found, used, or tampered with?"

Abdul's face was earnest. "No, Memattar-en. Not that I could tell. I have not been inside – I cannot go inside. But the doorways look to be intact."

Nikolas was nodding as the man spoke. "Good. You have done well. Please go and inform the others of the Ankh-el's directive. There is no need for us to assemble, but we will all need to redouble our efforts. Thank you, Abdul." He turned to Adam and Aletheia. "Come. It is time you saw."

Abdul smiled and excused himself. Nikolas ushered them out of the room and led them down a series of hallways deep into the castle. There were no more windows on the walls where they were, and despite the size and labyrinthine layout of the castle, Aletheia was fairly confident that they were now in areas that were actually inside the mountain, or close to it. They came to a library at the end of a long hallway and Nikolas led them inside. He walked to a bookshelf along the far wall and reached up to grasp a very old-looking book on the top shelf.

Aletheia was astonished when she got close enough to read the title of the book.

Aletheia.

The immortal pulled on the book and stepped back as the bookcase swung open to reveal a dark stairwell. Nikolas entered and as he did a light flickered on inside, revealing rough-hewn rock walls leading down. He paused a moment for the two of them to follow before disappearing down into the recesses of the stairwell. Aletheia looked to Adam and stepped forward, her fingers tingling with anticipation. The gravity of the moment was palpable.

They followed Nikolas down the stairwell to the bottom where it opened up into a large cavern. Aletheia wasn't sure, but from the direction they were facing she thought that this must have originally been a recess in the mountain and faced outward toward the plateau. Her eyes scanned the cavern in disbelief, and next to her she heard Adam curse under his breath.

The room was filled – *filled* – with treasures from ages past. These were not the relics from the castle above, but actual treasure. Gold and gems filled chests and adorned ancient weapons and armor, like a picture from a fairy tale. Aletheia gasped as she tried to comprehend the value of such treasures in the modern world. It was truly staggering. Adam was dumbfounded, staring open-mouthed around him.

Nikolas walked through the cavern without so much as a second glance, stepping over piles of gems that could have bought him the entire building he lived in, much less the penthouse. When he got to the far wall he brushed aside piles of gold and silver as if they were trash. Aletheia and Adam moved across the room, careful not to knock anything over, and joined him next to the wall. Seeing the looks on their faces, he grinned. "Do not fear. Much of it is fake. It is a ruse. The real treasure lies beyond."

Aletheia grimaced at the thought, turning around and looking at the room with different eyes. Adam looked decidedly disappointed as well.

"Stand back," said Nikolas. Adam and Aletheia backed up a step and the immortal reached his arms out to his sides as far as he could stretch, his fingers finding fine little cracks in the stone wall that they had not even realized were there in the dim light. His grip tightened and he seemed to tense as if he were exerting himself. Aletheia heard a deep, grinding sound as the cracks started to become larger. Aletheia's jaw dropped open.

"Holy shit," said Adam.

Nikolas continued to exert pressure on the massive slab of rock that he was pulling out of the wall. After a few moments, it came completely free. Adam grabbed Aletheia's arm and pulled her back a few steps reflexively, but the immortal seemed to handle the slab with ease, walking to the side and leaning it with a giant thud on the unchanged section of wall nearby.

"That thing must weigh tons!" exclaimed Aletheia.

"Yes," said Nikolas. "We have had some near misses over the millennia. The last was almost a century ago, during the Second World War. This area was overrun by Nazi Germany. You can imagine how hard it was for us to get here in the middle of a war zone, but we did what we must. We had already constructed this castle here – it is centuries old – but at that time all we had separating the rest of this cavern from what lay beyond was a brick and mortar wall. When we finally fought our way here, we found that the Nazi soldiers had invaded the castle, and found the secret staircase down here. They had even broken down the wall to reach what was beyond. We managed to re-take control of the castle and keep it safe and protected until the war was over, but the memory has taught us that we need to be more vigilant." He gestured to what lay behind the block he had just removed.

313

In the recess where the giant stone slab had been, a large, solid steel door sat nestled in the rock. The door had a biometric scanner like the one Nikolas had in his penthouse. On the surface of the door, engraved deeply into the steel, was a symbol. Aletheia recognized it.

"Isn't that the symbol for medicine and doctors?"

Adam's voice next to her was reverent. "Most people think so...but no. That's the Rod of Asclepius. It's a rod with a single serpent wrapped around it. This..." he pointed at the symbol, "...is the Caduceus. The symbol of the ancient Greek god Hermes. There's another one too..." He drifted off for a moment, no doubt sifting through piles of mental information about ancient mythology. "...Enki! It's also an ancient symbol for..."

Adam stopped speaking and turned to Nikolas, his eyebrows raised as his memory caught up with his words. "This...this is *your* symbol? Wait, does that mean the stories about Hermes were about you too?"

Nikolas chuckled. "No, to both, although they are both related. It is not my symbol. That is the ancient symbol of the Covenant."

"The Covenant between God and men? Like in the Bible?" asked Adam.

"The Covenant between the gods," said Nikolas. "A Covenant that was broken."

32

He saw the Secret, discovered the Hidden,
He brought information of the time before the
flood.
He went on a distant journey,
Pushing himself to exhaustion,
But then was brought to peace.
  -Epic of Gilgamesh, Sumeria c.2000 B.C.

Enki made ready to speak and said to his
servant...pay attention to all my words!
Flee the house, build a boat,
Forsake possessions, and save life.
  -Epic of Atra-Hasis, Akkadia c.1700 B.C.

I have saved thee.
Fasten the ship to a tree, but let not the water cut
thee off whilst thou art on the mountain...
...the flood then swept away all these creatures,
and Manu alone remained there.
  Satapatha Brahmana, India c.700 B.C.

And Noah went in, and his sons, and his wife, and his sons' wives with him, into the ark, because of the waters of the flood.
Genesis 7:7 c.700 B.C.

I do set my bow in the cloud, and it shall be for a token of a covenant between Me and the earth.
Genesis 9:13 c.700 B.C.

He looked at the symbol then, a distant look on his face. "Our people populated Eyid-en for thousands of years. As you know, we worshiped many gods; beings who visited us with fair regularity. Among the gods there were many types, which should be apparent to you because the legends of most of them are now your legends. Before the destruction of our home, I never really gave much thought to the differences or similarities between them. They just *were*. Then the Ankh-el took me and showed me truths I had never known. While it is true that some of them were Ascended, the beings we thought were gods were nothing more than members of races from other worlds that were far more powerful than ours. Once I began to see them as *species*, it became easy to see the similarities. I should have seen them all along. If you think about the ancient myths of this world, the races they derived from will become apparent to you."

He extended his index finger as if to begin counting. "The *Jaegintin*, are similar to us, but much larger and stronger. They are where your legends of giants come from; the Titans of ancient Greek lore and the Jotnar of the legends of the Norsemen. They carried great, powerful rods that were so large they would be the size of a staff to you or me."

He extended another finger. "The *Derk'won* are massive,

serpentine beings. Some are more like worms, while others have scales and wings. They are all immensely powerful. In your legends, you call them dragons."

A third finger came out. "The *Neta'rahen* are a race that remains rather mysterious to me. Even the Ankh-el are not comfortable with their level of knowledge regarding them. I do not know what their true form looks like, nor could the Ankh-el show me. When they visit a world, they take the form of beings that inhabit it, often mixing the features of several native creatures. When you look back through human mythology, you will see remnants of their memory in all the creatures and gods who have features of men and animals – or several animals – mixed together."

Adam's eyes had been getting bigger and bigger with each race Nikolas named, until it looked like they would pop out of his head. Unable to contain himself any longer, he blurted out, "You mean like the ancient Egyptian gods?"

Nikolas nodded. "Yes, some of them. And legends from many other parts of the world too."

"And you're saying that…giants…and dragons…exist too?

"Yes. I am not saying that they have ever set foot on this Earth. But yes, they exist…or at least, creatures like them do." He paused for a moment to let them process what he had just told them, and then extended his fourth and fifth fingers. "The Ankh, and the Dy'ibalis." He held up his hand, displaying the five fingers to Adam and Aletheia. "Five races that represented every god my people had ever worshiped."

"What were the other ones like? Besides the Ankh and the Dy'ibalis," asked Aletheia.

"I take it you are asking about their temperament. In truth, they were much like the Ma-en…and humans, in that they had individual personalities. There were benevolent gods among all three of the races I just mentioned, and there were cruel gods among them all as well. It is only among the Ankh and the Dy'ibalis that I see such uniform morality."

He looked back to the symbol on the door. "For thousands of years we lived that way, and although we fought among ourselves as much as humans do, among the gods there was relative peace. There would occasionally be a battle between two – a titanic event, from our perspective – but they were rare. Until the Dy'ibalis started to come in greater numbers. Many of the Neta'rahen gods – the most benevolent of them – removed themselves from the ensuing conflict. But the cruelest among them joined with the Dy'ibalis. It was a dark time. They waged war against the remaining gods across the heavens of Eyid-en. Eventually, those remaining gods forged a Covenant to fight against them."

He traced the pieces of the caduceus on the door, one by one. "The rod, for the Jaegintin. The serpents, for the Derk'won. And the wings, for the Ankh. Three races that we worshiped as gods, united to stand against the Dy'ibalis and their allies in order to protect our people and our world."

He looked to Adam. "The name Hermes is actually derived from a Ma-en word: *ermenhes*. It means 'messenger.' The stories of Hermes here on Earth are not about a single being; they are about the messengers between gods and Ma-en during the war. This symbol was a code; if they knew it, then the person receiving the message knew it to be true."

Adam sat transfixed as the immortal spoke. Nikolas turned to regard the symbol again. "We continued on that way for many years; war raging in the skies and sometimes spilling into our lands. We were truly at the mercy of all five races, for good or ill. The war raged for over two centuries, and the Covenant seemed to be winning. Gradually, our lands started to experience small stretches of peace again…until the Betrayal."

His fingers touched the serpents, lost in thought. "The Dy'ibalis broke the Covenant from within. The Derk'won betrayed us, or at least the most powerful of them did. That betrayal was bad enough. But along with them came another."

His fingers moved up to the wings atop the symbol. "One of the Ankh-el betrayed the Covenant as well, and took several of his brethren with him. It was a great blow to them; treachery such as his was unheard of in their race. He was also among their most powerful. There are only two that I know of who surpass him." He took his fingers from the symbol and seemed to return to the present. He turned to them with a sigh and said, "The Ankh-el, like the Derk'won, are individually incredibly powerful beings, but they were not great in number. The loss of the Derk'won, coupled with the loss of even a few Ankh, was too much for the Covenant to withstand. It was broken, and the tide of the war shifted. That was the beginning of the end of our world."

Aletheia stared at the symbol for a long time, trying to imagine what it must have been like to watch beings you called gods go to war over your world and your people. The thought made her feel small and insignificant, and not at all in control of her own destiny. She looked back at her great-grandfather, and not knowing what to say, said, "I'm so sorry."

He looked at her and smiled. "Thank you." He breathed deep as if trying to let go of the memory. "Come. It is time for you to see. It is your birthright." He looked to Adam. "In truth, it is the birthright of all of humanity. It is your story."

Nikolas placed his hand on the scanner and Aletheia heard a mechanical sound and then a loud 'clunk.' Nikolas reached out and pulled the massive door open. As it opened, Aletheia could see that the steel was at least a foot thick. Nikolas led them through the portal and as he stepped inside the chamber lights flickered on, filling it.

Inside was a large, natural rock cavern much like the one they had just come from. As she looked around Aletheia could see that it had once been a single large area that included the cavern they had just been in. There was not much to see in it, except for the massive structure standing in front of the far wall.

It looked like an arch, but a delicate one, perhaps fifteen feet tall and thirty feet wide. Aletheia walked closer to it, trying to discern what type of material it was made from. At first glance she thought it was some type of metal she had never seen before. It appeared hard, yet had a shiny, liquid quality like mercury in a thermometer. As she stepped closer she was no longer sure it was metallic, as it took on a translucent appearance like glass, or a gemstone, and as she moved it twisted with iridescent colors. She stood in awe. Nikolas' rich voice broke her out of the trance the arch had put her in.

"You cannot imagine what a war of beings that powerful looks like. The skies rained fire and lightning. Massive storms devastated entire cities. The land shook. Mountains erupted and fell. Both sides commanded the very power of Eyid-en and hurled it against the other." He looked into each of their eyes, his sky-blue stare piercing them. "The world was flooded and everything swept away. Many of the greatest and most powerful of our race were destroyed, either fighting against the dark gods or in the resulting cataclysm." A look of pain passed across the immortal's face.

"Among those of us who were left, there was a Ma-en named Noachtim. Just as the four of us were selected by the Ankh-el and given sacred duties, so was he. Noachtim was entrusted with gathering as many of our people as he could. He was told that the Ankh-el had found a way to save the last of us, and was given the location of our salvation. Noachtim led us out of our lands and up into the mountains just as the flood waters were sweeping away the last of our cities. It was he who explained the rules of passage to us, as the Ankh-el had explained them to him: to bring no weapons, no tools, and no books. To forsake all our worldly possessions in exchange for passage to safety."

Nikolas went to stand next to the arch. "It was Noachtim's duty to lead us to this." He gestured at the arch. "He called it 'The Preserver of Life.' The closest word we had for it in our language was *arku,* which means 'arc,' or 'bow.' But over the years our descendants have mostly referred to it as 'The Arc.'"

Aletheia stared silently at the arch in front of her, her mind and heart overwhelmed with the magnitude of what she was seeing. *This is the other half of my history. The history of the human race.* Adam was, predictably, enthralled with what stood before him. They all sat silently regarding it for some time.

"You should have seen it as we approached it," said Nikolas. He was speaking softly now, as much to himself as to them as he stared up at the arch. "It glowed like the sun along its length, except instead of one color the light that shone from it was a rainbow of colors. It was beautiful. We stepped under it in a dying world, and we stepped out of it here, on this mountain."

Adam was staring at the arch, his gaze moving along its length. "Noah. The flood. The ark. The rainbow. That is what we're talking about here, right? That's just...I don't know what to say. So people have been thinking it was a boat all this time?"

"Yes, almost since we first shared our story with them. They were never able to comprehend it as we told it. Over time our story spread all over the world, and the Arc became a boat. I believe it simply made more sense to them that a boat would be what is needed to save one from a flood. The first people we met called it an *arku* in their stories because they learned the word from us; it is where your modern words 'arc' and 'arch' are derived from. Others called it by different names. The Sumerians and the Hebrews called it by Noachtim's name for it: the Preserver of Life."

Adam was staring at the Arc as Nikolas related the story, and he was brought to life by the last thing the immortal had said. "Wait...the Hebrews? I thought they were the ones that called it an 'Ark?'"

Nikolas laughed. "The truth is truly stranger than fiction. The ancient Hebrew word for this device was 'tebah.' It meant, as you would expect, 'that which preserves life.' When the Hebrew Bible was translated into the English language, the word 'ark' was chosen instead."

"Why?" asked Adam.

Nikolas was grinning. "Turk may have had something to do with that particular translation. Do not forget, his duty is to preserve our history for the day when humanity is ready to learn it. He has worked diligently over the years to ensure those kernels of truth remain in place, so that when the day comes, people will be able to listen and understand, just as the two of you have."

Aletheia was deep in thought. Her brain understood everything she was being shown, but it was still overwhelming. She felt as though in the last week everything she had ever known had been turned upside down and thrown on its head. Still, one question stood unanswered in her mind, and she felt it was an important one.

"I know you said they are cruel, but why did the Dy'ibalis want to destroy you in the first place?" *Why do they want to destroy us?*

Nikolas sighed. "Not all answers have been shown to me. I know only this: the Ankh and the Dy'ibalis have been waging war across many worlds for hundreds of thousands of years. The Ma-en, and now the human race, are destined to play an important role in that war. The Ankh want to protect us and guide us towards that destiny...and the Dy'ibalis want to prevent it. That is all that has been shown to me."

Aletheia stared at the Arc deep in thought. She needed time to process all of it. She knew the things she had learned and been shown over the last week were enough to break her mind if she let them. She had no intention of allowing that to happen.

"I need time. I need to let this all sink in." Adam was nodding beside her, lost in a daze of his own. "Is there someplace we can go to just...think?"

Nikolas smiled. "Of course. Come...I will show you one of the places I go when I need to consider things deeply."

Aletheia looked to Adam and held out her hand. He took it and fell in step beside her, walking side by side as the immortal led them out of the cavern that held humanity's biggest secret.

They waited and watched in amazement as Nikolas lifted the massive stone slab again with ease and slowly slid it back into place, its sides grinding as he pressed against it until it finally seated once again with a deep, rumbling 'thunk.' The seams where it joined the walls were once again small and tight, disappearing in the dim light of the cavern. They followed the immortal in silence up the stairs and out of the small library, Aletheia considering the book that bore her name atop the bookcase as he closed it behind them. Her uncle had told her what her name meant once. Now, seeing it written on that book, she finally understood.

Nikolas led them back through the maze of hallways, up and up through several gracefully curving flights of stone stairs until she knew they must be nearing the top of the castle. They came to the end of a long hallway which had several doors connected to it and it opened into a large chamber. The chamber was nicely furnished from what she could see, but her attention was immediately drawn to the far wall. Where she would have expected to see more stone, or maybe a few windows, was instead a large wall made up of several panels of glass, with two large glass sliding doors placed in the middle. The glass was not tinted as the walls in the penthouse had been; it was clean and clear and sunlight spilled through it onto them.

Aletheia followed Nikolas out through the doors, hand in hand with Adam. She stepped out onto a large observation deck or patio of some sort. It was made from gray stone as was the rest of the castle, but it was all polished smooth, giving it a glossier appearance than the castle walls. Bone-white tiles, each two feet square and speckled throughout with gray, paved the patio all the way to the edges, which were enclosed by a waist-high stone railing. The railing itself was made from fluted columns of the same polished gray stone, lined up side by side and connected on their tops by a long, solid surface of the same white stone the tiles were made from. Vines and ivy were entwined in the railing, growing in and out of it like a neatly wrapped scarf keeping it warm from the crisp autumn air.

Nikolas led them up to the edge and they looked out upon the mountains. The view from the patio was magnificent, overlooking the mountaintops surrounding them, alive with fall colors. Directly in front of them, the view was dominated by one mountain, larger than all the rest, that soared up majestically towards the sky. White, puffy clouds danced through the field of blue, lit up bright as clean cotton by the shining sun. *Yes,* thought Aletheia. *This is what I needed.*

They stood there at the railing for a long time, not bothering to speak words that were unnecessary. Instead they breathed in the fresh, clean air, each deep in thoughts of their own. Finally, Nikolas' resonant voice broke the silence.

"I am sorry you two were thrust into this so quickly. No matter how you learn the truth, it always requires an adjustment. It is never the truth that changes. It is us who must change to accept it."

Aletheia was struck by the immortal's words. *He's right. I can't change this, no matter how hard it is for me to accept. I am the one who has to change.* She looked at Nikolas and found his bright eyes staring at her in return, as if reflecting the crystal blue sky above them.

"I think," he said, "it is finally time for us to begin your training." He adjusted his gaze to include Adam and added,

"Come. Both of you…sit."

Nikolas had them sit down, cross-legged, beside each other on a thick mat resting on the tiles that Aletheia hadn't really registered when she had first taken in the view. As she lowered herself onto it, it occurred to her that it must be where the immortal sat when he came to this place to think. Looking up from positioning herself, she realized they were still facing the mountain and the blue sky above it. Looking at it made her feel a myriad of emotions, chief among them humility. He sat down behind them both and started to speak, his rich voice low and relaxed, his words like velvet.

"You may keep your eyes open or close them, whatever feels best to you."

Aletheia glanced over at Adam to see what he was doing. *He must be loving this.* Her boyfriend had closed his eyes, and as she had predicted had a large, serene smile on his face. Bringing her gaze back to the mountain in front of her, Aletheia's thoughts were still spinning in her head. As much as it pained her to let go of the glorious view before her, she felt like she needed as little stimulus as possible. She gently closed the lids of her eyes. Aletheia was surprised that after a few moments she could feel the sunlight on her skin; its kiss warming her where it touched despite the cool breeze that blew around her. Behind her lids, her vision glowed pink as the sun shone through them, its light eradicating the darkness within her. She heard the immortal's voice from behind her, his soft words gently guiding her on her newest journey.

"It all begins with opening your mind…"

EPILOGUE

Aletheia looked at herself in the mirror, admiring her new hairstyle. Sam had arranged it for her, bringing a stylist to the penthouse after she had expressed displeasure with the hacked off, peroxide-bleached style she had been sporting for the last month. *I like the bob...it's cute,* she thought as she lifted the side of it and let the golden hairs bounce back into place. She had decided to stay with the blonde color; it disguised her appearance well and she had to admit she liked it on her. The stylist had done an incredible job of replacing her two-dollar bleach job with a gorgeous flaxen gold that was similar to her great-grandmother's.

She left the bathroom and went to the dining room to join the others. Walking into the room her heart lifted as she saw them. Besides her mother – who she had since been able to at least send a message to and receive one from – these were all the people she cared about in the world. Adam's smiling face looked up at her as she walked in. *He looks so handsome like that,* she thought as she considered his new hairstyle. Adam hadn't wanted to keep his bleached hair; the hairdresser had been able to return him to his natural brown, and had cut his hair in a short, clean style that somehow still looked moppy enough to satisfy him. Aletheia had to admit, as much as she had always liked his looks, she much preferred this new style to the longer one he wore before. It made him look more *together*, somehow.

Her uncle sat at the table with them, no doubt about to put them all to shame with his appetite. He had been eating voraciously as soon as he had been able, Sam explaining that she could only encourage his body to heal itself, which required a tremendous amount of energy. Alex's smile lit up when he saw Aletheia. As she sat down, her gazed drifted across her great-grandparents. In the last week they had both become more than family; they were now her teachers. She looked at both of them in admiration as she thought upon all that she had grown in that short time.

The conversation at dinner was pleasant, and more light than usual. The last few days had been spent discussing all that had happened as they continued their search for answers. Neither Nikolas nor Alex yet had an explanation for the GPS tracker that had been placed on her uncle's car, nor could they explain why the Dy'ibalis had behaved the way it had and left Adam and Aletheia alive in the first place. In addition, a new question had arisen as they recalled the events of that night in the aircraft hangar. As they lowered their heads and held hands to pray before their meal, the image of the Dy'ibalis appearing into view for a split second after it had attacked Alex flashed into Aletheia's mind. *Why did it show itself? Why not just remain unseen?* The implications were unsettling. Not for the first time, Aletheia shook the disturbing idea from her head that the creature had *chosen* to make itself known to her. As Nikolas finished the blessing, she looked up around the table at the faces of those she loved most and decided to enjoy the moment as it was. This was her new life, and it was a good one.

Ninety miles north of Aletheia, three figures lurked in an aircraft hangar, now empty for the night. They stared at a patch of the cement floor in front of a large mechanical bay full of equipment far too expensive for an airfield so small to afford. The patch was a slightly different shade than the rest, indicating it had been recently replaced.

Grylith regarded the spot with malice. All communication from Sh'ysistyk had ceased just over a week ago, the details of the other Dy'ibalis' death relayed in the final transmission. For the second time, Grylith mentally sent all the information from that last transmission to the more powerful female standing several feet away.

Sh'ysistyk was killed here. Death through violence. (Anger.)

The female's mental transmission came back immediately.

(Pain. Anger.) Arrogant fool. I warned you both against getting too close to the Ma-en. You underestimate him. Sh'ysistyk has jeopardized everything.

What is our strategy now?

We will adjust our plan. Go to more humans and implant these dreams in their minds. A barrage of images, feelings, and sensations flooded into Grylith's mind from the female's. When it subsided, the Dy'ibalis sent a feeling of understanding back in confirmation.

It will happen. (Pleasure. Anticipation.)

The female turned her attention to the human male standing

beside them. He looked at her, fear visible on his face. He was dressed in the human fashion of matching pants and jacket with a strip of cloth tied around his neck. When she sent her thoughts to the human, she shared them with Grylith as well.

Locate them, and this time, do not lose them. Do not fail us. Images of his targets flashed into the man's mind.

"I will not fail," he said.

Watching the exchange, Grylith considered the weak, puny human. *He thinks this will bring him power. It will not end as he thinks it will. Change is coming.*

ABOUT THE AUTHOR

Andrew Spencer's writing has been inspired by a wide variety of authors, ranging from J.R.R. Tolkien, Robert Jordan, and Michael Moorcock to Robert Fulghum and Ernest Hemingway. As an undergraduate, he majored in philosophy and psychology and continued his studies in psychology in graduate school. Andrew lives just outside Portland, Oregon with his wife and two youngest children. In his free time, he enjoys exercising, cheering on his favorite football team, spending time with his family, and consuming anything that either comes from a food cart or contains bacon as a key ingredient.

www.ingramcontent.com/pod-product-compliance
Lightning Source LLC
Chambersburg PA
CBHW071050250626
47159CB00002B/425